I0680366

YAYO

Lock Down Publications and Ca$h Presents

YAYO

A Novel by *S. Allen*

YAYO

Lock Down Publications
P.O. Box 870494
Mesquite, Tx 75187

Copyright 2019 S. Allen
YAYO

All rights reserved. No part of this book may be reproduced in any form or by electronic or mechanical means, including information storage and retrieval systems without permission in writing from the publisher, except by a reviewer who may quote brief passages in review.
First Edition September 2019
Printed in the United States of America

This is a work of fiction. Names, characters, places, and incidents either are products of the author's imagination or are used fictitiously. Any similarity to actual events or locales or persons, living or dead, is entirely coincidental.

Lock Down Publications
Like our page on Facebook: Lock Down Publications @
www.facebook.com/lockdownpublications.ldp
Cover design and layout by: **Dynasty Cover Me**
Book interior design by: **Shawn Walker**
Edited by: **Shawnon Corprew**

S. Allen

Stay Connected with Us!

Text **LOCKDOWN** to 22828 to stay up-to-date with new releases, sneak peaks, contests and more…

Thank you!

Submission Guideline.

Submit the first three chapters of your completed manuscript to ldpsubmissions@gmail.com, subject line: Your book's title. The manuscript must be in a .doc file and sent as an attachment. Document should be in Times New Roman, double spaced and in size 12 font. Also, provide your synopsis and full contact information. If sending multiple submissions, they must each be in a separate email.

Have a story but no way to send it electronically? You can still submit to LDP/Ca$h Presents. Send in the first three chapters, written or typed, of your completed manuscript to:

LDP: Submissions Dept
P.O. Box 870494
Mesquite, Tx 75187

DO NOT send original manuscript. Must be a duplicate.

Provide your synopsis and a cover letter containing your full contact information.

Thanks for considering LDP and Ca$h Presents.

Dedications

I would like to dedicate this book to my loving and supportive mother, Mrs. Karen Collins. Thank you for being by my side as I faced my trials and tribulations, and never leaving my side. I love you, ma,

To my beautiful daughters, Shamara and Shayla Allen: I love you both tremendously. I apologize for not being there, but I vow to make it up to you.

Shout out to Ca$h and Lock Down Publications for giving me a chance to speak to the world through my pen, and make something positive out of my life.

Peace.

YAYO

Acknowledgments

Shoutout to all my nieces and nephews, Laniya, Jacobi, Marcell, Man Man, Cynthia, Malia, Malani, and Eli. To my sister, Danielle Collins, I told you I was going to make it happen. Make sure you roll out the red carpet when I get to Florida. Shoutout to my lil' brothers, the TWINS. I got y'all. Sean, what's up with the Packers? To my sister, Demetria Collins, thank you for sacrificing for me, and being there when I needed you the most. You're a ridah! To Minister Barbera Becton, thank you for supporting me and keeping me focused with God's word when I was in some of my darkest times. I love you. To my brother, K-B, it's over, bro. All plans and goals we made are about to be executed to the fullest. The world is ours. To my partner, K-T a.k.a. Killa, you already know what it is. Words need not be explained. We coming. Shoutout to B-hustle from Killa City, Kansas. Smoke G, good looking out on getting my manuscript where it needed to be after that situation in Pollock. PML to Red G, respect to you, fam, and thank you for being a REAL brother to me when I needed one. To Lil' Man from Argyle Gardens, plenty much love. To OG-ED and Skateboard, much love. Shoutout to all my haters and adversaries. Thank y'all for giving me the fuel to drive my ambition into success. God bless y'all. Last but not least, I'd like to dedicate this book to myself for staying strong, mentally, physically, and spiritually, overcoming my obstacles, and still coming out on top. Now, turn the page and ride shotgun with me as I take you through one of the grimiest stories ever told!

S. Allen

YAYO

Chapter 1

"Yaton, I'm not gon' tell ya ass no more! Get up and get ready for school because we're running late!" Karen, Yaton's mom, screamed at him.

Yaton hated going to school. He was in the sixth grade, and didn't like the school because it was predominately white. Yaton stayed in a suburb north of Chicago called Aurora with his mother, his stepfather, Darrell, and his two half- brothers, Devon and Quavon. Yaton's mom remarried when he was just six months old, and growing up, he had little knowledge of his biological father.

Yaton reluctantly got up from his pallet on the floor, and started to get dressed for school. "Mama, I'm tired of wearing these old clothes. When am I going to get some new ones?" Yaton asked.

"Boy, I don't have no damn money for no new clothes. Ain't nothing wrong with the clothes you have. Some kids ain't got no clothes," Karen told him.

"Well, why Devon and Quavon always get new stuff, and I don't?" Yaton asked as he slid on his old Levi's.

"Because their daddy bought it for them," she said.

Yaton always felt mistreated because he wasn't Darrell's biological son. Darrell would treat him totally different from his brothers. When he would do something wrong, he would get severely punished. One time, Yaton came home late from school, and Darrell beat him so bad with an extension cord he urinated blood.

"Nigga, what took you so damn long to get home?" Darrell asked Yaton with vodka coming off his breath.

"I was just walking with my--"

"Shut the fuck up and go wait in the bathroom, and have all them clothes off, too." When Darrell came to the bathroom, he beat him for damn near an hour.

Yaton shook off the memory and put on his Green Lacoste polo and his beat-up Charles Barkleys, and was ready for school. Karen dropped him off at Georgetown Elementary School. Before he got out of the car, he said, "Mama, I want to go stay with my grandma in Chicago."

"Why, Yaton?" Karen asked.

"'Cause I don't like it at home."

Karen's face saddened and she felt hurt in her heart. She knew he was being treated differently, but she didn't have the courage to stand up to Darrell. She was a stay-at-home mom, and Darrell had her living in a nice condominium and driving a nice car. Karen figured one day, he would change his ways and start treating Yaton as his own.

"I know, baby. Everything is going to be alright. Just bear with me, baby," Karen said.

Yaton leaned over and kissed his mother on the cheek. "I love you, mama," he said and got out of the car.

"I love you too, baby, and be good at school," Karen said.

"I will, mama!" He screamed back and ran to catch up with some of his friends.

Karen sat there in her thoughts, thinking to herself things were definitely going to change.

Yaton was average at school. He wasn't really a people person, but he had a few friends. He got mostly B's and C's on his class work, he was good at sports, and liked to draw. The only problem was his attitude. He would sometimes get into fights with classmates, which got him suspended a few times.

He witnessed a lot at home. Yaton used to watch Darrell punch on his mother like a punching bag, and the next day, everything would be cool. This made Yaton hate Darrell with a passion.

In one incident after visiting his grandfather, Albert, Darrell had gotten completely drunk off of Crown Royal, and started talking shit about Alvin, Yaton's biological father.

"I wish the punk motherfucka would've survived that accident so he can come take care of his punk ass son. No driving clown. Nigga should've had a seatbelt on. He must've not seen the commercial, 'Click it or ticket.' Stupid ass nigga," Darrell said, slurring his words.

Yaton thought it was a good idea to defend his deceased father, so he spoke up from the back of the van. "Stop talking about my daddy!"

YAYO

Darrell pulled off the highway, parked, and exited the van. He violently yanked open the back door, pulled Yaton out of the backseat, and began punching him in the head and face. Yaton tried to fight back, but he was no match for Darrell.

Karen hopped out of the van, screaming for Darrell to stop the assault. "Stop! Stop!" She yelled.

"Shut up, bitch!" Darrell yelled as he turned and backhanded Karen, sending her down on the side of the road.

Karen apologized to Yaton. Even at his young age, he vowed to himself that one day, he would get back at Darrell for all the times he put his hands on him and his mother.

When Yaton's 12th birthday came around, Karen had a surprise for him. "Baby, look what I got for you," Karen said, smiling at her oldest boy while handing him a gift-wrapped box. "Hurry up and open it, boy!" She said, full of excitement.

When he opened the box, his jaw instantly dropped. "Whoooaaaa, mama, these are the new Jordans!" Yaton was so happy he had gotten some new Jordans. "Thank you, mama," he said and gave her a hug.

"You're welcome, baby. Call your granddaddy and thank him because he gave me half on them."

Darrell sat on the couch, clearly annoyed by Yaton's happiness. "You should've gotten his ass some Pro Wings. What the fuck you go and spend all that money on some shoes? You could've gave me some money for these damn bills."

"Darrell, please. It's his birthday," Karen pleaded. "Darrell, please."

"Bitch, what you just say to me?"

"Darrell, stop it. It's his birt--" Darrell jumped off the couch and punched her in the face, sending her to the floor.

"Mama!" Yaton yelled, and rushed toward Darrell, throwing a flurry of punches at Darrell's stomach and legs. Darrell punched him so hard he knocked Yaton out cold.

When Yaton came to, he saw two garbage bags filled with his belongings.

"Yaton, go get your coat. I'm taking you to the Greyhound station. You're going to Chicago to stay with your grandmother," Darrell told him.

"Where's my mama?" He questioned.

"She's in the back, so go say bye and come on, young nigga."

He ran to the back room and could hear his mother sobbing. "Mama, you okay?" He asked.

"Yaton, you're going to go and stay with your granny. She's gonna pick you up at the station when you get there. You be a good boy, alright? I love you, baby, and I'm so sorry. This is the best thing for you," Karen said as she cried.

"But mama, I want you to go, too."

"I can't right now. You go, and I promise I will come back for you," Karen said, trying to control her tears. He hugged his mother for dear life with tears streaming down his young face.

"I love you, too, mama."

"Now go. I'll call you tomorrow," Karen said and hugged her son.

Darrell stood in the doorway, annoyed. " Come on, boy. I ain't got all day."

Yaton walked past Darrell, grabbed his bags, and got in the car. The ride to the bus station was dead silent.

When they pulled up to the station, Darrell handed him a $20 bill and said, "This is for your ticket."

Yaton grabbed the money and his bags and got out of the car. He looked back at Darrell one last time and whispered, "I hate you."

Darrell pulled off from the curb, leaving the 12-year-old with two garbage bags of clothes and a $20 bill.

Chapter 2

Yaton had been staying in Chicago with his grandmother, Honey, for four years now. Honey stayed on the South Side of Chicago in the Englewood area on 69th and Wolcott. Honey was a devout Baptist, and had now taken on the responsibility of raising him. Honey obtained full custody for him.

At first, Yaton had trouble transitioning because Chicago's South Side was the total opposite of the suburbs. The suburbs were quiet and peaceful, while 69th and Wolcott was full of drug dealers, prostitutes, dope fiends, gang bangers, and a lot of other things he'd never been exposed to. Yaton had transitioned from right off the front porch to the gangsters on the corner selling drugs. They interested him the most: the way they dressed, the cars they drove, and the jewelry they wore.

Yaton sat on the porch with his best friend, Pudge, who stayed next door to Honey.

"Man, you see that car right there?" Yaton pointed to the '87 Cutlass with 20-inch rims. "That's my car right there."

A blue Chevy Malibu drove past with a bangin' system, and Pudge yelled out, "Nigga, that's my car!" The two would claim cars all day long.

"Yaton!" Honey yelled from inside the house.

"Yes, grandma?" Yaton responded.

"Baby, go to the store for me." Yaton went into the house to retrieve the money and the shopping list.

He liked living with his grandmother because she spoiled him. He had changed dramatically since moving. The way he spoke, walked, and dressed was like his peers. He loved the hood.

"Aye, Pudge, walk to the store with me, fam," Yaton said. Pudge followed.

Yaton and Pudge started their journey to the corner store called Moe's located up the block.

While walking to the store, an Astro van pulled up with four men occupying it. The passenger window rolled down and the man yelled out, "ATG, nigga! Against the Grain 'til the world blow!"

Then, they drove off.

"Man, I don't like them dudes," Yaton said while mean mugging the van.

The ATG gang was from a different neighborhood, and they were beefing with Tha 69th Street Gangsters, so he felt loyal to his neighborhood gang.

While walking back to the hood, Yaton and Pudge took a shortcut on 72nd Street and walked through a dark alley.

"Man, you know Rachel who sits in front of you in class?" Pudge asked.

"Yeah. What about her?"

"Nigga, I think she choosing," Pudge said as he kicked an empty wine bottle.

"Yeah, right, fool. That girl don't want you! Look at your shoes," Yaton said, laughing.

"What, nigga? I'ma get some more shoes. My mama gonna get me the new Jordans when they come out," Pudge said, sticking his chest out.

Out of the blue, a rat the size of a cat ran across the alley behind a garbage dumpster.

"Damn! What the fuck was that?" Yaton screamed, never seeing a rat so big in his sixteen years of life. His eyes followed the rat all the way to the dumpster, but his eyes locked on the black bag near it, and his curiosity got the best of him.

"Man, what's that?" Yaton said, pointing at the bag. He picked it up and unzipped it. When he looked inside, his face was a mix of excitement and confusion.

"Man what the--" He started as he pulled out a .25 cal automatic handgun.

"That's a thumper, fool!" Pudge said, more excited than Yaton.

Yaton then grabbed a bundle of white stones in individual plastic bags. "Damn!" They both said at the same time.

"Pudge, hold this," he said, handing Pudge the white stones, while he admired the shiny handgun in his hands. There were all kinds of emotions running through him, but what he felt the most was a sense of power.

Yaton placed his finger on the trigger and tried to pull the slide back.

Blocka!

The gun went off, and him and Pudge took off running toward 69th and Wolcott.

When they got back to his house, Yaton gave Honey the groceries, and him and Pudge headed downstairs to the basement where his bedroom was.

"My nigga, did you hear how loud that shit was?" He asked Pudge while pulling the gun from his pants pocket.

"Yeah, nigga! That shit scared the shit out of me, but what's all those white things in this plastic bag?" Pudge said, pulling them out of his pocket.

"I don't know, but I'ma ask Jug-head tomorrow," Yaton said, examining the rocks himself.

"Nigga, you don't even know Jug-head," Pudge said dismissively.

"Man, I don't care. I'ma holla at him anyways."

Jug-head got his nickname because he had a head the size of a Kool-Aid pitcher, but he was a balling ass nigga from 69th, and the head chief of the 69th Street Gangsters. Jug-head also had a stone cold reputation for letting his gun go off. In other words, Jug-head was *that nigga,* and Yaton looked up to him. He had closely observed the man's moves from his porch and the window. The cars he drove, the way he dressed, and the women he rolled with made Yaton want a piece of that world.

The next day, Yaton was on the porch when he saw Jug-head pull up in his pearl white Range Rover sitting on 26-inch Lowenhart rims. He was dressed in an all-white Pelle Pelle leather jacket, all-white Prada jeans, and some all-white Mauri gators. His jewelry shined off of his white outfit.

Jug-head walked to the corner to greet his workers and fellow gang members.

Yaton ran in the house and down to the basement to grab his new gun. He threw it on his waistband, then grabbed the plastic bag with the stones and put it in a brown paper bag, and ran out the door to catch Jug-head. His heart was beating out of his chest as he made his way over.

"Aye, Jug-head. What's up?" He said, trying to sound cool.

"What's up, shorty?" Jug-head replied, looking down at Yaton.

"Fam, I need to holla at you. It's kinda important," Yaton said nervously.

"Aight, let's head over here," Jug-head said as he led him into a gangway. "What's good, shorty?" Jug-head asked, curious about what the young boy had in mind.

"What's this shit?" Yaton asked as he pulled out the Ziploc bag and handed it to Jug-head.

"Shorty, this is power," Jug-head continued, "This is respect, lil' nigga. This is crack cocaine. Where did you get this from?" Jug-head asked.

"I found it on 72nd and Marshfield," Yaton stated, still nervous.

"Shorty, this is money. You trying to make some money?" Jug-head asked.

"Yeah, I'm ready to get some money."

"Well, in order to get money with this, you gotta protect it with this," Jug-head said, pulling out an all-black Glock .40 cal from the holster inside of his jacket.

Yaton grabbed the plastic bag from Jug-head and said, "Well, I already got one of them," and took out the Chrome .25 from his waistband.

Jug-head stared at Yaton for a minute before he spoke. He saw the hunger of a lion, and at that point, he knew Yaton was going to be a force to reckon with on the streets. "Listen, shorty, what's your name?"

"My name is Yaton."

"Where you live at?" Jug-head questioned.

"I live right there on the corner with my granny," Yaton responded.

"Yaton, listen, this block is hot. Never walk around with that much work on you. You got about $1,500 worth of crack in that bag. If you get bumped with that, you going to the Audi jail," Jug-head said. "Bring out a few bags at a time. If somebody asks you whose work you got, tell 'em it's mines. Stack ya bread up. And if you're serious, I'll give you the game and put you on ya feet, feel me?"

Yaton couldn't believe his ears. He was talking to one of the illest niggas on the South Side, and he looked at this as the opportunity of a lifetime. It was his chance to get everything he ever wanted. The money, power, and respect would all come from this crack cocaine.

"What I gotta do?" He questioned.

"Lil' nigga, just let the work work for you. You found this shit, so everything you make is profit. These are dime rocks, so give motherfuckers two for $10. Tell your clientele to always meet you at 71st and Justine when they want something. That's also my block, but I'ma see what you do, if you really trying to hustle," Jug-head said. "Holla at me when you finish dumping the work." Yaton shook Jug-head's hand and walked off.

At 9 o'clock that night, Yaton snuck out of the house with his black Carhartt hoodie pulled over his head, and headed toward 71st and Justine. The block was quiet and nobody was out. He saw how the drug dealers did it on his block, and followed suit by posting up on the corner. After about 10 minutes, a red Chevy TrailBlazer pulled up to the curb and rolled down the window.

A female voice spoke, "Excuse me, shorty. Who got some work out here?" she asked.

He knew exactly what she was asking for, and told her to park. Once she parked, Yaton made his way over to the passenger window. "What up? What you trying to get?" He asked while observing the light-skinned lady who didn't look like the crack addicts he was used to seeing in the hood. He actually thought she was somewhat attractive.

"Just a dime, sweetheart," she replied as she went into her purse to retrieve a $10 bill.

Yaton had 10 bags of crack in his mouth. He spit two of them into his hands, and handed them to her. In exchange, she handed him the $10 bill.

"Damn, baby. I get both of these for $10?" She questioned.

"Yeah."

"Do you be over here all the time?" She asked.

"Yeah, Ms. Lady, I'm out here all the time."

"Okay, then. I think I just found my new D-boy. By the way, my name is Joyce," she said in a sweet voice.

"Yeah, I'll be around here. My name is--" He stopped and thought about it for a second. He thought about his favorite movie, Scarface, and how Tony Montana kept calling cocaine "yayo," and then it hit him. "Yayo. My name is Yayo," he replied.

"Aiight, then, Yayo, I'll probably see you in a few," Joyce said.

"Aiight," Yaton said, still clutching the $10 bill in his hand as Joyce drove away. Yaton had just made his first serve. At that moment, Yayo was born.

Chapter 3

It had been 3 months since Yayo had sold his first bag to Joyce on 71st and Justine. Since then, Yayo had started posting up at Joyce's crib on 51st and Aberdeen. Joyce's crib was slumping. She had traffic coming in and out, and Yayo and Pudge were making all the money. Yayo and Pudge were running through 9 ounces of crack a week.

Jug-head was fucking with Yayo hard, giving him 9 ounces of hard for $4,800. Jug-head even taught Yayo how to cook the work to maximize his profits. Yayo and Pudge pulled in at least 10 grand a week. To be 16 years old, that was considered "getting it."

The only problem was they were in Moe Town, a hood ran by the Black P Stones, a ruthless street gang known for putting in work. Joyce's son, TJ, was a member of the gang, and Yayo was cool with TJ, selling him 8-balls of crack for $80. Joyce also had a 16-year-old daughter, Shakira. Shakira was dating one of the P-Stones, Ameen.

Yayo and Pudge were sitting in Joyce's crib, getting high as a kite.

"My nigga, shorty playing games," Yayo said, referring to Shakira as he inhaled smoke from the kush blunt.

"Man, shorty fuck wit' the Stone nigga, don't she?" Pudge asked.

"That nigga ain't getting no money," Yayo said, pulling out $3,500 from his Red Monkey jeans.

Yayo stayed fresh. He was killing the game with the black, red, and blue Red Monkey outfit with the all-red ACG Nike boots.

"You a fool, nigga," Pudge said, handing him back the blunt.

"Where my money? I need, I need." The sound of his Rick Ross ringtone had Yayo reaching in his pocket for his Nextel phone. It was Jug-head. "What up, Joe?" He spoke into the phone.

"Ain't shit, just checking on you, fam. I ain't heard from you in a couple of days."

"I've been trappin', G, but I'ma get at you when I get back to the hood," Yayo said.

"I'm in for the night, shorty. Just hit me in the AM."

"Aiight, G, love." Yayo hung up.

"Who was that?" Pudge asked.

"That nigga, Head, just calling to see what's up," Yayo said. "Aye, I'm 'bout to run to the car and grab some more blunts. I'll be right back."

Yayo walked to his car, a clean, all-gray Box Chevy. Yayo was planning on going to the Three Amigos store on Western to cop some 24-inch rims next week. Yayo pulled out his car keys and hit the button to open his door, retrieved the Philly blunts out of the glove box, and started back toward the house.

When he made it to the back door, a dope fiend was standing in the yard. "Shorty, you got some hard?" He asked Yayo.

Yayo was high out of his mind, and not wanting to turn away money, he said, "Yeah, school. What you looking for?"

"Let me see what your dimes looking like," the skinny crack-head asked.

Yayo reached into his hoodie and produced 10 dimes from a plastic bag.

"Yeah, school. Fuck with me," he said. "This straight drop."

The dope fiend grabbed Yayo by the throat with one hand and the drugs with his other hand. Yayo reached into his pocket and pulled out his .25. The crackhead saw the gun and went for it. Yayo and the crackhead were wrestling for the gun. Yayo managed to hold on to the gun and squeezed the trigger. *Blocka!* A loud pop cracked through the night air.

The crackhead's eyes rolled in the back of his head, then another pop, and the crackhead fell on his back and started twitching. Yayo felt some wetness on his neck, looked at his hand, and saw blood. The sight of blood on his hands brought back memories, and he visualized Darrell lying on his back, coughing up blood.

Yayo aimed the .25 at the crackhead, and let off two more shots to send him to his maker. Yayo ran into Joyce's house frantically.

"Pudge! Pudge!" He called out.

"What's up, Yayo? I heard some gunshots!" Pudge said, scared to death.

"Come on, fam. Go grab the work. We gotta go."

Pudge went to Joyce's bedroom to get the two ounces they had left, while Yayo ran to Shakira's room and hid the gun under her mattress. Luckily, nobody was home. They both ran out of the house, jumped in the Box Chevy, and pulled off in complete silence. Pudge didn't know what to think, and he definitely didn't know his homie just caught his first body.

When Yayo pulled up on the block, there were a few hustlers out selling crack.

One of the hustlers, named TB, flagged Yayo down. Yayo pulled up to the curb and rolled down the window. "What up, G?" He said to TB.

"Shit, what up, shorty? Be careful out here. Batman and Robin been cruising," TB told him.

"Good looking out," Yayo replied, knowing Batman and Robin were the gang task force.

Yayo parked on the next block, turned off the engine, and began rolling up a blunt of kush.

Pudge broke the silence. "Aye, G, what was that shit at Joyce's house 'bout? What the fuck happened?" Pudge asked, looking concerned.

Yayo finished twirling the blunt, and fired it up. "Crackhead tried to rob me, I went for the banga, and I busted," Yayo said as he blew out the smoke from his nostrils.

"You think they gonna ask Joyce and 'em about that shit because it happened in her backyard?" Pudge asked.

"Shit, nigga, I don't know. What you scared for? You making me nervous," Yayo said and passed Pudge the weed.

"I'm just saying, nigga," Pudge said, trying to choose his words wisely as he thought of how much his homie changed since he first moved to the Chi.

"Man, just chill, G. It was only me and him out there. The only people who know what happened is me, him, and God."

Pudge gave Yayo some dap and hopped out of the Chevy. Yayo was still puffing on a blunt inside his Chevy when his phone rang. He saw it was Joyce calling and answered. "What up?" Yayo said.

"Yayo, don't come over here tonight, bae. There's police every-damn-where. These crazy ass niggas done killed somebody in my backyard. When Shakira and I came back from the grocery store, they rushed me, asking all types of questions about the man who was murdered. I told them I never seen him a day in my life. I know one thing for sure, I'ma move from this crazy ass neighborhood."

"Auntie, just chill out. I'ma holla at you tomorrow," Yayo said as he blew out the smoke.

"Aiight, boy, you just make sure you be safe out there," Joyce said and ended the call.

Yayo sat in the car and meditated on the night's events. The feeling of power invaded his thoughts and engulfed his being. The thought of getting away with murder seemed to have empowered him, and the feeling was somewhat intoxicating.

When Yayo walked in the house, Honey was sitting on the couch, watching a Christian show called Awakening.

"Hey, Yaton," Honey said as she stood up and hugged her grandson. "Boy, you smell like that stuff," she said with a funny look on her face. Yayo took a seat on the couch next to her.

"Yaton, your mother called here for you today. She said for you to call her, and she loves you and misses you."

"She sure don't act like she loves me," Yayo said sarcastically. "She said she was gonna come back for me, and she never did."

"Yaton, your mother loves you, so don't act like that," Honey continued. "I hope you're not out here running around with these thugs. You need to live your life for the Lord because you are going to be judged by your deeds. You understand?"

"I understand, Granny, but I'm tired right now, and I wanna go to sleep," Yayo said as he got up off the couch, hugged his grandmother, and went downstairs to his bedroom.

Honey sat on the couch and said a silent prayer, asking God to look over her grandson. Chicago was a crazy place to live. A lot of people got killed every day due to street violence. There had already been 300 murders, and the year was hardly over. She prayed he doesn't end up becoming the 301st murder of the year.

Chapter 4

The dispatch came over the radio. "224! We have a call of shots fired!"

"This is 224. What's the location?" Batman said to the dispatch as he smoked on his Newport cigarette.

"Dispatch to 224. Shots fired in the Englewood area on 53rd and Aberdeen."

"This is 224. Clear. Over," Batman said.

"What the fuck? These lil' niggas over here is crazy. That's the third shooting in that area today," Batman said to his partner, Robin.

Batman and Robin had been partners on the homicide unit for fifteen years. They were nicknamed Batman and Robin because they were always up for fighting crime.

As a rookie, Batman a.k.a. Lloyd would patrol the streets of Chicago with one mission in mind, bringing gang members to justice. Lloyd was a good cop. He had no kids or wife. He was dedicated to his job. He would put in endless hours and bring ideas to the table of how to take the streets back. He was liked by all of his peers and the 51st precinct. Lloyd was on his way to becoming one of the best cops on the South Side, until one incident took him in a totally different direction.

One night, while patrolling the Englewood area, Lloyd was driving behind a green, two-door Cutlass, which was occupied by three black males. The one in the backseat looked back. Lloyd took this as the guy being nervous about something, and pulled them over.

Lloyd got out of his squad car and approached them. "Driver's license and registration, please," Lloyd told the driver.

"Man, what the hell you pulling me over for, pussy ass cop?" The driver aggressively said.

"Okay, driver, step out of the vehicle," Lloyd responded.

"Yeah, aiight," the driver said and stepped out of the car.

"You two don't make a move," Lloyd told the passengers with authority. When Lloyd wasn't looking, the guy in the passenger seat made his move and went for his 9mm on his waist.

When Lloyd noticed what was happening, it was too late. The slugs from the semi-automatic weapon tore into Lloyd's chest. The impact knocked Lloyd on his back, and he was gasping for air and holding his chest. The men took off on foot and fled into the darkness of the grimy streets.

When Lloyd looked at his hands, he didn't see blood. At that point, Lloyd knew his issued vest had saved his life. At that point, Lloyd wanted revenge. He raged a war on all gangsters and drug dealers. An attempted murder on his life would have Batman dancing to a different tune.

Robin, whose real name was Jeffery Washington, was a 40-year-old loose cannon. Jeffery was married for eight years with two daughters, Tracey and Lindsey, who were his world. Jeffery grew up in Waukegan, Illinois, to two rich parents. He was the star running back for his high school, got all the pussy, and didn't have a worry in the world. Jeffery's dream was to go to the NFL and play professional football.

All of Jeffrey's dreams were shattered when his parents were murdered in their home by two masked gunmen looking for money and jewelry. The double homicide rocked the town of Waukegan. Jeffery took his parents' death hard. He stopped caring about sports, and poured his sorrows over a bottle of Dimitri gin. He would drink day in and day out. Tammy, his soon-to-be wife, cleaned him up and helped him finish college. When Jeffery and Tammy had their first child, he vowed he would never let anything happen to his family.

After college, Jeffery got into law enforcement and took his job seriously. He would go extra hard on street thugs, reminding him of the ones who murdered his parents. Sometimes, he would blank out for no reason, and go into a rage. Tammy got Jeffery to go to counseling sessions, but that didn't help.

Jeffery had two sides to him, a loving husband and father to his family, and a vengeful Chicago police officer who was trying to bust some ass. Jeffery looked at criminals like they were the scum of the earth, and he would treat them as such.

Jeffery took pride in police brutality, planting drugs on gang members and shaking down dealers for their drugs. In Jeffery's sixth year at the 51st precinct, he was promoted to the homicide unit. That's when he met Lloyd, and the two become partners in crime on the second shift.

The two detectives became a force to be reckoned with. Every hoodlum in Chicago knew about the crooked dynamic duo. They were feared throughout Chicago, and the streets named them Batman and Robin. Batman and Robin were known for extorting drug dealers, and sending young black men to prison on bogus charges.

During one incident, Batman and Robin got some information from a confidential informant about a house where heroin was being manufactured and distributed. The house was ran by a vicious gang called the Vice Lords. Batman and Robin knew the house was bringing in no less than fifty thousand a week, and they couldn't resist the temptation of a bonus.

Batman and Robin kicked in the door to the trap house with vests on and AR-15s aimed at the suspects.

"Chicago police! Everybody lay on the fucking ground, now!" Robin yelled while pointing the assault rifle at the four men who were in the front room, sitting on the couch counting stacks of money and smoking weed.

Batman moved with stealth and speed as he cleared every room in the house. When Batman came back to the living room, all four men were on the floor, handcuffed. Batman and Robin took all of the money and searched the house for drugs. They recovered $28,000 and five handguns, but no dope.

"Where the fuck are the drugs?" Batman sneered through clenched teeth. Batman's whole persona was intimidating, standing at 6'3''and 250 pounds of pure muscle from countless hours at the gym. He wasn't playing any games.

"Man, ain't no drugs in here. Y'all got everything," One of the four men said.

Robin slammed the butt of his rifle into the man's face, crushing his cheekbone.

"Motherfucka, we not gon' ask you no more. Where the fuck is the dope?" Saliva ran from the corner of Robin's mouth.

One of the men looking at his bleeding homie yelled, "It's under the stove!"

Batman went to the kitchen, moved the stove, and found bundles of heroin. Batman and Robin left the men handcuffed, and left the residence like two professional armed robbers. This was just one of the many capers the dynamic duo pulled.

***

Batman floored the Crown Vic. "Another shooting today. These niggas is wild. It's like Iraq around this motherfucka," he said as he zoomed to the scene.

"Yea, these damn gangbangers lost their mind out here. They should put all their asses in a pile and burn their asses up like the Germans did the Jews," Robin said.

Robin was a bonafide racist, but tried his best to conceal it around his partner. But they both hated two kinds of people, drug dealers and gangbangers.

When the duo pulled up to the crime scene on 53rd and Aberdeen, the block was full of people. When they got out of the car, they saw a few more homicide detectives from the 51st precinct.

"What do we have here?" Batman asked Detective Royce.

"I don't know, Lloyd. Seems like somebody shot this old dude. He was hit twice in the head and twice in the upper chest," Detective Royce told Batman as he lit his cigar.

"Any witnesses? Batman asked Royce.

"Nope, just a lady who stays here. She said she came home from the store, and when she looked out the back window, she saw a body lying in her yard."

"Man, those lil' dudes over here are tripping. Somebody over here knows something about this murder, but everybody on that no snitch shit," Batman said, pulling out a pack of Newports.

"Detective, I want this whole neighborhood swept. Anybody standing on these blocks, bring 'em in. Anybody on file for being a Black P Stone, bring 'em in. Not a bag gets sold over here until we get a suspect," Detective Royce told Batman.

YAYO

For the next few weeks, from 53rd all the way to 61st was hot, and Batman and Robin jumped out on gangsters, bringing them in for questioning. They raided drug spots, searching for weapons and drugs. Batman and Robin were bringing havoc to the streets, and still didn't have a lead on the suspect.

S. Allen

Chapter 5

It was September 3rd and 102 degrees in the city of Chicago. Yayo and Pudge were on the porch, kicking it and smoking a blunt.

"Aye, fam, how much work we got in the stash?" Yayo asked Pudge.

"We got about 3 ounces left," Pudge said while taking a hit from the blunt.

"Aye, look, my nigga, we gotta step our game up. That nigga Jug-head just copped that H2 on some 28s, while we still riding around in this Box Chevy. Plus, my birthday is coming up. I'm trying to jump in something fresh," Yayo said while grabbing the weed back from him.

"Yeah, we both need whips. I like that Dodge Charger. I'ma put 4's on that bitch. These hoes gon' go crazy, fool," Pudge said, breaking down another blunt.

"I like the Camaro," Yayo responded. "They only want $15,000 for that."

"How we gonna pull that off? Jug-head only letting us get 9 ounces at a time. What's the plan, nigga?" Pudge said.

"Listen, fam, we gonna put up 12 G's and try to get a half a brick, and ask Jug-head to front us the other half. Then, we'll have a whole thang to work wit'. We'll cook it up and bag up the whole brick. Off of that, we should make 54 stacks, pay Head back his 12, and we off to the lot. What up?" Yayo said as if he had it all figured out. He was only 16 years old, and already had the mind of a drug dealer.

"That's what's up. We back at Joyce's crib or what?" Pudge asked.

"Hell, yeah. You know them niggas got their block, but the fiends want Yayo!" He said as he took a hit from the blunt. Yayo grabbed his cell phone and called the big homie, Jug-head.

"What up?" Jug-head answered.

"What's up, Joe? What's the bizness?" Yayo asked.

"I ain't on shit, just ridin' and shinin'. Why, what up?"

"Aye, fam, I'm trying to go to the store," Yayo replied.

"Where you at, shorty?"

"I'm at the crib. Slide down on me."

"Aight, give me thirty minutes," Jug-head said, and then hung up.

"Fam, that nigga on his way. Let's go down to the basement and get this paper right," Yayo said.

When they got in the basement, Yayo went into one of his shoe-boxes and started pulling out knots of money. He sat at the foot of his bed and counted $8,200 in small bills.

"Pudge, how much do you got at the crib?" Yayo asked while putting thick red rubber bands around the stacks he already counted.

"I got about six stacks. Why? How much you need?"

"Grab about 4 G's, aiight?" Pudge got up to go get his money.

Yayo looked down at the knots of money on his lap and thought, "I came a long way from them old Charles Barkleys." Yayo now had a slew of the newest shoes like Jordans, Timberlands, and Air-Maxes. He had all kinds of designer clothes, like Red Monkey, True Religion, and Pelle Pelle. He stayed fresh, and all of this was achieved by selling crack cocaine. Now, he was determined to step his game up and grab a whole kilo, which is every drug dealer's destiny.

Yayo's plan was to stay at Joyce's crib until him and Pudge sold every last bag of crack. They wouldn't leave the house for anything until the whole kilo was gone. If Yayo had it his way, they weren't leaving there with nothing but empty Ziploc bags and 54 thousand in cash.

About 15 minutes later, Pudge entered the basement and threw a wad of money on the bed next to where Yayo was sitting. As if right on time, Yayo's cell phone rang.

"Hello?" He answered.

"I'm outside, shorty," Jug-head said, and quickly hung up.

"Look, Pudge, I'm 'bout to go and bend a block with Head. I'ma hit your phone as soon as I get back," Yayo said while stuffing the money into his pants.

"Aight, bet," Pudge replied.

They gave each other dap and then left the house. When they

got on the porch, Jug-head was parked across the street in his new H2. The 28s were still spinning as they walked off the porch toward the sidewalk.

"Damn, that nigga on one," Pudge said, admiring the SUV.

All Yayo could think was, "Nigga, we 'bout to be on one, too," as he walked toward the truck. He hopped in the passenger seat and greeted his big homie.

"What up, fam? This motherfucka serious!" Yayo said as he looked around at the interior and noticed the words "I'm a boss" stitched into the headrest of the cocaine white leather seats.

"What up, shorty?" Jug-head said, shaking Yayo's hand. Jug-head was iced out. His wife beater was brand new, and his Prada jean shorts were creased to the max. The diamonds in Jug-head's bracelet and earrings played peek-a-boo with Yayo's eyesight. The nigga was a walking slot machine, but at the same time, the Glock on his waist also made him a walking gangsta.

"Man, shorty, you trying to do the same 9?"

"Nah, fam, I'm trying to get some real money. I got 12 G's to get a half a brick, and I was wondering if you fuck wit' me enough to front me the other half."

Jug-head just sat listening and observing his young G.

"I'ma have that bread for you," Yayo continued. "I'm just trying to elevate and ride like you, G."

Jug-head looked at Yayo, and knew this lil' nigga was a true money getter from the first time he met him on 69th and Wolcott. He had been fucking with Yayo ever since, and the young nigga never came short on some paper.

"So, you really trying to get it, shorty?" Jug-head asked.

"Yeah, G," He replied.

"Aiight, look. I'ma do that for you cause you been loyal since day one. You a real lil' nigga, and I told you from jump if you proved ya'self, then I'ma put you on. So far, you've been handling your business, so I'ma keep my word. Just stay focused, and keep ya circle tight," Jug-head said.

"Aiight, love," Yayo replied, absorbing the game he was given.

The H2 made its way down Lakeshore Drive, and the bang coming from the six 12-inch Rockford Fosgates in the back of the truck had Yayo on 10 as Jeezy rapped on "Hypnotize." "Can't explain the feeling when I'm ridin' in a Chevy, I'm on top of the world, 26 inches got me deep in ya girl, I command you niggas to get money," Yayo rapped along, knowing in a month, he was gonna be like Jeezy and Jug-head.

Jug-head dropped Yayo off in front of his crib on 69th and told him he'd be right back.

When Yayo walked into the house, he smelled the welcoming aroma of Honey's fried chicken and macaroni and cheese. Honey was busy talking on the phone and barely noticed Yayo enter the kitchen. "Hey, grandma," he said, surprising her.

"Boy, you scared the mess out of me!" She said turning around to greet her grandson. "Girl, here go this child right here," she spoke into the phone before passing it to Yayo.

"Hello?" he spoke into the phone, already knowing who it was.

"Hey, boy!" Karen said with excitement in her voice.

"Hey, ma. What's up?" Yayo replied in a dry tone.

"Boy, what you mean, 'What's up?' What you been doing?" Karen said, sensing a change in her son since she spoke to him two months ago.

"I'm straight. I've been doing good."

"Yaton, your grandmother told me that you ain't been going to school. So what the hell have you been doing that's so important you ain't been in school?"

"I ain't been doing nothing. Why ain't you come see me yet?" Yayo said, switching up the conversation and putting the spotlight back on her.

"I asked you what you been doing, and why you ain't been in school. Don't try to turn this around on me. You wanna run them streets. Is that what it is? You wanna be a street thug? Because that's not how I raised you, Yaton. You need to get your ass back in school and get your shit together," Karen said with authority.

"Whatever, mama," Yayo said in his defense. "You let Darrell kick me out and send me down here with a garbage bag full of

YAYO

clothes. You don't care about me. All you care about is him, Devon, and Quavon. You don't love me, so how you gonna tell me what to do?" Yaton said, finally letting his mother know how he really felt.

"Yaton, you gotta understand I did what was best for you at the time. If I did something wrong, God will deal with me on Judgment Day, but that still ain't no reason for you to not be in school."

Yayo could hear the trembling in his mother's voice. A big tear fell from his eye because he loved his mother, and he needed her in his life.

"Aiight, mama. I love you," he said, trying to fight his emotions. "Here, grandma," he called to Honey and passed her the phone.

"Yaton, you hungry?" Honey asked.

"Nah, not really, Grandma. I'ma eat when I come back in the house later on."

"Aiight, baby. You be careful out there, and don't be coming in this house too late, ya hear me?" Honey called out to Yayo as he left out. What she said fell on deaf ears. Yayo's phone rang and it was Jug-head.

"What up, shorty? I'm outside," Jug-head said, then hung up.

When Yayo got outside, Jug-head was sitting in an all-black Ford Focus with tinted windows. He hopped in the car and greeted Jug-head. They pulled off and parked in a dark alley not far from 69th. Jug-head reached into the back seat and grabbed an army fatigue backpack and handed it to Yayo.

"Shorty, this the whole thang in there. Be smart about this shit, and you gonna make a lot of paper. You got that 12 for me?"

Yayo went in his pocket and handled the bundles of cash to Jug-head.

"Do I gotta count this?" Jug-head said with a half-smile on his face, but Yayo knew he was dead serious.

"It's all there, fam, but I understand the rules of the game," Yayo said.

"Nah, I know you good money, shorty. Just hit me back with that other 12 ASAP, aiight?"

"For sure. I got you, big homie," Yayo said as he exited the car and headed back toward his crib.

Once he got to his room, Yayo opened the backpack and placed the kilo on his bed. He just sat and stared at it for a moment as chills ran through his entire body. Yayo started seeing dollar signs. He knew he was going to be just like Jug-head, if not better. Not many grown men ever had a kilo in their possession, let alone a 16-year-old. The game god had blessed him, and that god was Jug-head.

Yayo picked up his cell phone and called Pudge.

Pudge answered on the third ring. "Yo, what up?"

"Tha eagle just landed, my nigga. Come through first thing in the a.m. We got work to do."

"Aiight, love," Pudge said and hung up.

In the morning, him and Pudge would cook the whole brick and bag it up in dime bags. Their next destination would be Joyce's crib to open up shop. The thought of all the money to come made a devilish grin appear on his face. Yayo was making his mark in the streets of Chicago, and he was going to be a force to reckon with.

***

As expected, Pudge knocked on Yayo's door after Honey left for work that morning. It was time to punch the clock, and they had a long day ahead of them.

"What up, my nigga?" Pudge said as he gave Yayo a pound.

"Ain't shit, my nigga. Time to get this paper," Yayo said as he led Pudge downstairs to the basement. When they reached his room, Yayo grabbed the backpack and pulled the kilo out.

"Damn, my nigga, that's a lot of cake!" Pudge said with excitement.

"Yeah, we gotta hurry up and cook this joint before my Granny gets back. We'll just bag it up at Joyce's crib."

Him and Pudge made their way up to the kitchen to start the process. Yayo grabbed a plate, a Pyrex container, and a box of baking soda and put them on the table.

"Oh, shit." He remembered the digital scale he left in the basement and went to go get it. After returning, he unwrapped the kilo and started breaking it down. He weighed the first ounce and put it in the container. He then took 7 grams of baking soda and used the cake mixer to mix the two together. Then, he put enough water in the container to cover the powder, and put it in the microwave for 2 minutes. Yayo watched as the heat from the microwave broke the coke down into an oily substance. He then removed the container from the microwave and hit it with a little cold water while mixing it little by little. The substance instantly turned hard.

"Yo, Pudge, grab that newspaper and spread it on the table for me," he said as he prepared to dump the crack from the Pyrex onto the newspaper so it can dry. He then weighed the finishing product to see if he gained or lost grams in the process of cooking it. He repeated the same process until the whole kilo was cooked and weighed up. The whole process took about 4 hours, but it was worth the money to be made.

"My dude, we gonna see a lot of paper off of this shit. Look how much crack we got! We gotta get to Joyce's crib ASAP," Yayo told Pudge. They put all the work inside a Ziploc freezer bag, cleaned up the house, and made their way over to Joyce's crib on 53rd and Aberdeen to set up shop.

When they arrived at Joyce's crib, the block was in full swing. Everybody was outside, from the little kids that were playing in the sun to the drug dealers and crackheads.

Shakira was sitting on the porch with two of her friends, Candy and Jessica. When they hopped out of the Chevy, Shakira noticed how attractive Yayo looked in his Pelle Pelle short outfit and the army fatigue backpack hanging from his shoulder. "What up, Shakira? Where ya mama at?" Yayo asked.

"Nigga, I don't know. She sure as hell ain't in my back pocket," Shakira responded with attitude and sass. She knew that Yayo and Pudge sold her mother drugs. "Matter of fact, I need to holla at you anyways," Shakira said.

"About what?" Yayo asked, sounding concerned.

"Just come in here," she said as she led Yayo into the house, leaving Pudge on the porch with Jessica and Candy.

Yayo took notice of how hard Shakira was switching in her Ed Hardy jeans. The jeans were so tight, it looked as if they were painted on her curvaceous body. Yayo had a thing for Shakira, but she wouldn't give him the time a day because he was only 16. Her boyfriend, Ameen, was 19. Yayo followed Shakira into her bedroom, then watched her go into her closet and retrieve his .25 from one of her coats.

"Lil' nigga, is this your gun?" She asked as she spun around with the Chrome banga in her hand. "Why would you put this shit under my bed? I know it's yours because my man don't carry no gun."

"Yeah, it's mines. I know it ain't ya man's cause your man is a goofy. You need to get wit' a boss. If you don't, then you taking a loss," Yayo said as he grabbed his gun out of her hands and put it in his pocket.

"Boy, please. You still a virgin," Shakira said, laughing him off.

"Yeah, I'm still a virgin, until you let me hit that," Yayo replied smoothly.

"Whatever," Shakira said, once again brushing him off. "What you got in that bag?"

"Don't worry about it, cause when I get done wit' what in this bag, ya gonna be breaking ya neck to let me hit that," Yayo replied smoothly.

"Whatever, nigga. I'm 'bout to go back outside. My mother should be back in a few. Stay the hell out of my room," Shakira said, walking back toward the front door.

For the next few hours, Yayo and Pudge sat at Joyce's kitchen table and bagged up the whole kilo. When they were done, they had two freezer bags full of dime bags. They heard a knock on the window and slid the curtain back, and it was an old, bald man.

"Let me get 3 dimes," he said. Yayo collected the $30 and gave him four dimes. "Damn, shorty, good looking out," the man said. "This how y'all doing it?" He questioned happily.

"Yeah, tell everybody I said it's buy one get one free before 9 o' clock."

"Aight, bet," the crackhead said, and then he was off to spread the word.

YAYO

Within the next few hours, Joyce's crib was cracking. Everybody in the hood was trying to get the buy one get one deal. Joyce had finally come home and was happy they were there. She sat in the front room with a few of her smoker buddies and got high off of the crack they had given her.

Yayo watched from the kitchen as Joyce carefully placed a piece of rock in her pipe and lit it up. She inhaled the smoke, held it for a sec, and then exhaled. It was as if she had a brain freeze.

She got back to her senses and said, "Damn, boy, this some good shit. This shit so good, it got my pussy wet."

Yayo and Pudge looked at each other, confused. They never heard Joyce talk like that before. "She must've been tweaked out of her mind," Yayo thought. She got up and walked into the kitchen where Yayo sat counting the day's profits.

"Can you come in my room for a second?" Joyce said. "I need to holla at you." Yayo got up and followed her to her bedroom. Once inside, she closed the door and locked it.

"What's up, Joyce? Why you locking the door and shit? What type of time you on?" Yayo asked nervously.

Joyce responded by pulling down her Levi's jeans and taking off her top to expose her big melons.

"Come here, Yayo. Let me suck ya dick," Joyce said, sounding hungry. Yayo was speechless. He had never had sex before, but looking at Joyce's naked body made his dick hard. She unbuckled his belt and slid his shorts to the floor. His manhood popped through the slit in his boxers and she dropped to her knees and engulfed him in her warm, wet mouth.

"Mmmm, you got a big ol' dick with ya young ass," Joyce said in between moans. She was in her zone as she sucked his dick from the side while massaging his balls. Yayo eyes rolled to the back of his head as he grabbed a handful of her weave and pumped himself deeper into her mouth.

"Daammmn, Joyce, this shit feels soo good," he said as he felt a strange feeling coming from deep within his groin. It was unmistakably the best feeling he ever felt. He couldn't control it any longer.

"Aaaahhhhhh, shit, Joyce!" He said as he exploded in a shivering jolt. Joyce held on to him and continued to suck as he spasmed and released his fluid in the back of her throat.

She swallowed all of his semen, then got up and wiped her mouth with the back of her hand. Joyce grabbed her clothes and started to get dressed. "Let me get another dime, Yayo," she said as she fastened her Levi's. "I know you gonna look out."

Yayo reached into his pocket and handed her a dime. "Thank you, nephew," she said, and headed back to her smoking gallery with the rest of her buddies. Yayo just sat on the bed smiling from ear to ear. He had busted his first nut, and he got it off on a crackhead.

***

"You can't fuck with me! I was built for this!" Yayo said as he punished Pudge in Madden on the PS3. They had been at Joyce's crib for a few weeks, and the money was still coming faster than they could count it. It seemed like all the fiends were coming to Joyce's to shop with them because they had the best work and the biggest bags.

"My nigga, light that up," Yayo said, motioning to the blunt on the table.

"We running through these bags. Shit moving like hot cakes," Pudge said. "How much bread you think we got saved already?" Pudge asked while blowing out a thick cloud of smoke.

"We got about fourteen stacks so far. I'm telling you, man, we gonna stunt for my birthday," Yayo said, excited. "I'm trying to come through on 24s, straight up."

"How we gonna get the whips?" Pudge asked.

"We gonna give Jug-head the money, and let him grab 'em for us."

"You heard from him lately?"

"Yeah. I spoke to him yesterday. He called to make sure we were straight over here. He wanted to know if these niggas were trippin' about us slangin' stones on their block. I told him we cool because we fuck with Joyce's son, and he's a Stone."

That's what's up," Pudge said, grabbing the blunt back from Yayo. "We need to go shopping. We've had these clothes on for like a week now," Pudge said, looking down at his wrinkled up Akademiks jeans.

"We definitely gonna do that, but first, let's finishing stacking this paper. We'll have plenty of time to shine later."

"Why y'all lil' bad ass niggas always in here smoking that stanking shit in my mama's house?" Shakira said as she walked into the living room followed by her boyfriend, Ameen. "Y'all need to take that shit outside on the porch."

"Shorty, chill out. We always smoke in here. Joyce ain't saying nothing 'bout it, so why you trippin'?" Yayo said as he continued to play the game without looking at her.

"Because this is my motherfuckin' house, and you don't live here," Shakira said in a rude tone.

"What's up, lil' niggas?" Ameen finally spoke up. "All well," he said, throwing up his gang sign.

"Nah, man. We ain't in no gang," Yayo said.

"Well, where y'all from, shorty?"

"We from up on 69th and Wolcott."

"69th and Wolcott?" Ameen said. "Them gangsters over there, but fuck them hoe ass niggas. It's all well till the world blow," he said, mean mugging them before he walked to the bedroom with Shakira.

Yayo and Pudge looked at each other until Yayo broke the silence. "Man, fuck that clown. That bum ass nigga ain't on shit." Yayo made a mental note about the disrespectful shit Ameen just pulled, and decided to bust his head when the opportunity presented itself. Yayo learned   money and blood don't mix from the fiend jumping him in the backyard.

"What's up, niggas?" TJ said as he came in and sat down on the couch beside Pudge.

"Ain't shit. Just beating this nigga's ass in Madden," Yayo replied.

"Man, y'all got this motherfucker on fire! I smell that good-

good. Where it at? Roll up. Let me inhale it," TJ said, trying to get high.

"Man, you just missed out. That was our last blunt, but we 'bout to grab some more in a few."

TJ had grown closer to Pudge and Yayo since they started hustling out of Joyce's crib. He knew they sold her drugs, but he ain't give a fuck because he served her, too. TJ liked them because they were paper chasers, and he made money fucking with them.

"Where Shakira at?" He asked.

"She in the room with that goofy ass nigga," Yayo replied, full of disdain.

"Man, I done told that nigga already he's too old to be fucking with my lil' sister. He needs to find a girl his own age," TJ said, heated.

At that moment, Shakira came out of her room, followed by Ameen.

"What up, Moe? All well," Ameen said as him and TJ threw up their gang signs.

"Ain't shit, but check this out," TJ continued. "I thought I told you Shakira's too young for you. So why you still fuckin' on my sister?"

"TJ, stay out of my business," Shakira said in her own defense. "You ain't my mama or my daddy."

"But I'm your older brother, and you gonna start listening to me when I tell you shit, and that nigga's too old for you."

"I ain't gonna start doing shit. What you gonna start doing is staying the fuck out of my business," Shakira said matter-of-factly.

"Aye, Moe, I ain't gonna tell you no more," TJ said, turning his attention to Ameen. "On Stone, you better leave my sister alone."

"Or what, nigga?" Ameen said through clenched teeth.

TJ knew Ameen had a bad reputation in the hood for putting in that work, and all of his crew were certified goons. They were the type of niggas who looked for drama.

"Man, I'm just saying, Moe," TJ said, trying to stand his ground in his crib.

"You ain't sayin' shit, nigga. Stay the fuck out of my business before I punish ya lil' ass," Ameen sneered. He stared TJ down for a second and then made his way out the door with Shakira following him. TJ was visibly upset.

"Aye, TJ, fuck that goofy. That nigga gonna jump out there one day, and we gonna put this on his ass," Yayo said as he pulled out his Chrome .25 automatic from his pocket, letting TJ know he had his back and he was down to ride for him.

"Man, fuck all that," Pudge said. "What y'all niggas got on this weed?" He asked, breaking the tension in the air. "Fuck that nigga. Let's grab some more weed, get high, and finish getting this money."

Later that night, Yayo, Pudge, and TJ were sitting at the kitchen table, chopping it up, smoking on kush, and serving the fiends who came to the window. Suddenly, Shakira came busting through the door crying, and went straight to her room.

"What the fuck wrong with you?" TJ called out, standing from the kitchen table. She didn't answer. "Shakira! Shakira!" He called out again, but there was no response. He walked to her room and opened the door. "Girl, what's wrong with you?"

Shakira just sat on the bed sobbing and covering her face. TJ noticed that her eye was swollen shut, and her lips were bleeding.

"Who the fuck did that to your face?" TJ said, full of anger and concern.

"Just stay out of my business, TJ. It ain't got nothing to do with you," she said with tears streaming down her face.

Yayo approached the doorway and instantly went crazy seeing what happened to Shakira. He was unable to hold back his anger. "Who the fuck did this to you?"

Even though him and Shakira argued all the time, she surely couldn't miss the signs that the young boy had a crush on her. The angry expression on his face was a dead giveaway that he cared about her.

"Shakira, who did this to you?" Yayo repeated.

Shakira seemed to get angrier. "Could y'all please leave me alone and get out of my room!"

"TJ, let me holla at you in here," Yayo said. TJ followed him down the hallway and back into the kitchen.

"I know this faggot ass nigga done laid hands on my people," TJ said, trying to contain his emotions. "I swear on Stone I'ma hurt that nigga."

"Nah, nigga, *we* gonna hurt that nigga. Where that clown at, anyway?"

"He be right around the corner on 53rd and Troop."

Pudge finally spoke up. "Fuck all this talking. Let's go take a look at this nigga."

All three of them left the house on a mission. Yayo popped the trunk of his Chevy and grabbed a Louisville slugger and a tire iron. He handed the baseball bat to TJ and the tire iron to Pudge, and they made their way over to Troop Street.

"Listen, niggas. If this goofy over here right now, there's no talking. Just walk up and work his ass. Anybody jump, this .25 gonna pop off," Yayo said, taking the small, but deadly firearm out of his pocket and cocking it.

When they hit the corner of 53rd and Troop, there was a crowd of teenagers in the middle of the street, most of them wearing red and black, the Black P Stones' colors. Ameen was in the middle of the crowd, smoking a blunt and talking to a thick redbone when they approached him.

"What up, Moe?" TJ said as he swung the bat at Ameen, striking him in the head. "Hoe ass nigga! Put your hands on my family again if you want!" He continued to swing the bat at Ameen, making cracking sounds with each hit. "Bitch ass nigga! You think this shit sweet! I told your chump ass to stay away from my sister!"

One of Ameen's homies tried to come and defend him, and Yayo quickly drew his gun and pointed it at the goon. "Go ahead, nigga. Go ahead, and you gonna make the news out this bitch," Yayo said with a sinister look on his face.

Pudge grabbed TJ and said, "Come on, y'all! Let's get out of here. These people probably called the police."

Ameen was laid out on the street, covered in blood. TJ gave his the ass-whooping of a lifetime. Yayo walked over to Ameen, who was bleeding profusely from his head, and stood over him.

YAYO

"Come on, Yayo!" Pudge yelled, trying to get his attention.

Yayo pulled the .25 out, aimed it at Ameen, and pulled the trigger twice, hitting him twice in his buttocks, then jogged up the street to catch up with Pudge and TJ.

***

They were all full of adrenaline when they got back to Joyce's crib. TJ headed straight to the bathroom to clean the blood off of him.

"Nigga, you crazy as shit!" Pudge said. "Fuck you shoot him for? You probably killed that nigga!"

"Yo, Pudge, shut ya scary ass up. That nigga ain't dead!" Yayo said, trying to justify his actions. "I only shot him in his ass a couple of times because the nigga disrespected me. He lucky I ain't kill 'em for putting his hands on Shakira."

Yayo had no idea Shakira was standing in the doorway listening. She couldn't believe TJ beat up Ameen with a bat and Yayo shot him. She confirmed that Yayo cared about her and had feelings for her, and the thought turned her on, knowing he was willing to bust that thang for her.

Shakira walked into the living room while Yayo was rolling a blunt and said, "Yayo, can you come here so I can holla at you?"

Any other time, he would've told her to wait or said something smart to get under her skin, but she sounded serious, so he got up and followed her to her bedroom.

He sat at the edge of her bed, anticipating the conversation. He couldn't help noticing the bruises on her face.

"Damn, shorty, he fucked you up and almost lost his life behind it."

"Did you really shoot him?" Shakira asked. "Why did you do it?"

"I shot that nigga because he was disrespectful and put his hands on you," Yayo said as he lit up his blunt and inhaled it deeply. "Now, answer my question," he said with authority. "Why did he do that to your face?"

"He tried to make me have sex with his friend, Torry, and I wouldn't do it, so he started punching me in my face. I jumped up, got out of there, and ran home," Shakira said as tears rolled down her cheeks.

"Well, you ain't gotta worry about him anymore. If he tries anything again, I'm gonna murk his ass next time."

Shakira was at a loss for words. She felt so protected and sheltered by him, knowing he just shot someone over her.

She got up off the bed, leaned over to him, and kissed him gently on the lips. Yayo responded back by kissing her on her neck. She let out a soft moan and grabbed the back of his head as he continued to place kisses all over her face and neck. She couldn't take anymore foreplay and pushed Yayo back onto the bed and pulled her Von Dutch shirt over her head. She unsnapped her bra and invited Yayo to pleasure her waiting nipples.

Yayo had no problems following directions as he sucked on her hardened nipples. "Aaaahhhhhh, Yayo, that feels sooo goood. Suck the other one, too," Shakira moaned.

He did as he was told. Shakira stopped him, stood up, and started taking off her Ed Hardy jeans, showing off her flawless skin and shapely thighs.

"What, you gonna just sit there?" She asked him with pure lust in her eyes. "Oh, I forgot. You ain't never had no pussy before."

"Come here," Yayo said and started back at her titties and made his way down to her stomach and waist. Shakira started unbuckling his belt and helped him out of his jean shorts. When she pulled down his boxers, his dick was ready. Shakira laid back on her bed, peeled her panties off, and threw them on the floor.

Yayo climbed on top of her and into her waiting arms. She took hold of his manhood and guided him to her.

"Oohhhh, shit," Yayo said as he felt her warm wetness. It was a feeling he never felt before, and he wished that he could live inside of her. She clenched his backside and pulled him deeper into her, working up a rhythm. As Yayo got the hang of it, he started to pump faster.

"Damn, Yayo, why you doing me like this?" She moaned.

Her moans excited him more, and he started savagely pounding her tight pussy.

"Hold up baby, hold up," she said as she got up and got on all fours, wanting it doggy style. She had been fucking since she was 12 and had a body like she was 23. She definitely had enough experience to know what made her cum.

Yayo entered her and used every inch of his shaft. He was working for what seemed like an eternity, until he felt that familiar feeling building up in his groin. He knew he was about to explode, and he put more power into his thrusts. "Aaaahhhhhh!" He moaned as he exploded inside of her wetness.

"Damn, lil' boy, that was some grown man dick," Shakira said, wiping the sweat off of her forehead. The both of them laid in her bed, spent from the session.

"Aye, Shakira, you still gonna fuck with that nigga when he gets out of the hospital?" Yayo asked as he lit up his blunt.

"Hell, naw, I ain't messing with no nigga who put his hands on me. I don't deserve that shit. I want a boss, a nigga who cares about me and respects me. I'm a black queen, and I need a king in my life," she said as she laid her head on his chest.

"So, basically what you saying is you want a nigga like me?"

Shakira looked up at him and into his eyes. "Boy, you had me a long time ago. You just ain't know it." She kissed him on his cheek with her swollen lips.

"Shakira, just give me a minute. You'll see. I'm 'bout to be that nigga out here. Mark my words," Yayo said, "I want you to be my wifey and get up out the hood with me."

"Damn, boy! You movin' kinda fast, ain't you?"

"I've been moving fast ever since my mother sent me to Chicago."

"Well, if you play ya cards right, I just might be ya wifey," she said and gave him another kiss on his cheek, then rested her head back on his chest.

"That's what's up," Yayo said.

They laid up for a few minutes, lost in their thoughts. Then, Yayo got up and started putting on his clothes.

S. Allen

"Where you going?" She questioned with sleepy eyes.

"I'm going back out here to holla at Pudge and TJ. Why, what's up?" He said, buckling his belt.

"Nothing," she replied.

When Yayo walked into the living room, all eyes were on him. Joyce was home, and TJ and Pudge already gave her the rundown about what happened to Shakira and what transpired after that.

"Where's Shakira at?" She asked Yayo.

Before he could reply, Shakira entered the room behind him, smiling from ear to ear. TJ, Joyce, and Pudge looked at each other, confused.

TJ looked at Yayo and smiled. He knew Yayo had feelings for his sister, and tonight, he proved it. TJ knew Yayo was on a come up, so it was cool to say his sister had fallen for a real nigga.

***

It had been three weeks since Yayo and Pudge had come to Joyce's crib to dump the work, and they had accomplished their goal and stacked the whole 53 G's. Shakira and Yayo had been fucking around hard since he shot Ameen, and she stayed up under him at all times. She even started smoking weed, and he taught her how to roll his blunts for him.

On occasion, when he left and went back to Honey's on 69th, she would sell his drugs for him and make sure his money was right while he was gone. She was falling head over heels for him, and he felt the same way about her.

Yayo called Jug-head. "Aye, Head, what's good with you? You plus 12, big homie."

"Damn, shorty! You move fast! Where you at?" Jug-head asked.

"I'm on 53rd and Troop. I need you to slide on me."

"Aiight, give me 'bout 30 minutes."

"Aiight, G," Yayo said and ended the call.

"What's good with Head?" Pudge asked.

"He coming through in 30 minutes, I'ma give him his bread and let him know we trying to grab them whips by my birthday next week. We gonna stunt, ya feel me?"

"Hell, yeah, G!" Pudge said in agreement.

Yayo picked up his phone and dialed Shakira's number.

"Hello," she answered on the second ring, knowing it was him.

"What up, boo?" Where you at?" he questioned.

"Coming from Dominick's with my mother. Why, what's up?"

"Baby, me and Pudge gotta take care of something. We'll be gone for a few days, but I'll be back for my birthday. I'm gonna take you out, aiight?"

"Oh, yeah?" She said, sounding excited.

"Baby, I'ma show you what bosses do, straight up."

"Aiight, baby, I hear that. Love you, and make sure you call me later on."

"I'll do that. I love you, too," Yayo said, then hung up.

Jug-head pulled up in front of Joyce's in his all-white Range Rover sitting on Asantis.

"Who's that?" TJ said, eyeing the Range.

TJ's reputation was on a million after they put work in on Ameen. Word got out that Ameen was laid up in the Cook County Hospital in ICU, so now, TJ had a bunch of flunkies trying to be under him.

"Yo, TJ, I'm 'bout to bounce up outta here. I'ma hit you up later," Yayo said as he reached out and gave TJ a pound.

"Aiight, fam, hit me up. I'm out here," TJ said, sounding like a soldier on guard duty.

Yayo and Pudge jumped in the Range. "What's the bizness, Joe?"

"Ain't shit, shorty. Just trying to duck these suckers in a land full of lollipops, you heard?" Jug-head said and pulled away from the curb.

"Yeah, I hear that," Yayo said as he handed Jug-head $12,000 in cold, hard cash.

A big smile spread across Jug-head's wide lips. "You lil' niggers something else. Fire that weed up," Jug-head said, pointing to the freshly rolled blunt in the ashtray.

After Yayo lit the blunt, he passed it to Jug-head.

"Aye, Jug-head, Pudge and I need a favor."

"What's that, lil' G?"

"We trying to get some whips."

"What y'all trying to get?" Jug-head said and passed the blunt to Pudge.

"We trying to ride that Charger," Yayo stated.

"How much doe y'all got?"

"We got like 42 stacks. My birthday's next week, and we trying to stunt, ya feel me?"

"You lil' niggas getting that bread, so it's only right you flex, but check this out. Keep your money. I need to holler at you, but I wanna holler at you on the solo. No disrespect to you, Pudge, but everything ain't for everybody, feel me?" Jug-head said.

Pudge nodded his head like he understood. Him and Yayo were a team, and now all of a sudden, Jug-head and Yayo were on some secretive shit.

Jug-head pulled the Range in front of Pudge's crib and Pudge hopped out.

"I'ma hit you when I get back, Pudge," Yayo said.

They gave each other dap, then Pudge waited as the clean ass Range Rover bent the corner on Wolcott.

Jug-head drove down Halsted Street, as "H.A.M." by Jay-Z and Kanye West blasted through his subwoofers. Yayo was crazy high after smoking two blunts of kush with Jug-head.

Jug-head pressed mute on his Navi Screen console. "Yayo, I got a lil' problem I need you to fix," Jug-head said as Yayo attentively looked on. "You see, these ATG niggas are starting to get a lil' bold. They done started selling their work on my turf, which is fucking up my paper. Now, I got killers on my payroll who murk for a lil' bit of nothing, but I'm trying to bring you all the way on as a 69th Street Gangsta! I kept my word, and I'ma put you on."

Yayo nodded his head in agreement as Jug-head spoke. "Now, I need a favor from you. I need you to go over there and put one of them niggas on ice."

Jug-head glanced over at Yayo to see how he was taking it all in, not knowing Yayo already had experience.

Yayo saw this as a chance to make his presence known on the streets. Niggas would know Yayo would bust his gun, plus he had money to back him up. This was his chance to be his boss' right-hand man.

"I got you, Jug-head. When you want it done?" Yayo said, staring out the window.

"Tonight, shorty. Go over there and let them know 69th 'bout that murda-murda. Take care of ya business, and I'ma put you and Pudge in them whips."

Yayo looked at Jug-head, who resembled Satan himself, as his diamonds shined off of his neck. "Aiight, bet, I'ma take care of it," Yayo said.

"That what's up. Where you want me to drop you off?"

"Drop me back at Joyce's crib. I gotta go grab my Chevy."

When they pulled up in front of Joyce's crib, Shakira was sitting on the porch with Candy and Cristina.

"Open the glove box, shorty," Jug-head said.

Yayo opened the glove box and saw a chunky Glock 9mm with a .30 round extended clip attached to it. Yayo grabbed the 9 out the glove box, and placed the clip in one pocket and the gun in his other.

"Don't drive your car," Jug-head warned. "Use a bike or something. It's hot outside, so they should all be at Murray Park. Go over there, give their asses the issue, and hit me up when the mission is complete."

"Aiight, I got this," Yayo said as he jumped out of the Range.

"Who's that in the truck?" Shakira asked as he approached the porch. "Where you coming from? I thought you was gonna be gone for a couple of days," she questioned.

"Baby, just come in the house for a second. I gotta holla at you," he said, ignoring her brief interrogation.

"Hold up, y'all. Let me go see what this boy wants," Shakira said to her friends as she got up and followed Yayo into the house. When she reached her bedroom, Yayo was laying on her bed, lighting up a blunt she had in the ashtray.

"What's up, bae?" She asked, waiting for an explanation.

"Come here, girl."

Shakira walked over to him, and he put the blunt back in the ashtray and started kissing her passionately on the lips. She submitted to his kisses as he slid his hand under her shirt and squeezed her tender breasts.

"Oohhhh, baby, that feels so good. What you trying to do to me?" She questioned in between moans.

Yayo pulled her top over her head, then quickly tugged at her Seven jeans, sliding them off her curvaceous frame. He kissed her all over her flat stomach while pulling off her thong. After sliding out of his clothes, he got on top of her and eased inside of her wetness with a long thrust.

"Aaaahhhhhh, shit!" Shakira cried out from the pain and the pleasure. He continued to work her until he got the reaction that he was looking for. "Oohhhh, I'm 'bout to cuummm. Baby! Oohhhh! I'm cummmin!" Shakira cried out, coating him with her love juices. Yayo went into overdrive and got his off as well, making her orgasm for the second time before he got up and quickly got dressed.

"What's up, baby? Why you not talking to me? What's wrong with you?" Shakira asked.

"Nothing. I'm good," Yayo said, double-checking the Glock before walking toward the door.

Shakira jumped up, quickly threw on one of his T-shirts, and tried to catch him, but by the time she got to the front door, he was already in his Chevy. She felt in her heart something was wrong. His whole demeanor was different. She badly wanted to know what was on his mind.

***

When Yayo pulled up in front of Pudge's crib on 69th and Wolcott, he was chilling on the porch with a few dudes from around the block. They were sitting there, lying about all the girls they had sex with, when Yayo came up.

"What's up, fam?" Pudge said, cutting the chatter short and acknowledging Yayo.

"Ain't shit. 'Bout to run in the crib real quick. I'll be right back."

When Yayo entered the house, he was greeted by Honey, "Hey baby," she said, reaching out to hug him.

"Hi, Granny," he said, embracing her.

"Where you been, Yaton?" Honey asked, full of concern. "I was calling your phone."

"I'm sorry, Granny. I've been with Shakira and I had my phone turned off," he said as he took a seat on the couch.

"Child, don't be out there making any babies with your lil' grown tail," Honey said jokingly, but he knew she was dead serious. "You better be wearing a condom because I ain't taking care of any more babies. After you turn 18, my days of raising kids are over," she said, smiling at the thought of how much Yayo had grown up.

She knew Yayo was in the streets, but what could she do? All she could do is pray for him and let him grow into the man he was destined to be.

Yayo and Honey sat up talking for about 45 minutes before she went upstairs and got ready for bed. "I'll see you in the morning, and stay ya butt in this house tonight," she said as she made her way upstairs to her bedroom.

"Okay, Granny. I love you," he called out to her.

After his grandmother went upstairs, Yayo went downstairs to his bedroom and changed into a pair of black Dickies and his black Carhartt hoodie. He grabbed the Glock, threw it on his waist, and threw the extended clip in his back pocket. Yayo knew Pudge was still on the front porch, and he'd have a million questions, so he grabbed his bike off the back porch and started his journey through the back alley. His first destination was 71st and Winchester, the hood known as Murda Town, and the home turf for the ATG gang.

As Yayo rolled through the dark alley on 71st and Winchester, across the street was a clear view of Murray Park, also known as Murda Park.

There were plenty of people at the park drinking, smoking, and chilling out.

Niggas were sitting on their cars, people were barbecuing, and hoodrats were flirting with ballers. It was hot outside, and the park was in full swing.

Yayo pulled his hoodie over his head, took the Glock from his waistband, and inserted the 30-round clip. He walked up to the top of the alley to get a better view of his prey. He knew he came too far to turn back now, plus he already gave Jug-head his word that he would handle his business.

"Fuck it," Yayo said as he stepped out the darkness, raised his Glock, and pulled the trigger.

After the first shot, Yayo watched as the crowd ran frantically in different directions, which only boosted his adrenaline. "69th Street Gangsters!" He screamed as he fired "ATG, killa!" He said as he continued to fire at any and everyone.

After airing the park out with 9mm bullets, Yayo jumped on his bike and rode off into the darkness, leaving the alley filled with gun smoke, thirty 9mm shell casings, and his second body, a 5-year-old named Jasmine Walker.

**

"This is WGN News at 9. Today's top story: Last night, a shooting on Chicago's South Side in the Englewood area left a 5-year-old dead and 4 others seriously wounded. Five-year-old Jasmine Walker is the city's 301st homicide since the beginning of the year. Let's go to Tarsha Walbert, who is live on the scene at Murray Park."

"Thank you, John. What seemed to be a normal family BBQ at Murray Park last night turned into a horror scene when gunfire erupted. A gunman fired multiple shots from a semi automatic weapon, hitting Jasmine Walker in the head and upper body. The 5-year-old's mother, who was with her at the time of her death, was cutting the child a piece of cake when the gunfire erupted, killing Jasmine, and wounding four others who are currently at Mt. Sinai Hospital in critical condition. Police say the shooting appears to be a gang-related dispute amongst the 69th Street gang and the ATG gang, who are known to frequent Murray Park. As of right now,

police do not have a possible suspect, and they are following all leads. If you have any information, please contact the Chicago Police Department. Thank you. John, back to you."

Yayo cut the TV off and ran to the bathroom to throw up. He'd been throwing up ever since he found out he was responsible for the death of an innocent, young girl. He had called Jug-head numerous times, but his phone kept going to voicemail. Yayo had received a call from Pudge, informing him the block was hot because of what happened.

Yayo decided to stay in the house and lay low. He needed to spend some quality time with Honey anyway. His birthday was in a few days, and his only concern was staying out of jail.

S. Allen

Chapter 6

Jug-head felt like he was on top of the world. He had accomplished a lot in his 35 years of life. He grew up in the poverty-stricken project on the city's South Side. He rose from the ranks in the 69th Street Gangsters organization, and built a $100,000-a-week drug turf. He kept most of his enemies at bay by applying pressure through automatic weaponry and kidnappings.

As the chief of the 69th Street Gangsters, Jug-head had a squad of wild goons willing to give their lives for him. Everything was going well for him. He had money, power, and enough cocaine and heroin to supply the whole city of Chicago.

The only problem he had was the ATG clique, a ruthless gang of killers itching to make their presence felt in Chicago's drug trade. They had a nasty reputation, and were known for robbing and killing drug dealers to eliminate competition. They had tried Jug-head's hand a couple of times by shooting at his crew.

Their actions had started getting on Jug-head's nerves, and now, it was time for a reaction. That's why Jug-head had given Yayo the mission to lay the murder game down at Murray Park. Jug-head knew it was time for Yayo to make his impression in the gangster underworld.

Yayo had proven to be official with the hustle. If Yayo completed the mission, he would bring Yayo all the way in and groom him to be the next don.

Jug-head was in the comfort of his downtown condo off of Lakeshore Drive, getting some head from a 25-year-old Dominican chick named Ashley in his living room.

"Damn, baby, suck this dick," Jug-head said as he grabbed the back of Ashley's head, pushing her head down further on his 10-inch pole, making the model-looking girl gag.

"Ahh, shit, girl," Jug-head moaned as he cummed in Ashley's warm mouth.

Ashley swallowed every bit of nut and wiped her mouth with the back of her hand, all while staring Jug-head in his eyes. Jug-head watched as Ashley got up and walked to the bathroom and closed the door.

Jug-head got up from the couch, put on his polo boxers, and walked over to his exclusive bar to pour himself a shot of Remy XO. Walking back to the couch, he grabbed the remote and turned on the 60-inch Visio plasma, catching the end of the Bulls Heat game. He changed the channel and caught the beginning of the news.

"This is WGN News at 9. Today's top story: Last night, a shooting on Chicago's South Side in the Englewood area left a 5 year-old dead and 4 others seriously wounded. The 5-year-old Jasmine Walker is the city's 301st homicide since the beginning of the year. Let's go to Tarsha Walbert, who is live on the scene at Murray Park."

Jug-head dropped his drink in his lap as the news continued.

"Thank you, John. What seemed to be a normal family BBQ at Murray Park last night turned into a horror scene when gunfire erupted as a gunman fired multiple shots from a semi-automatic weapon, hitting Jasmine Walker in the head and upper body. The 5-year-old's mother, who was with her at the time of her death, was cutting the child a piece of cake when the gunfire erupted, killing her, and wounding four others who are currently at Mt. Sinai Hospital in critical condition. Police say the shooting appears to be a gang-related dispute amongst the 69th Street gang and the ATG gang, who are known to frequent Murray Park. As of right now, police do not have a possible suspect, and they are following all leads. If you have any information, please contact the Chicago Police Department. Thank you. John, back to you."

Ashley came out of the bathroom. "What the fuck? What's wrong, baby?" Ashley said as she watched Jug-head get up and put on his Armani jeans.

"Ain't shit up. Get your shit. I'm about to drop you off."

Jug-head had a million things going through his mind. The police said they didn't have any witnesses, but they knew about the gang war. Police would definitely have 69th on lock and key, jumping out on anybody in the hood, trying to find out who fired the fatal shot that sent Jasmine to her grave.

YAYO

He threw on his all black Pelle Pelle leather jacket, grabbed his 40-caliber Glock from the closet, and put it inside his jacket.

After he dropped Ashley off, he got back on the expressway and headed toward the block. His Blackberry went off. He looked at the caller ID and saw it was Yayo calling, but he sent the call straight to voicemail. "What if those people got him?" He thought to himself as he took a long pull from his Newport. Jug-head definitely was paranoid. He had to find out how much the law knew about the shooter, and he definitely wasn't trying to rap with Yayo right now.

As he exited off on 63rd, his phone rang again, and it was Yayo.

He pulled the Range Rover over in front of Harold's Chicken to use the payphone. He dialed Yayo's number.

"Hello. Who dis?" Yayo asked.

"Man, shorty, what's up? I saw the news. What the bizness?" He said.

Yayo hearing Jug-head's voice let him know police were all over Wolcott. "Man, Head, I fucked up. I didn't see shorty out there. I fucked up," Yayo said with tears streaming from his eyes.

"Shorty, listen, calm down, and don't call me from your phone no more. Use the payphone. I know you're scared, Yayo. Just chill out and let the heat die down, and keep your fucking mouth closed. Always remember, silence and secrecy. You all good, Yayo. They ain't got no clue, so keep it that way, alright?"

"Alright, family," Yayo said, feeling a little bit better.

"You good over there, Yayo?"

"Yeah, I'm good, my nigga."

"Alright, hit me tomorrow," Jug-head said and hung up the phone.

Jug-head got back in his truck and started to roll a blunt of weed. He didn't know what to do. The way Yayo was acting on the phone made him think Yayo wasn't strong enough to hold water if the police was to knock him off and get him in the infamous interrogation room. Jug-head figured he would play it by ear.

He pulled away from the curb, taking the 40 from his waist and putting it on his lap, hoping he wouldn't have to use it to spill Yayo's blood. He liked Yayo, but in situations like this, it was life or death. Before he did 50 years for Jasmine's body, Yayo's soul would leave his body.

***

A few hours later, Batman and Robin sat in a black, unmarked Crown Victoria a block away from 69th and Wolcott. Since the deadly shooting at Murray Park, homicide detectives wanted all the gang members from 69th to 71st brought in for questioning.

For 3 hours, police officers jumped out on anyone standing on those blocks, arrested them, and brought them in. The block was like a deserted island.

"So you think anybody's going to give us the scumbag who shot that innocent girl?" Robin asked his partner as he pulled a pack of Kools from his vest pocket.

"Whoever was firing that gun had to be a 69th street gangster. The punk was pulling on the trigger like he was possessed or some shit. Damn cowards these days won't even walk up and shoot the person they're trying to get. Instead, they stand across the street. Scary motherfucka. I can't wait to catch whoever did that. I'ma make sure they get a hundred years and end up in the penitentiary," Batman said.

Batman had been on a rampage since the shooting on 53rd and Aberdeen. He was jumping out on suspected drug dealers without cause, harassing any and everybody connected to the streets. Him and Robin still had no leads in the suspect, and now this. Chicago was cursed with murder.

All of a sudden, a white Range Rover with rims drove past them. The driver seemed to be talking on his cellphone. When the Range drove past, Batman could see the 15-inch screen on inside the SUV.

"Will you look at that? Range Rover with the rims, TVs, and shit. I wonder how much crack he sold to get that pretty mother-fucker. Looks like a dope boy to me," Batman said.

"Well, let's pull him over and ask him," Robin said as he took a pull from his cigarette.

YAYO

Batman brought the Crown Victoria to life, pulled out of the vacant lot, and got behind the Range. Once behind the Range, Robin activated the blue and red lights.

***

Jug-head had just turned on 69th and Wolcott and was creeping slowly down the block, noticing it was deserted. Jug-head drove down Wolcott when his Blackberry started to ring. When he picked up the phone and saw it was one of his goons, he answered.

"What up, fam?"

"Shit, big homie. Just calling to make sure you straight. Police done snatched up like five of the guys. They got Earl, Trouble, Pee Wee, and Rob Base from right off the block. You hear they turned up about that little girl getting murked at the park?"

While Jug-head was getting the 411 from him, he made a left turn onto Wolcott when he noticed an unmarked car jump behind him. "Fam, good looking out, but these people just got behind me. I'ma hit you in a minute."

"Alright, be safe," he told him and ended the call.

"Fuck these clowns!" Jug-head said out loud while pulling the Glock 40 from his waist and putting it under his seat. He had his license and registration, so he wasn't tripping.

All of a sudden, they put on their blue and red lights.

"Driver, pull your vehicle over," Jug-head heard over their loudspeaker. He watched through the rearview mirror as Batman and Robin got out of the Crown Vic.

"Put your hands where I can fucking see 'em! You make a move, I'ma put your brains on that dashboard!" Batman said through clenched teeth as he pointed his 17-shot Sig at his head.

"Man, what's this all about?" Jug-head asked as sweat poured from his forehead.

"Get your black ass out the truck nice and slowly, boy, or you will never ask another question in your life!" Robin barked, holding his Colt .45, hoping Jug-head would make a move so he could make him a statistic.

When Jug-head got out of the whip, Batman holstered his weapon, grabbed Jug-head by the neck, and forced him toward the cruiser.

"What the fuck y'all on? I ain't do shit." A strong right-hand jab landed dead in his grill, forcing him to spit out three of his pearly whites.

As Jug-head continued to spit out blood, Batman proceeded to search him. He pulled a quarter ounce of weed out of his Pelle Pelle leather jacket, $2,600 in cash, and Jug-head's driver's license out of his Armani jeans.

"Jerome Fields, huh? Thirty-five years old, 1156 South Ashland, huh?"

"Jerome a baller, Robin. Look at all this cash, and he got drugs on him," Batman said with a smirk, stuffing the money in his pants pocket.

"He's a baller, huh? Well, looks like he gon' be an inmate at a correctional institute. There's a loaded firearm here," Robin said, holding up the evidence bag with the gun inside of it. "Well, Mr. Fields, you are under arrest for the possession of a firearm and the possession of marijuana."

Jug-head was read his Miranda rights, put in the Crown Victoria, and taken to the 51st precinct. When they got there, Batman and Robin took him to a desk, handcuffed him to the bench, and proceeded to run his name through the database.

"Mr. Fields, released from Centralia Correctional Facility four years ago, was in for attempted murder. Prior arrests for manufacturing and delivering cocaine, possession of heroin, two counts of battery. God damn, nigga! You one of them tough niggas, huh?"

Batman continued to go through the database. "Gang affiliations, 69th Street Gangsters! Yeah? That's interesting, Mr. Fields. Maybe you can tell us who the fuck shot that lil' girl at Murray Park? Was it a 69th Street Gangsta who pulled the trigger?"

"Man, fuck you. I don't know who shot that lil' girl," Jug-head said through his swollen, bloody lips.

"Well, Mr. Fields, it seems like you're on parole. You're definitely going back for the weapon charge. You niggas never seem to amaze me. Y'all sell all that poison to our people, then use the money to go buy Range Rovers and shit. You come back to the ghetto, where our people are struggling to survive in an economy that's going down by the minute, to come floss your rims and shit. Then, you bitch ass niggas shoot and kill our black youth. Mother-fucka, she was 5 years old, and you don't know shit? You hear me, nigga, you hear me? Nigga, a 5-year-old! Mr. Fields, if I could get away with it, I would kill you, your momma, and everything you stand for!" Batman said, meaning every word.

"Man, fuck you, pig. I ain't shoot no lil' girl," he said.

Detective Royce came in the office and said, "Detective, bring this man to the holding cell in the front. We have somebody saying this man is the one who pulled the trigger at the Murray Park incident."

Batman led Jug-head to a holding cell in front of the police station and uncuffed him.

An hour later, two black thugs came into the station. When he saw their faces, Jug-head knew there was some bullshit going on. The tall man with the long dreads was the nigga, Truck, from the ATG. Truck had some rank, and was Jug-head's archnemesis.

Jug-head had sent his men a few times to kill Truck and each time, they failed. It was like Truck had nine lives and refused to die. Truck orchestrated the robberies of many drug dealers on the South Side of Chicago and commanded murders. Truck was also the one who sent his people to sell heroin on Jug-head's turf.

Jug-head and Truck locked eyes for what seemed like an hour until Jug-head broke the silence. "Nigga, I'ma bury your soft ass," he said as he mugged Truck.

Truck looked Jug-head up and down and laughed. "Nigga, how you gon' bury me through a prison wall, my nigga? You can't go around shooting babies and shit. That ain't how gangsters get down," he told Jug-head and walked off to the front desk.

Detective Royce walked up and shook hands with Truck. "How you doing, Mr. Patterson?"

"Same ole shit, Royce. Trying to stay ahead of y'all and get a lil' paper," Truck said.

Jug-head couldn't believe his eyes. The nigga he was warring with was working with the police. Truck was a fucking rat.

"So, you say you can ID the shooter in the Jasmine Walker homicide?"

"Hell, yeah. That's his goofy ass in that bird cage. That's Jerome Fields, a.k.a. Jug-head. The nigga drives an all-white Range Rover, and he got a Hummer H2. He's the shot caller for them 69th Street Gangsters. He was the shooter. I'd seen him in the alley getting off."

"Muhfucka, you ain't seen me do shit!" Jug-head yelled.

"Mr. Patterson, I need you to sign your statement." Detective Royce passed Truck the clipboard and watched him sign the dotted line.

"Thank you, Mr. Patterson, for your intel and cooperation."

"Anytime, Detective Royce," Truck said and proceeded to walk out the door, him and his goon laughing all the way. "Checkmate, nigga," Truck said as he walked past Jug-head's cell and out the door.

Batman and Robin walked to Jug-head's cell and read him his Miranda rights.

"Mr. Fields, you are being charged with the murder of Jasmine Walker, possession of a firearm by felon, and possession of THC of over 5 grams," Robin said.

"I didn't shoot that lil' girl. Y'all gotta believe me." Jug-head was scared shitless knowing he was being charged with murder.

Robin continued, "You will be transferred to the Cook County Jail in the morning. Your black ass will probably cop up to 80 years or 85%, so that means you gon' pull about 75 years in the can, and 15 years behind a maximum security prison. Your cellmate will probably be about 350 pounds and likes men. With your smile and flawless skin, he probably gon' fuck you in your ass and make you his bitch. Then, you gon' start wearing Kool-Aid on your lips and sucking penis for cigarettes for the rest of your life."

Jug-head put his head in his lap. He was being charged for a murder he didn't commit. He had grown fond of lil' Yayo and respected his gangsta. Yayo was on the path to be a boss, but Jug-head could either spend 75 years in Menard, or snitch on Yayo and continue to dress fly, get money, and push fly whips. It was either him or Yayo, and Jug-head chose Yayo.

"I know who shot the lil' girl," Jug-head said as a tear fell from his left eye.

"And who might that be, Mr. Fields? We've got somebody making you the suspect," Batman
said, lighting a Newport.

"Listen, this lil' nigga from my hood did the shooting." Jug-head told the detectives everything he knew except him motivating the shooting. He told them Yayo had called and confessed to shooting Jasmine, and he gave them Yayo's cell phone number and his grandma's address on 53rd and Aberdeen. Jug-head also told them Yayo might still have the murder weapon, and if they let him out, he could get Yayo to bring him the gun.

"Well, Mr. Fields, you might have just saved your own life. If you can get the gun, you probably will be able to stay on the streets until somebody puts a bullet in your square ass," Batman told him. "Now get that gun."

Batman gave Jug-head his cell phone and Jug-head called Yayo's number. Yayo answered on the third ring.

"Hello?"

"What's up, shorty. This Jug-head."

"What's good, big homie? Whose number is this?"

"This my lil' bitch's number, but check it out. We need to get rid of that banga you used, fam. I'ma need you to meet me somewhere."

"Aiight. Where you want to meet at?"

"Shit, meet me at the Grant Mall on 47th in about 45 minutes."

"Aight, fam. I'm on my way."

Jug-head hung up the phone, feeling like the scum of the earth because he had just made a deal with the devil, and there was no turning back. He had just set up his lil' homie with some crooked cops on a murder.

"Good work, Mr. Fields. It seems like you may have a lil' sense in that bald ass head of yours," Detective Robin joked.

"Just being curious, but how old is this guy, Yayo?" Batman asked.

Jug-head put his head down. "Shorty like 16 years old," he said.

"Sixteen years old?" Batman and Robin said at the same time with confused looks on their faces. "And where on Aberdeen is he?"

"Man, he be on 53rd at Joyce's crib," Jug-head said.

"Now why does that name and street go together like that?" Robin asked.

"Because that's the house where old dude was found in the backyard!" Batman stated. "Well, let's go get this fucker off the street! We running late!"

Chapter 7

Yayo was a nervous wreck. He was chain-smoking Newports, and smoked a quarter ounce of hydro since the shooting.

Shakira knew something was wrong, and he eventually told her what was going on. Yayo was high out of his mind when he told Shakira. He even told her about the man he murdered in the back-yard a few months ago. Yayo told Shakira everything, including the reason he got sent to Chicago.

When he was done, she hugged him so hard. In spite of being shocked by his revelations, she was sympathetic. "Baby, don't worry. Everything's going to be alright." Her words were warm and soothing to his ears. He felt he could trust Shakira, and she felt the same way about him.

"Shakira, I gotta go meet Jug-head at the mall."

"At the mall for what? The mall is closed." Shakira was concerned about why he was going at 4:30 in the morning.

"Jug-head called. I gotta go meet up with him real quick," Yayo said, caressing her smooth face.

"Well, do you want me to go with you?" Shakira asked, letting Yayo know that she was on some ride or die shit for her man.

"That's okay, boo. Just stay here 'til I get back. I'ma go drop this off and come right back," Yayo told her and planted a kiss on her lips. He went to her room and grabbed the Glock, put it in his pocket, grabbed his keys, and left the house.

Yayo was in the Chevy on the way to the mall. He had a weird feeling in the pit of his stomach, but ignored it. The sound of Rick Ross' "White House" filled the Chevy as Yayo pulled on his New-port cigarette. When Yayo pulled up to the parking lot, he could see Jug-head's Range Rover and parked on the side of it. He got out, and undercover cops swarmed him like bees on honey.

"Get on the ground, now! Get on the ground!"

Yayo didn't know what to do but lay his face down on the pave-ment. The police went over to Yayo, rolled him over, took the Glock from his waist, and handcuffed him.

While in the backseat of the squad car, he let the tears roll from his hopeless eyes. He knew he was in deep shit, and the reason he was getting arrested was because of one man, the man he looked up to and trusted.

When he got to the precinct, he was charged with first-degree murder for the slaying of Jasmine Walker. While going through the interrogation process, Yayo remained silent. He didn't give the police anything, but they already had enough. They found the murder weapon on him with his prints on it. It was a wrap.

Detective Royce gave Yayo his one phone call. Yayo grabbed the phone and dialed his grandmother's number.

"Hello, Grandma. It's me, Yaton."

"Boy, where have you been? I've been calling you!"

"Grandma, I'm in jail," Yayo said in a whisper.

"Jail? What you mean you in jail? In jail for what, Yaton?" Honey asked.

"Grandma, they say I killed somebody…"

Yayo couldn't even finish his sentence when Honey broke down.

"Lord, Jesus! Noooooo! God, not my grandson! God, please! God, please!" Honey couldn't control her emotions as she cried into the phone.

Detective Royce grabbed the phone from Yayo. "Ms. Anderson? Ms. Anderson?"

Honey tried to calm herself down as she listened to the detective tell her about his charges.

"Ma'am, your grandson has been charged with the killing of Jasmine Walker at Murray Park yesterday. He will be transferred to 11th and Hamilton to the Juvenile Detention Center where he will await trial. You can call down there and find out when visits are, and get other information you may need concerning your grandson and his case," Detective Royce said and hung up the phone.

Yayo was taken to a holding cell where he was kept for about three hours until the detectives transferred him to 11th and Hamilton, also known as the Audi Home for Boys.

To make matters worse, it was his birthday. Him and Pudge had big plans for the day. They were going to cop whips, go get fresh, and ride around and stunt. Instead, he was on 11th and Hamilton going through a booking process. The whole procedure took two hours. After Yayo was fingerprinted and taken to see the nurse, he was taken to the third floor, Unit 3F.

3F was a unit for Chicago's most dangerous youth. Most of the juveniles on 3F had cases like robbery, assault, rape, and murder. They were all on a sure ride to the Department of Corrections. The officer gave Yayo some brown khaki pants and a T-shirt, and told him he would be in room 12. Yayo looked around the dayroom and saw a lot of dudes sitting at tables, playing cards, dominoes, and board games. A lot of guys were mean mugging Yayo, trying to size him up.

When he went to his cell to make up his bed on the concrete slab, a light-skinned dude with braids approached his cell.

"What you locked up for, fam?" He questioned.

"I'm locked up for murder," Yayo said, making his bed.

"Damn, doe. What you is?"

"What you mean what I is?" Yayo asked.

"I'm a BD from the Calumet, building C. What you is?"

I'm from 69th and Wolcott. I'm a Gangsta," Yayo told him.

"Yeah, y'all niggas over there about that murder shit. Y'all into it with them ATG cats over there at Murda Park. Y'all be putting in that work. Matter of fact, a lil' girl just got bodied over there..." He stopped in mid-sentence and stared at Yayo. He had just seen Yayo's face on the news that morning.

"Man, you're that nigga who was shooting at Murray Park and hit that lil' girl," he said. "Aye, fam. What's your name? My name's Chaos."

"My name is Yayo." The two gave each other a pound.

"Aye, they about to call gym in like 30 minutes. I'ma introduce you to some of my guys," Chaos said.

Within the 30 minutes before gym was called, every inmate knew Yayo was locked up for the Jasmine Walker murder. Some guys gave him head nods while other guys continued to give him stares and mean mugs. In the Audi home, if you had a murder case, it gave a lil' clout, but at the same time, it brought envy and enemies.

There were a lot of killers in the Audi home. It was considered "gladiator school," as Yayo would soon find out.

While in the gym room, Chaos introduced Yayo to a lot of guys from the Englewood area. Some were even from his hood, like Drake, Tees, and Dope Boy. They were all 69th Street Gangsters. Drake, Tee, and Dope Boy were 17 years old and about to get an automatic transfer to Cook County Jail. All three of them were co-defendants on a robbery at a gas station on 55th and Halsted, and were looking at prison time.

"Aye, Yayo, there's a few niggas on your unit from 71st and Winchester, and they probably gon' be on some bullshit with you. I wish you were on our unit," Drake said.

"Man, fuck them clowns. They come at you sideways, put this in their ass," Dope Boy said, passing Yayo a six-inch shank.

The four teens continued to converse throughout the rec session. Yayo told them about what was going on in the hood, and how Jug-head had set him up with the police. They all saw Jug-head in a different light, because they all looked up to the big homie. And now, he had violated the number one street law, silence and secrecy.

"On my mama, fam, the punishment for that shit is death. Motherfucka need to watch that shit," Tee said.

While the three talked about money, murder, and revenge, Yayo soaked it all in, listening and taking notes on everything. At that point, Yayo made a vow to himself that if he ever got out of jail, he was going to rob and kill Jug-head for violating the law of the streets.

When Yayo and Chaos came in the unit from gym, it was an hour before lockdown.

"Aye, Yayo, you better go get your shower shit and get ready to get in that water, cuz niggas gon' be crowding the showers, straight up."

"Aight, bet." Yayo walked past a table in the dayroom.

Four dudes was sitting at the table playing dominoes. They were mean mugging Yayo. Yayo knew these dudes were ATG gang members. He saw the Against the Grain tattoo on one guy's neck in big, bold cursive letters.

YAYO

The boy with the tattooed neck's name was C-note. C-note was 16 years old, and had been in the Audi home for two years, fighting a double homicide, and was on his way to a life sentence. His case involved an armed home invasion. Him and his crew tied up the victims. After only retrieving a half pound of weed, they executed the victims. C-note had left DNA on the scene and was apprehended.

C-note was 6'1'' and weighed 220 pounds. He knew he was going to prison, so he did countless pushups to build his frame into pure muscle. C-note was a loose cannon with nothing to lose, and he had just found food in Yayo.

When Yayo came out of his cell, he had on his shorts, a T-shirt, and his Jordans. He had his shower shoes and his towel in his hand with the shank under his towel. Yayo entered the shower and was uncomfortable from the jump. He had never showered with other men, and the sight before him was abnormal. He proceeded to the shower. There were ten shower heads in the shower and five people were in there, including Yayo.

He grabbed his soap and started lathering up his washcloth when C-note and two of his flunkies came into the shower room. The other inmates saw C-note come in the shower and they all cut their showers short and started making their exit. C-note took the shower next to Yayo. Yayo's heart was pumping through his chest. He knew he had the shank, but he had to get to the stall where he had his clothes. The shank was in his Jordans.

"What up, shorty? You the lil' nigga who shot that lil' girl in my hood, huh?" C-note asked Yayo.

Yayo didn't respond, and kept washing his body.

"Nigga, you heard me! Fuck 69th, nigga! You cowards are at the bottom of the food chain out there!" C-note punched Yayo in the jaw, sending him to the shower floor. C-note and his homies proceeded to punch and kick Yayo in his face until the correctional officers ran in to break it up.

"Break it up! Break this shit up!" Officer Hightower yelled.

Officer Hightower grabbed C-note and threw him against the wall, and his flunkies fled the scene. When Yayo got off the floor, the only thing he noticed was a busted nose and hurt jaw.

"You alright, boy?" Officer Hightower asked.

Yayo didn't say shit. He just walked to the stall, holding his nose, got dressed, and went to his cell.

"Aye, fam, you cool? Niggas say C-note and them just punished you," Chaos said, standing at the door.

"Man, I'm cool. It's all good."

"You gon' get some get back or what?" Chaos asked.

"Naw, I'm good. It's all good."

"Aiight, fam. I'ma holler at you tomorrow." The two gave each other a pound.

"Lock it down! Lock it down!" The officer yelled over the intercom.

Yayo laid on the concrete slab in deep thought. He had told Chaos one thing, but was thinking of something else. In the morning, he was going to make a scene in the dayroom.

***

At approximately 6:30 in the morning, the first shift officer started opening up the doors. Ms. Henderson had been working at the Audi home for the past eight years and loved her job. When she got up to Yayo's cell, Yayo was already up. He had been up for the last five hours, doing pushups and plotting on his enemy. Most of the inmates after would sleep until 7:15 and come to breakfast. Ms. Henderson popped Yayo's door and he was standing there.

"Good morning," she said with a beautiful smile. Ms. Henderson was 50, but was drop-dead gorgeous, standing at 5'5'' and 130 pounds of pure chocolate. Yayo stepped out of his cell.

"Good morning, Ms. Henderson," Yayo said as she continued to unlock the doors.

Yayo went to the washroom, brushed his teeth, and washed his face. When Yayo went back to his cell, Ms. Henderson had already popped everybody's door. There were only a few other inmates in the dayroom. Yayo knew C-note was in cell #20 sleeping, and thought this was the perfect time to make his move.

YAYO

"I'ma catch this nigga sleepin'," Yayo thought to himself. When he left his cell, he had his shank in his pocket.

Yayo was nervous as hell and had sweaty palms. He proceeded to C-note's cell. When he got to C-note's cell, he saw him asleep with the blanket over his head. He looked around to make sure no one was watching.

Then, in one swift motion, he slid into C-note's cell and started repeatedly stabbing him in the neck and the back of his head.

C-note didn't know what was happening as he woke to the piercing feeling from the cold steel in his flesh. With all the strength he could muster, he got Yayo off of him and made a dash for his cell door with Yayo behind him.

"Aaaahhhhhh, help! Get him!" C-note yelled as he ran and fell onto the dayroom floor.

Yayo got on top of C-note and continued to stab C-note, catching him in the face and the forearms.

Ms. Henderson let out a scream. "Oohhhh, my God!" She hit the panic alarm on her walkie-talkie.

In minutes, officers swarmed unit 3F and rushed Yayo, who was still stabbing C-note. C-note was stabbed 35 times. It was a miracle he still had a pulse.

All the other inmates were at their doors, watching everything play out. This scene would be something they would never forget.

Yayo was hauled off the unit to 4J and put in confinement for 14 days. Yayo had been in the Audi home for only two days, and had already made blood spill.

While Yayo was in confinement, he had gotten letters. He had gotten a letter from Pudge asking him what to do with the money they had stacked up, and advising him to call his mama's house if he needed anything.

"Man, that's my nigga," Yayo thought as he folded the letter and put it under his mattress.

He also got a letter from Shakira, which said:

"Hey baby. I'm just writing to let you know how much I miss you. Yayo, you are my everything. I don't know what to do without you. Please call me or something. I need to talk to you."

Yayo missed Shakira, too, and from the looks of it, he wouldn't see her for a long time.

The third letter Yayo got was from his grandma, Honey. She told him she found out he was in confinement for stabbing another inmate. Honey told him to pick up his Bible, and put his situation in the Lord's hands, and that God would make everything all right. As Yayo read further into the letter, his eyes lit up like a Christmas tree.

"Yaton, when you get out of confinement, your mother and I will be there to see you."

Yayo couldn't believe it. He was going to see his mama for the first time in four years. He couldn't wait to hug her.

Yayo had been through so much since he had left home. He had become everything his mama didn't want him to be. He had become a drug dealer, a liar, and had killed two people, and he was only 16 years old. Yayo thought about how life had dealt him a bad hand as he was constantly abused physically and mentally at home.

"I never did anything wrong," Yayo thought to himself as the tears began to fall from his eyes. "Why me, Lord? Why me?" Yayo asked aloud. "What have I done, God, to deserve this?" Yayo said through his sobs. Then the tears stopped falling. Yayo rolled over on his bunk and drifted off to sleep.

Two weeks went by, and Yayo was let out of confinement and sent back to 3F. When he got back to his unit, all the inmates was giving Yayo what's up and head nods. C-note was still in intensive care recovering from his stab wounds.

Chaos walked up to Yayo.

"What up, fam? Good to see you again. Niggas been talking about how you punished C-note the whole time you been gone. You definitely got the juice in here," Chaos said.

"Yeah, forget that clown. He got what he deserved," Yayo responded.

"That's what's up. Come in the dayroom and holler at us when you make your bed and shit. I need you to be my spades partner."

"Aight," Yayo said and went to his room to think about the new status he had just established in the unit.

YAYO

***

It had been a week since Yayo had gotten released from confinement. He had gotten a letter from his grandmother telling him on the first Sunday of the month, her and Karen would be there to visit him. Today was that day.

Yayo just got his hair braided in six braids to the back from a dude named Trent, who was official with the braids. Yayo's khakis and white T-shirt were creased to the max. Visiting hours started in an hour, and Yayo was beyond ready.

"What's up, Yayo? You getting ready for a visit? I see you all crispy and shit," Chaos said as he walked up, drinking an orange soda.

"Yeah, my granny and my moms are supposed to be coming to holler at me," Yayo said as he wiped his Jordan Retro 4s with a damp rag. Yayo was excited to death.

"Man, you lucky you got your peeps, pimp. My people don't even fuck with me. My moms smoke that shit, and that's all she got time for. That's why I just do me," Chaos said with a sad look on his face.

"You straight, fam. Real soldiers stay grounded," Yayo told him and gave his friend some dap.

While Yayo and Chaos were kicking it, a slew of visitors walked up to the front desk.

"Meeks, Dobson, Banks, Smith, Edmonson, Briggs. You have visits," the officer said over the loudspeaker.

Yayo watched as the visitors took seats at the tables in the dayroom to wait for their loved ones.

"Damn, my people ain't even come," Yayo said sadly.

"Fam, you tripping. Visiting ain't over till 4:00. It ain't shit but 12:00," Chaos said as he got up and went to his cell.

Yayo sat in the TV room watching Gangland for another 30 minutes until he heard the loudspeaker. "Yaton Anderson, you have a visit."

Yayo jumped up from his seat and walked toward the dayroom. When he passed Chaos' cell, he was standing in his doorway. "See, nigga? I told you they was coming!" He gave Yayo a smirk.

When Yayo walked into the dayroom, he couldn't believe his eyes. At the table was Karen, Honey, Pudge, and Shakira. When Karen saw Yayo, a tear escaped from the corner of her eye. She couldn't believe how much Yayo had grown.

"Mama!" Yayo yelled and ran into his mother's warm embrace.

"Baby, I missed you so much!" Karen said through her sobs. "Boy, look at you! You done got so big! Give your mama a kiss!" Karen said as she kissed Yayo on his lips. Yayo held on to his mama for dear life as his tears started to fall. Yayo let go of Karen, ran to his granny, and gave her a huge hug.

"Grandma, I'm so sorry," Yayo said as he put his head in her chest.

"Yaton, it's okay. God gon' make everything alright, baby. Just have faith, Yaton," Honey told him.

Pudge stood up from the table and gave his comrade a pound. "What up, fool? Got yourself in a lil' trouble? You got me coming to the Audi home to see you and shit!" Pudge said with a smile.

"Pudge, I messed up, fam, I messed up. It's not supposed to be like this. I let you down, my nigga," Yayo said as he stared Pudge right in his eyes.

"Fam, you ain't never let me down. You're my right-hand man, Yayo, You can never do no wrong. I'm riding wit' you regardless of right or wrong. If you're wrong, we'll deal with the consequences afterwards," Pudge said and hugged Yayo.

Yayo and Pudge were a two-man movement, and their loyalty for each other could never be broken.

When Yayo broke from Pudge's bear hug, he looked at Shakira, standing there looking sexy as hell. She wore some gray, skin tight Deréon jeans with a matching sweater. A pair of dark gray Jimmy Choo high boots completed the outfit. Her long hair was straightened and layered. She looked like a young Kelly Rowland. Shakira ran to Yayo and gave him a passionate kiss. "Baby, I missed you!" She said, planting kisses all over his face.

"I missed you too, boo!" Yayo said as he stared in her brown eyes.

YAYO

Karen couldn't believe her eyes. Yaton had a beautiful girl-friend who was in love with her son.

The five of them talked for about an hour. Karen told Yaton that Devon and Quavon wanted to come and see him, and they're always asking about him and talking about him. She also told him she got a job working at Walmart on the 1st shift, and things were starting to look up.

"Yaton, you want something from the vending machine?" Honey asked and grabbed her Dooney and Bourke purse.

"Yea, granny. Thanks," Yayo said.

"Pudge and Shakira, why don't y'all come with me so y'all can help me carry some of this food?" Honey knew Yaton and his mama needed some time alone. When the three left, Karen broke the silence.

"Baby, how you doing in here?"

"I'm alright. I got into a fight when I first got here, but I'm fine now."

"Listen, I don't know what's going on in your life, but they're saying you shot a lil' girl. I'm not asking if you did it or not. You are my son and I'm with you through everything. I'm in it for the long haul. You are my baby," Karen said with tears falling from her brown eyes.

"Well, why you let Darrell kick me out? You said you was gon' come back and get me, ma. Now, you're telling me you're in it for the long haul?"

"Yaton, I'm sorry. I had to do what I had to do. I am coming back for you, but I have to get myself together first, Yaton. Sometimes, it takes time for a person to get their self together. Baby, I'm sorry, but I am your mother, and I love you. You are so strong, Yaton, and right now, regardless of the past, I need you. You're my oldest son, and you have to stand up and face whatever comes your way. Yaton, you are not a lil' boy anymore. You are a grown man facing grown man situations. Never let them see you sweat. Whatever you do in life, if it's good or evil, you make sure you be the best. You hear me?"

Yayo looked at his mama and said, "I love you," and he got up and hugged her.

"Love you, too, baby."

While the two were having their emotional moment, Honey, Pudge, and Shakira came back with all kinds of snacks. They brought chicken wings, cheeseburgers, fries, Doritos, and Yayo's favorite, Reese's' cups. For the next two hours, they ate, talked, and offered their support. Yayo asked his mother and granny to let him, Shakira, and Pudge have the last 30 minutes to talk.

"Okay, baby. I love you, and I will be here next month to see you," Karen said and got up to hug her son. "And don't be getting in no fights, and remember what I said, Yaton."

"I love you, momma," Yayo said, then hugged his grandmother. "Granny, I'ma call you next Sunday."

"Okay, Yaton. Be good." Honey kissed her grandson.

When Karen and Honey left, Pudge, Shakira, and Yayo were seated at the table.

"Aye, fam, here," Pudge said as he handed Yayo an ounce of granddaddy kush.

Yayo looked around nervously, then stuck the ounce in his boxer briefs.

"Listen, fam," Yayo said. "My public defender is saying the state is looking to give me juvenile life, which means I'ma go to St. Charles till I'm like 21 years old."

"Damn, nigga! That's like 5 years," Pudge said with a disgusted look on his face.

"It is what it is, Pudge. Take that bread and get on. Fam, make sure my granny's straight, and make sure Shakira and Joyce are good, too. Do your thang, Pudge, and always remember, don't trust nobody because trust will get you in here with ya boy," Yayo told him.

"You got that, Yayo. You not gonna want for nothing while you in here. Trust." The two gave each other a brotherly hug.

"Look, my nigga, I'ma let you and Shakira have the rest of the time. You be cool in here, fam."

"No doubt," Yayo said as he watched Pudge leave.

"Yayo, that detective came by our house last week asking my

momma about you and the man who got killed in our backyard. They asked my momma if you knew the man, and if she ever saw you with a gun."

"What did Joyce say?"

"She told them she never saw you with a gun, and she didn't think you knew the man who got shot."

"Tell your momma I love her," Yayo said and moved his chair closer to Shakira. "I know we ain't been messing around that long, but Shakira, I love you. When I get out, I'm coming for my wifey," Yayo said as he caressed her face, drying the tears that were now rolling down her cheeks.

"Yaton, I love you, and I'm not going anywhere. Do you hear me, boy? You are my man, and I'm not leaving you. When you get out, we can start a family, get married, and all that good shit." Shakira kissed Yayo, giving him a mouthful of her warm tongue. Yayo's dick got brick hard as he kissed his girl.

"Visits over! Visits over! Visitors, please exit the unit. Please exit the unit," the officer said over the loudspeaker.

Shakira and Yayo were so caught up that the officer had to come over and break it up.

"Miss, Miss! Visits are over. Please exit the unit."

Shakira broke from Yayo's embrace and mouthed the words, "I love you," and walked toward the exit. Yayo watched his beautiful, thick girlfriend all the way down the hall.

"Damn," Yayo thought to himself, "I'ma miss the shit out of her."

***

"What up, nigga? How'd the visit go? I see you getting your freak on and shit," Chaos said, giving Yayo his props.

"Yeah, everything's all good. Got a chance to see my moms and shit," Yayo said and threw Chaos a pack of Reese's cups.

"Good looking, Yayo."

"Naw, thank me after we smoke some of this." Yayo pulled out the ounce of kush. Chaos' eyes lit up.

"Lil' nigga, you something else," Chaos told him.

"So I've been told. Chaos, close my door and put that towel under it. Let's get high."

***

It had been six long months for Yayo. He had started lifting weights in the gym room, and he was cut up to death. He had earned the respect of his peers and the officers.

Karen had come to see Yayo a few times since the last visit, and so did Shakira. Pudge kept Yayo with the newest shoes, and the best magazines like *Hip-Hop Weekly*, *F.E.D.S.*, and *Straight Stunting*. Pudge was doing well, and living his life for the Lord. Honey would come up to see Yayo often and preach about the Bible, trying to get Yayo to change his life.

Today was Yayo's sentencing. All of Yayo's people sat behind him in the third row of the courtroom. Joyce and TJ also came to show their support. When Yayo looked back, he also saw Batman and Robin looking like two big cats that caught a mouse.

Yayo was sitting before the honorable Judge Kelly. Judge Kelly was extra hard on violent offenders due to her daughter being car jacked and shot to death on Chicago's West Side. Now, she was about to sentence a 16-year-old juvenile in the midst of a violent gang war. The state prosecutor made Yayo sound like a vicious animal.

"Your honor, Mr. Anderson seems to have no value for human life. He pulled the trigger on that gun 11 times that night. He didn't care who was in sight. He just kept shooting, hitting Jasmine in the head. Then, on top of that, Cook County juvenile disciplinary records show Mr. Anderson stabbed another inmate not once, but 35 times. This kid is a monster with no regard for human life. The state of Illinois is recommending Mr. Anderson be released to the Department of Corrections for the rest of his juvenile life."

The judge looked at Yayo for what seemed to be an eternity.

"Ms. Stockdale, do you have anything?" The judge asked Yayo's public defender.

YAYO

"Yes, your honor, thank you. Your honor, Mr. Anderson has come so far since he has come to the detention center. He has been going to school, taking counseling sessions, and has maintained good behavior since the stabbing incident, which for the record was self-defense due to him being jumped by the inmate. Mr. Anderson is definitely remorseful for the death of Jasmine Walker, and is taking full responsibility for his actions. Before this, Mr. Anderson has had no previous engagement with the law. I feel that Mr. Anderson is a product of his environment, where disputes are settled with automatic weapons and violence. Instead of sending these young men to prison, where they will be warehoused with a bunch of criminals and wrongdoers, we should help them by sending them to treatment, take them out of these violent ghettos they call home, and show them a different way. It's our recommendation that Mr. Anderson be permitted to the Maryville Home for assessment to find out what kind of treatment he can receive to help him and monitor his behavior."

"Thank you, Ms. Stockdale," Judge Kelly said, then turned her attention to Yayo. "Mr. Anderson, would you like to say anything to the court before I impose sentence on you today?"

Yayo stood up and straightened his khaki pants. "Your honor, I am terribly sorry for shooting Jasmine. It was an accident. I know what I did was wrong, and I accept full responsibility for my actions," Yayo said as he paused and looked behind him at his mom, who had tears rolling down her cheeks with her hands over her mouth.

"Your honor, I am trying to change my life for the better. I would just like to ask the court to have leniency on me today. Thank you," Yayo said and sat back in his chair.

"Alright. Thank you, Mr. Anderson. It's good to know you are remorseful and sorry for firing the fatal shot that killed Jasmine. But unfortunately, it's a little too late to be sorry. Jasmine is gone, Mr. Anderson, and she can never come back. You see, guns and bullets are real, not like a cartoon where you can take back what you did. Mr. Anderson, you have serious issues that need to be addressed. You are a violent teenager with ties to a gang that is responsible for at least 60% of the shootings and murders on the South Side. You knew what you were doing that night, and why you were doing it. You broke the law by committing murder. You will be sentenced to serve the rest of your juvenile life at the Department of Corrections St. Charles home for boys. You will be released no sooner than your 21st birthday. Good luck, Mr. Anderson," Judge Kelly said and hit the gavel.

Yayo stood up and was walked out of the courtroom by the bailiffs, leaving his loved ones in tears. Batman and Robin gave each other high fives.

Chapter 8

It had been 5 years since Judge Kelly sentenced Yayo to juvenile life. Yayo had transitioned into prison well. He received his high school diploma, and also stayed on the weights, which turned his 6'1'' frame to pure muscle.

Shakira stayed by Yayo's side all the way through, sending him money and sneaking drugs into the prison for Yayo to get money with. Shakira proved herself to be a ride or die bitch, and earned her title as wifey. Honey and Karen visited Yayo frequently to give him their support.

Pudge was on the streets doing his thing. He was flooding Chicago with high-grade marijuana. Pudge kept his word, and sent Yayo whatever he needed to make his situation comfortable. Pudge had a team of young wolves, and they anticipated Yayo's release.

Joyce was still smoking crack, and doing anything to get it. TJ was still in the hood thuggin' it, and trying to keep his head above water. He would send Yayo pictures of him and different women at the club.

Yayo was in his cell, thinking about his people, and how fast five years had gone by. In 2 years, he would be released back to the streets of Cook County, the same streets that claimed the lives of so many young black males like himself.

During the whole 5 years at St. Charles, Yayo thought about getting money, and most of all, revenge. Jug-head had to pay for his actions. Yayo's plan was to get out of prison and hit the streets hard. He was going to rob Jug-head for everything he had, put a hole in his head the size of a bo-dollar, and then, he would put his hood on.

"Stand for count!" The pale-faced guard said as he proceeded to walk down the tier for the 9:00 count.

Yayo jumped off of the top bunk and stood by the back of the cell to be counted.

"Aye Yayo, my mans is trying to grab some smoke. How much you want for a cap?" Yayo's celly asked as he got off the bunk for count. Yayo's celly was from the West Side of Chicago, from the Henry Hornets projects, and had been his celly for the past 5 years.

His name was Rex, and he was being transferred in the next few months. Rex was a Four Corner Hustler, a vicious gang from the West Side. Rex was doing time for a heroin charge. Him and Yayo were as thick as thieves.

"Shit, I need fifteen a cap. I need all commissary, but if he sends it to my books, I'll give him a play for ten a cap," Yayo said as he jumped back on his bunk as he watched the guard walk past.

"Aight, I'ma holla at dude tomorrow, and see what he's talking about," Rex told him and started to roll himself a cigarette.

"Yayo, you know we get out about the same time. What you gon' do when you touch?" Rex asked Yayo as he took a deep pull and blew a cloud of smoke into the air.

Yayo stared at the ceiling, pondering the question. "My nigga, I'ma get out and get a lot of money. I'ma put my people on and get my moms a crib. That's what I'ma do when I touch. Anybody who gets in the way of that is going to the cemetery, and that's on my life," Yayo said and took a pull of the cigarette.

Prison had turned Yayo's heart cold as ice, and made him a force to be reckoned with.

"I hear that, my nigga. Just be safe out there. Niggas getting rocked to sleep. Friends is killing friends, so watch your crew," Rex said and grabbed the cigarette back from Yayo.

"Lights out!" The officer yelled before the lights went out. Yayo and Rex talked about the streets and future plans for the next hour until they fell asleep. Yayo drifted off thinking about how he was going to take Chicago by storm and force.

***

Pudge sat in his black-on black Cadillac DTS with 24-inch Forgiato rims at the White Castle restaurant on 115th and Halsted, waiting on one of his workers, named PK, to show up. PK owed him $8,500 for a pound of kush he had fronted him the week before.

Pudge had come a long way since Yayo got locked up. Pudge was getting money with a Jamaican from the North side of the Chi who had enough kush to supply the whole country. Pudge, at the age of 19, had the streets on lock with the kush. He had the city, and all the women loved his swagger. Pudge jumped out of exclusive whips, sitting on no less than 24s, dressed head-to-toe in Gucci, True Religion, or Prada. Women lusted in the clubs as niggas plotted and schemed on the hood trap star.

Pudge's cell phone sprung to life with Rick Ross' "9-piece" ringtone.

"What's good, fam, where you at?" Pudge said.

"I'm pulling up right now. What car you in?" PK asked, knowing Pudge had about 8 different cars.

"I'm in the DTS, nigga."

PK pulled up in a Ford Expedition being driven by a redbone who resembled Lisa Raye. He jumped out of the truck and slid into the Cadillac with Pudge.

"Pudge, my main man. What's up, baller?" PK said and gave Pudge some dap. The woman in the truck put the vehicle in drive and pulled off, which rose Pudge's suspicion.

"What's up with your ride, fam? Where's she going?" Pudge asked, raising an eyebrow.

"Aye, Pudge, I got half the money right now, but my lil' cousin got the other half. He out West, so we gotta go get it," PK said, lighting a Black and Mild.

"Why you ain't tell me that shit on the phone? I could have met you out west."

"My fault, big homie. Shorty wasn't trying to give me a ride out west," PK said. "We gotta go to the Village projects off of Roosevelt."

The ride out west was quick as Pudge glided the DTS down the Dan Ryan expressway. Pudge listened as PK talked his ear off about opening up shop on the West Side and upgrading from a pound to two pounds. Pudge knew PK was a fuck up and not D-boy material, but on the strength of his girlfriend, Mariah, he tried to put PK on. Mariah was PK's older sister. Pudge got off on Roosevelt.

"Turn at the light," PK told him.

Pudge took note of all the niggas standing on the corners. He knew these projects were ran by the Black Gangsters, and cursed himself for not bringing his cannon with him. He felt naked and out of his element.

"Park right here, my nigga," PK said.

Pudge parked on the side of Madill Elementary School and killed his lights. PK grabbed his cell phone and dialed a number.

"What up, lil' cuz? Come outside. I'm in a black DTS." PK hung up the phone.

In less than three minutes, the back door of the Cadillac opened up and a masked gunman jumped in.

"This a robbery, nigga! Don't make it a homicide! Come up off the jewelry and money!" The gunman sneered through the mask.

"Aight, chill," Pudge said to the masked man. Then, all of a sudden, the masked man hit Pudge in the back of the head with the butt of the .44 revolver he was holding. The back of Pudge's head cracked open, and warm blood flowed from the wound. Pudge pulled off his 32-inch diamond encrusted chain with the money bag charm and gave it to the robber, all the time eyeing PK, who had his hands on the dashboard. Pudge knew it was a setup, and if he made it through this robbery, PK would be murdered by sunrise.

"Where the fuck the money at, nigga?" The masked man yelled.

Pudge reached in his Red Monkey jeans and threw a wad of cash to the robber with a mean mug. The robber put the chain and money in his black hoodie, then cocked the hammer to the .44 and pulled the trigger, blowing Pudge's brains on the steering wheel.

"Come on, let's put this nigga in the trunk," PK said and got out of the car.

The masked man pulled off his mask and got out with PK. The two hoodlums put Pudge's dead body in the back of the trunk and drove to Washington Park. After wiping the car down for fingerprints, the two assailants left the car in Washington Park and disappeared into the darkness like   ghosts.

Pudge's body was found the next morning by Chicago police officers after they received a call for a suspicious vehicle in the park.

"Nineteen-year-old Jarvis Blake was claimed Chicago's 420th homicide," the news reported, using Pudge's government name.

***

YAYO

Yayo had just come from the gym room, doing his daily routine of 1,000 pushups, 500 squats, and hitting the bench, and decided to call his wifey. After Yayo dialed Shakira's number, she answered on the third ring.

"Hello," Shakira answered the phone in a sad tone.

"What's up, baby? Why you sound so sad?" Yayo asked, concerned.

"Baby, they found him dead," Shakira said through her sobs and tears.

"They found who dead, Shakira? What the fuck is you talking about, baby?" He asked as his heart started pounding under his wife beater.

"Boo, they found Pudge. Baby, they said he got shot in the head at Washington Park."

Yayo let the phone fall from his hands and fell to his knees. "Nooooooo!" Yayo screamed, feeling like a piece of his soul had just left him.

Shakira yelled Yayo's name into the receiver to no avail. Rex came to the dayroom, grabbed him off the floor, and took him back to the cell.

"Yayo! What's up, my nigga?" Rex asked.

Yayo was in a vicious rage. "These hoe ass niggas killed my mans, Pudge! These niggas killed Pudge!" Yayo said over and over again. Yayo was seeing red as he started throwing his belongings around the cell and punching the air. Rex waited for his opportunity, then rushed Yayo and put him in a bear hug.

"Yayo! It's okay, baby boy. Calm down. It's gon' be all good, my nigga. Just calm down and think, Yayo. Think," Rex said as he held Yayo in his arms.

"Rex! They killed him, Rex! My man gone! He's gone!" Yayo said through his tears. "I swear on a stack of bibles I'ma murder every nigga who had something to do with it. Any nigga who ever did something to me is going to hell. I swear to God, Rex!"

"It's all good, fam. Just calm down," Rex said as he felt his celly's pain.

***

It had been two weeks since Yayo found out about Pudge's murder. Yayo had learned through TJ that Pudge was set up by PK. He also told Yayo that PK was apprehended and was in Cook County Jail for Pudge's murder. Mariah had told the authorities that her brother had something to do with Pudge's homicide. PK was caught with Pudge's chain and the murder weapon.

Yayo sat in the cell, looking at Pudge's obituary that Shakira sent him. "Don't worry, my nigga. I'ma make the streets pay for you not being here. I love you, Pudge. I'ma make you proud. That's on us, fool," Yayo said, then put the obituary back under his mattress. Yayo then got up and put on his workout clothes and proceeded to the yard to hit the weights. All while thinking, "Two more years, Yayo. Two more years."

***

It had been a long two years, but now, the time had come. In the morning, Yayo would be released to the free world. Yayo had gotten a letter from Rex, wishing him well:

"What up, Yayo?

Remember, my nigga, be careful out there, and remember what I said about the lion: To be a lion, you must know who and what you are. Once you figured out the character in yourself, then you must know your abilities and your struggles, or strengths and weaknesses. Once you've obtained that, you must determine how to carry out your character, either aggressive or aggressively, which means all the time or some of the time, but you got to keep your mind focused. You are the king of the jungle, and it's in your nature to be aggressive, or the jungle will swallow you whole. But be well respected throughout the world, and that's in any jungle and universal code. To carry out the laws of the land, you got to be the king of the jungle, the beast! My nigga, stay focused on your objectives, and move in silence. I got love for you. I touch next month. If you ever need me, hit my line, 773-874-1124. Your boy, Rex."

Yayo respected Rex's gangster, and had learned so much from his celly for almost 6 years before Rex was sent to Harrisburg prison. Tonight would be the last night he slept in St. Charles. As Yayo laid on his bunk deep in thought, he focused on what awaited him in the streets of Chicago. Yayo was about to jump ten toes down in a battlefield known as Chi-Raq.

***

"Yaton Anderson, report to the administration with your property. Yaton Anderson, report to the administration with your property," the C.O. yelled over the loudspeaker.

As he approached the door, the whole unit had wished him well with head nods and salutes. Yayo left the unit well respected. After Yayo checked in with the lieutenant and was cleared, he was free to walk.

Shakira was outside of the prison, looking beautiful as ever, with a clothing bag from J-Bees in her hand. When she saw Yayo step out the door in his all-grey jogging suit, she almost lost it. Shakira dropped the bag and ran over to her man, almost knocking him over as she leaped into his arms.

"What up, boo?" Shakira said and slid her tongue in Yayo's mouth.

Yayo and Shakira kissed passionately for what seemed to be an eternity until they broke each other's embrace. The two walked back to Shakira's Toyota Camry.

"Here, boo, this is for you." She gave Yayo the clothing bag. Shakira had bought Yayo a pair of Mauri jean shorts, Mauri sneakers, and a white T-shirt with Pudge's face on the front. On the back, it read, *"Forever loved and never forgotten. R.I.P. Pudge."*

Yayo changed his clothes in Shakira's car. As she pulled out the lot of the prison, she went in her Jimmy-Choo handbag, and handed a blunt of kush to Yayo. He grabbed the blunt and fired it up, taking a deep pull, holding it in before blowing the smoke through his nostrils.

Shakira got on I-94 and headed toward Chicago. During the ride, Yayo couldn't help teasing Shakira's wet pussy with his fingers.

"Boy, stop! You gon' make me crash this motherfucka. Baby, we about to get a room and do us. Hold on, baby," Shakira said, smiling from ear to ear.

Yayo loved Shakira. She had stood by his side the whole bid without missing a beat. He was high as hell. They had already smoked two blunts by the time they passed Elgin.

Thirty minutes past Elgin, Yayo could see the Chicago skyline through his bloodshot eyes. He was now home, the city where a nigga would meet the graveyard before he graduated high school.

Yayo looked at Shakira. "Baby, you get it for me?" He asked.

"Yea I got you, baby," she replied, and gave Yayo her Jimmy Choo handbag.

Yayo looked in it and retrieved the shiny chrome 9mm Taurus with the two 17-shot clips. Yayo put one of the clips in the semi-auto and cocked it, chambering a round. He was finally home, and a lot of niggas were going have to tell it to the 9.

Chapter 9

Yayo couldn't believe how much the city had changed. Driving down the Dan Ryan on Chicago's South Side seemed unreal to him. All of the projects had been knocked down and turned into condos. When Shakira got off on 69th, reality set back in for Yayo as he saw cars with big rims blasting the latest rap music from their subwoofers. Homeless men stood on corners, walking up to the vehicles asking for change and food. Yayo noticed dudes on the corners in packs like wolves with hardened looks on their young faces. Women walked down the street with little to no clothes covering their bodies.

"I'm definitely back in Englewood," Yayo thought to himself.

When Shakira turned down on 69th and Wolcott, it was 7:00 in the evening, and the block was in full swing.

"So, what's up, birthday boy? What you thinking about over there? You all quiet and shit," Shakira said, rubbing the back of his neck as she parked the car in front of Honey's house.

Yayo's mind was going in a million directions as he watched a group of men on the corner flagging down cars to sell drugs.

"Shit, baby, I'm just glad to be home," Yayo said and kissed Shakira on her soft lips.

When Yayo knocked on Honey's door, he studied the group of men standing across the street. Yayo didn't know any of them. Then, he glanced next door at the house Pudge used to live in, and a chill ran down his spine.

Honey opened the door. "Thank you, Jesus! Thank you, Jesus!" Honey screamed as she grabbed Yayo, hugging him. "Karen! Come here, girl!" Honey yelled as she continued to hug her grandson. When Karen came to the door, she screamed with joy.

"Yaton! Oh, my God!"

"What up, mama?" The two embraced each other. Yayo stepped in the house. It looked the same as when he left. On Honey's entertainment center were countless pictures that he had taken in prison during visits with his family. Honey also had all the cards Yayo had mailed her. Also, there were a lot of pictures of Pudge.

"Boy, we did not know them peoples was gon' let you out to-day. We could have had you a meal cooked and everything. We ain't even got a cake, boy! Today is your birthday! Happy birthday, grandson!" Honey said as she started pulling meat out of the freezer.

"Thanks, granny. It don't matter if y'all ain't got no food cooked for me. I'm just glad to be home," Yayo told Honey as he took a seat at the kitchen table.

For the next couple of hours, Karen sat at the table, bringing her son up on the current events, while Shakira braided his hair.

Honey made Yayo's favorites, fried chicken, baked macaroni and cheese, and collard greens. They all sung "Happy Birthday" to Yayo, and ate an immaculate meal Honey prepared.

"So, Yaton, what are you gonna do? Now that you're home, I hope you plan on getting a job because it's hard out here, baby," Karen said as she stared in her son's eyes, trying to read him.

"Momma, I'ma do what I have to do to survive and get you a crib. You not gon' have to worry, or need Darrell. I'ma have you right. Just give me a lil' minute," Yayo said and kissed his momma on her cheek.

"Yaton, don't worry about me, boy. You just take care of yourself, and don't be out here doing no stupid shit. These niggas is crazy, and they playing for keeps. Do you hear me, Yaton? I'm not gon bury you like Barbara did Pudge. Do you hear me?"

"I'ma be alright, momma. You raised a soldier," Yayo said with a smile.

It had gotten late, and Yayo had plans for Shakira's body. It had been 7 years. Yayo had to release some built-up tension.

"Momma, I'm about to go, but I'ma see you in the morning."

"Alright, boy. Be safe. Shakira, call me tomorrow."

"Okay, Karen," Shakira said. Karen followed them as they left the house, and stood on the front porch.

"God, please look over my son. Please, God," Karen silently prayed.

***

YAYO

Shakira and Yayo got a room at the Congress Hotel in downtown Chicago. The room was stunning. It had marble floors, and it was fully furnished with a 50-inch Vizio TV. She had planned this night for the last 7 years. Tonight, she was going to give Yayo all of her.

When Yayo stepped into the hotel, he was mesmerized by the large room. Yayo grabbed Shakira and pulled her close to him, and kissed her on her soft lips. Shakira was full of passion as she pulled away from Yayo to admire him. Yayo proceeded to take off his shirt, showing his muscled chest and six pack. Seven years of prison treated Yayo well.

Shakira pushed Yayo on the bed and climbed on top of him, planting kisses on his neck, chest, and stomach.

"Damn, baby," Yayo moaned as he grabbed the back of her head. She sucked on his six pack, and then proceeded to pull off his boxers and jean shorts. His dick was rock hard, almost hitting her in the face when it sprang from his boxer briefs. Shakira stared at it for a minute before she attacked it as if it was the last time she would get to have this moment. She slowly wrapped her lips around his engorged meat and slurped it noisily.

"Ahh, Shakira, baby. I love you, girl. Do that shit for daddy," Yayo said, going crazy from the warmth of Shakira's mouth. She sucked Yayo with everything she had before he pulled away from her.

Shakira got on all fours and arched her back to give her man full access to her fat pussy. He got behind her and slid in her, almost about to bust due to her tightness. He started slow at first.

"Baby, fuck me. This is your pussy, boo. This always gon' be yours," Shakira said through clenched teeth as Yayo pounded her from the back with long, strong strokes. "Yayo, I'm about to cum, boy. You making me cum!"

Yayo was on the same page as they both climaxed at the same time.

"Ahh, shit, girl. I swear you got the best sex in the world," he said as they laid in each other's arms, soaking with sweat from the passionate love making. Shakira reached in her Jimmy Choo hand-bag and pulled out a cigarillo stuffed with kush.

"Here, baby. Fire this up." She passed Yayo the potent marijuana.

Yayo lit the blunt and inhaled the herb, blowing the smoke through his nostrils.

"So, birthday boy, now that you done had some birthday sex, what's next on your agenda?" Shakira asked and grabbed the weed from him.

"Shakira, you already know what I'm on. I been on the same shit for the past 7 years. Ain't shit changed. I gotta get on and get my shit together out here," Yayo said, looking Shakira in her brown eyes. "You seen Jug-head lately?" Yayo asked.

"Yeah, but he don't be around the hood like that. I think he moved to the suburbs or some shit. After he got you locked up, Pudge and his crew was trying to catch him slipping, and he moved, but the nigga still getting money, and he got a few workers on Wol-cott," Shakira stated and passed Yayo back the weed.

What Shakira had just told him was music to his ears. Yayo hit the weed and let his mind drift to thinking about Pudge. It had made him proud to know Pudge was trying to bring Jug-head an ugly move. "I miss you, my nigga," Yayo thought to himself as he took a pull from the blunt.

"Baby, do you love me?" He asked Shakira.

"Of course I love you, nigga."

"Will you die for me, shorty?" Yayo asked.

"Yes, baby, I would," Shakira said, trying to figure out where Yayo was going with the conversation.

Yayo looked into her curious eyes and asked, "Would you kill for me?"

Shakira stared at Yayo for what seemed like forever and a day, and answered, "Yes, baby. I would do anything for you."

Yayo knew at that moment, Shakira was all he needed. She was the poster child for the phrase, "down ass bitch."

"Baby, I need you to get close to that nigga Jug-head so I can flatline his rat ass."

YAYO

"How am I supposed to do that?" She questioned, looking astonished.

"I'll tell you in a minute," Yayo said and laid Shakira on her back, parted her thick thighs apart and started to suck on her clit.

"Yayo, I love you, boy. Oooh, shit, baby. Eat this pussy. I love you, Yayo. Ooh, I love you."

Yayo looked up and gave a sinister grin. His plans were about to be executed. Jug-head was a walking corpse, and Yayo was going to make sure he was laid to rest.

***

The next afternoon, Yayo and Shakira checked out of the Congress Hotel because she had to work at Sears.

"Yayo, you can keep the car until I get off. I know you got some running around to do," Shakira said as she pulled onto the Dan Ryan expressway.

"Yeah, that's what's up. I gotta go back to the hood and see what's going on," Yayo said.

After Yayo dropped Shakira off, he jumped on the expressway and headed to 69th and Wolcott. When Yayo pulled up on Wolcott, the block was in full swing with every D-boy in the hood outside, selling kush, powder, crack cocaine, and ecstasy. Yayo parked Shakira's Camry in front of his grandma's house, turned the engine off, and watched the dealers on the corner get their grind on.

Times had definitely changed since he had been in prison. Yayo scanned the crowd, looking for familiar faces, but was to no avail. After about 15 minutes of checking out the competition, Yayo went in his grandma's house. Honey was watching her daily soap opera when Yayo walked in.

"Hey, Yaton. I was wondering when you were going to stop by," Honey said, standing up to give her grandson a welcoming hug.

"What's up, granny? You know I had to stop by and check on you," Yayo said, giving her a kiss on the cheek. Honey made Yayo some food, and the two sat and ate while Honey asked Yayo a lot of questions.

"So, Yaton, are you going to be staying here, or what? What's going on, and what are your plans?"

"I'm going to be staying with Shakira, and I'm going to try and get a job," Yayo lied.

"I hope so, Yaton, because I don't want you out here running these streets and getting into all kinds of trouble. Your mother is trying to get her own place, and she don't need to be worrying about you."

The mention of his mother needing to find a place made Yayo even more determined to get his money up.

"Don't worry, granny. I'm all good, and I'ma help momma get a crib," Yayo said and headed toward the kitchen to use the house phone to call TJ.

"Who dis?" TJ asked after he picked up on the third ring.

"What up, nigga? This is Yayo. What's the bizness, bro?"

"Yayo! What's up, bro? I was wondering when you was gon' hit my line. Where you at?"

"I'm at my granny's house. Where you want to meet?" Yayo said.

"Shit, meet me on 53rd. You know where the house at," TJ told him.

"Aiight, I'm on my way," Yayo said and hung up the phone.

When Yayo got to TJ's crib, he pulled up and saw TJ on the porch, smoking a blunt. TJ met Yayo on the sidewalk and the two gave each other an embrace.

"Damn, nigga, you got big as hell!" TJ said, playfully throwing a two-piece combo at Yayo's stomach.

"Been hitting them weights. You gotta keep your body up to par. Gotta stay ready so you won't have to get ready, ya feel me?" Yayo said, dropping a jewel on his homie.

"I feel you, my nigga. Come on inside. I gotta holla at you."

When they got inside the house, Yayo was tripping because the inside of Joyce's house looked exactly how it looked the night Yayo left to meet Jug-head at the Grant Mall.

"Where's Joyce at, fam?" Yayo asked TJ.

"She's at work. She got a new job at the Jewel grocery store.

YAYO

She works nights," TJ said and passed Yayo half of an ounce of blueberry kush. Yayo and TJ sat at the kitchen table, rolling up the $250 bag of weed.

"Man, listen, Yayo," TJ started, "There's a lot of shit going on in these streets. It's murkin' season. Them ATG niggas on 71st are clapping shit in Englewood. They got a nigga named Fatboy calling it for them, and he be on some savage shit, trying to extort niggas and shit."

Yayo fired up a blunt and took in everything TJ was saying. "So what's up on Wolcott? I see a lot of niggas on the block getting money, and I don't know none of them," Yayo said and blew out a thick cloud of smoke.

"Them a bunch of young niggas. They freelancing over there. Ain't no structure or no old heads to guide them, so they just doing them. It's every man for themselves," TJ said and grabbed the blunt from Yayo.

"What about Jug-head? What he been on?" Yayo asked.

"The nigga got work in the hood, and he overtaxing niggas for the coke. He charging 30 a brick for some banged-up coke," TJ said.

"Where he be kicking it at, fam?" Yayo asked.

"Dude, he be everywhere. He just don't be in the hood like that no more. He be clubbing though. Nigga always at the new club, 50 Yard Line, trying to stunt."

"Man, fuck that nigga. He a rat. He don't deserve to breathe the same air as me," Yayo said and pulled his 17-shot 9mm off his waist and put it on the kitchen table.

"Listen, TJ, this nigga Jug-head violated a universal street law. I used to look up to this lame. He was my mentor, and a father figure to me. I went on a move for him, and he set me up and got me sent to prison for 7 years. I can't let that ride," Yayo stated.

"So, what you on, bro? I'm with whatever you on, bro. All you got to do is give the word."

"That's all I need to hear," Yayo said and gave TJ a pound.

TJ got up from the table and walked to the basement. When he returned, he had a black Nike duffle bag.

"I know you got a strap already, but I was saving this for you.

Pudge had me hold it, and I never got a chance to give it back," TJ said and unzipped the bag, pulling out an all-black, 32-shot Mac 11, and passed it to Yayo.

Yayo grabbed the light submachine gun, admiring the Austrian-made firearm before placing the clip in and cocking the side. A feeling came over him, the same feeling he had when him and Pudge found the .25 automatic in the alley when he was only 13 years old: the feeling of power. Yayo put the gun on the table and took a long pull from the kush blunt and exhaled.

"TJ, we about to come up, and we gon' do it like this." Yayo proceeded to tell TJ his plans of how he was going to take over the grimy South Side streets of Chicago. The streets were about to crown a new king.

Chapter 10

Jug-head had just left an important meeting with his Italian plug, Ricardo, and was in a good mood. Ricardo had dropped the price on the kilos he was copping every month. At first, he was getting the birds for $25,000 a piece, after proving to Ricardo that he was a monster at the game, by offing 100 keys a month. Now Jug-head was getting the rawest form of cocaine for $10,000 a brick.

Jug-head glided his all-white Bentley Continental through the rush hour traffic on his way to Ford City Mall to cop a few outfits. It was Friday night, and he felt like flossing.

Life had been good to him, and he had gained so much. Jug-head also had a few enemies. The ATG clique was on his bumper, and had made a few attempts on his life. Pudge's clique of goons was also on some bullshit with him because he had ratted on Yayo.

The money Jug-head was getting kept him invincible, and allowed him to relocate to the suburbs of Chicago. Jug-head had gotten all of his vehicles bulletproofed, kept a vest on his chest, and moved through the city with caution.

It was 6:00 when he got home from his small shopping spree. He pulled the Bentley into the spacious four-car garage next to his Hummer H2. When he went inside the small mansion, he was greeted by his pitbull, Dollar. After making himself a Remy and coke, Jug-head sat at his table, emptied about a quarter ounce of cocaine, and took a big hit from the small pile. He felt the effects from the drug almost instantly and had a good drain.

The sound of Jay-Z's "Streets Is Watching" ringtone blasting through his Android brought him out of his trance. "What up? Who dis?" Jug-head said, not noticing the number on the caller ID.

"This Monk, nigga. What you on, killa?" Monk was one of Jug-head's workers who sold crack for him on 69th and Wolcott.

"Man, I ain't on shit. I'm about to get dressed and probably hit the club. A nigga need some companionship, you feel me?"

"Yea, big homie, I feel you. But check, I got that lil' bread for you. I'm trying to get it right," Monk told him.

"I gotchu when I come back outside. I'ma hit your phone when

I come south."

"Aight, G. I'm out here," Monk said and they ended the conversation.

After Jug-head got out the shower, he got dressed. He was going to kill the game. He was dressed to the tee in a silk, jet black Davoucci button-up with platinum cuff links. His wore black Mauri jeans with black Mauri gators to match. To set the outfit off, he threw on his 32-inch platinum Cuban Link chain and his platinum Breitling watch, and was out the door.

It was 11:00 when he got to the 50 Yard Line club. It was packed to capacity with every crook, hustler, dope boy, and gold-digging woman the city had to offer.

Jug-head walked to the crowded bar and ordered a double shot of 1800 tequila and a Corona. He was paying for his drinks when somebody tapped him on his shoulder. When he turned around, he was greeted by a beautiful redbone. Her one-piece Baby Phat dress hugged her curvaceous body. The gloss from her MAC lipstick made her lips look so inviting. The Jimmy Choo 6-inch pumps with the matching Jimmy Choo handbag showed she had a knack for fashion. "She is definitely a bad bitch," he thought to himself.

"Excuse me, I'm trying to order a drink. It's so crowded in this place. A girl can't even get to the bar," she said to Jug-head.

"Lil' mama, you can have the world if you let me buy you a drink. My name's Jug-head, but you can call me Head. What's your name, sweetheart?"

"My name's Trish. It's nice to meet you, Head, and if I was you, I wouldn't promise things you can't give," Trish said with a slight smile. Trish was definitely turned on by the baller in front of her. Jug-head's jewelry glowed in the dimly lit club. Trish knew Jug-head had money, and a lot of money at that.

"Baby, I don't promise things I can't deliver," he said as he downed his shot of tequila.

"Well, Mr. Baller, for starters, can I have a long island iced tea?" Trish asked and took a seat at the crowded bar.

Jug-head and Trish sat at the bar for about an hour getting to know each other. He found out that Trish had no kids at 22 years old, was in college, and single. Both of them were feeling the effects of the alcohol. He knew if he played his cards right, he would be between Trish's warm, thick thighs at the end of the night.

"Do you smoke, lil' momma?" Jug-head asked.

"Smoke what?"

"Weed, shorty, that kush!"

"Not really. Why, you got some?" Trish asked.

"Yeah, let's get up out of here and go blow," he said and led her outside to his pearly white Hummer H2. Trish let her body sink into the plush, peanut-butter leather seats, as she marveled the interior of the roomy vehicle.

"Damn, boy, I see you riding good out here," Trish said, giving him his props for the whip with the 26-inch Giovannis. He rolled a fat blunt of the kush, lit it, and passed it to her. Jug-head let his eyes scan Trish's toned thighs.

"Lil' mama, it's hard to believe you ain't got no man. Any real nigga would be truly blessed to have someone like you by their side," he said and put his hand on Trish's warm thigh.

"There's a lot of boys out here. I need a grown man to tame me. I need a nigga with some stamina." She grabbed Jug-head's hand and put it between her legs. His dick was hard as he used his index finger to slide her thong to the side, all while putting his middle finger inside of Trish's warm pussy. Trish slipped off her heels and planted one of her legs on the dashboard, giving Jug-head full access. He then raised her dress and pulled her thong completely off. Trish was in a daze from the kush already and now Jug-head was sucking on her pussy lips.

"Damn, girl. You taste so good," he moaned.

Trish grabbed his bald head and arched her back, letting him have his way with her. "Oooh, shit, Head. Eat this pussy, nigga," Trish said in a whisper.

Jug-head got up and unfastened his belt and pulled his pants down, exposing his long, thick shaft. Trish stared at the black anaconda before she grabbed it with both hands and massaged it with slow strokes. Jug-head was about to bust. Trish leaned over and took the head of his dick into her warm mouth.

"Ahh, shit, girl. Suck this mothafucker," he said as Trish used her tongue to lick the sides of his monster, making him go crazy. "Karinne Steffans ain't got shit on her," he thought to himself as Trish took all of him into her mouth while looking directly into his eyes.

"If this was the type of shit the drug game brought, then I'ma die in it," he thought to himself. Trish knew she had him with her head game.

"Baby, I'm not really the type to be fucking in a whip. Why don't you take me somewhere so I can show you how I get down for mine?" Trish said, planting a kiss on his lips.

"Don't trip, ma. We can go to my crib. Roll this up," he said and passed Trish a quarter ounce of weed and a cigarillo.

Jug-head had just struck gold. He knew he was going to fuck Trish the moment he saw her. "That's the thing about being a boss. Bosses do what they want, and boys do what they can," he thought to himself as he pulled the Hummer H2 into traffic. He was on cloud 9 from the kush, and the head.

***

Yayo, TJ, and Monk sat across the street from 50 Yard Line, parked in a Buick Lacrosse, watching the pearl white Hummer. Yayo had found out everything he knew about Jug-head from Monk. Monk was a loyal soldier to Pudge's squad. After Pudge got killed, Monk started working for Jug-head. Monk wasn't happy with his current situation because Jug-head was overtaxing him.

Yayo had seen Monk on the block, and Monk had remembered Yayo from back in the day. Monk had heard stories about Yayo. At a young age, Yayo was already a street legend in the hood. When he saw Yayo on Honey's porch, he recognized him and jumped right in line with him. The information Monk gave to Yayo made his plan that much easier. Monk had told Yayo that Jug-head would be going to the club. It was time for Yayo to execute his plot.

When the Hummer pulled off in traffic, TJ started the Buick and slid right in traffic with the Hummer. Jug-head wanted to stunt so hard, he didn't want to take Trish to a hotel. He wanted her to see his lavish estate, though it was not something he'd normally do. Tonight, he threw caution to the wind.

It was 4:30 in the morning when they got to his house. Trish had fallen asleep due to the effects of the bomb ass weed.

"Wake up, lil' mama. We here," Jug-head said.

He led Trish into his immaculate home and straight to the master bedroom. Trish took off her Jimmy Choo pumps and slid on the king-sized bed with heightened seductiveness.

"Shorty, you want something to drink?" Jug-head asked.

"Yeah, some orange juice would do, thank you," Trish said, giving him a seductive smile.

Jug-head went downstairs to get Trish some juice. When Trish saw Jug-head go downstairs, she grabbed her handbag, pulled out her Blackberry phone, and sent a text.

Yayo was sitting in the back of the Lacrosse when his phone vibrated.

Yayo read the text: "He's the only one here. We're upstairs in the bedroom. Please hurry up!"

"Let's get this shit over with, y'all. Everybody knows their job. Let's get this paper," Yayo said, and all three men pulled down their black ski masks, cocked their hammers, and stepped out into the darkness.

When Jug-head came back to the bedroom, Trish was laying on the bed with only her thong and bra on.

"Damn, baby, what took you so long? I was starting to get lonely," Trish said as she slid two fingers in her pussy.

Jug-head sat the glass of orange juice on the dresser. Like magic, he got out of his clothes, climbed on the bed, and started kissing on her neck. He unsnapped her bra, freeing her big titties, and took one of her long, brown nipples into his mouth and sucked on it.

"Ahh, boo, that feels so good," Trish moaned as she reached down and grabbed Jug-head's dick. "Boo, you got a condom?" Trish asked.

Jug-head got up, walked to the dresser to retrieve a Magnum

XL Gold condom, and slid it on his shaft.

"Shorty, bend that thang over and let me hit it from the back." She obeyed. With long deep strokes, he pounded Trish like he was trying to make a baby with her.

"Fuck me, daddy. Fuck me! Ooh, shit! This dick so good. Damn, baby!" Trish moaned as Jug-head pounded her.

Jug-head plowed into Trish for 10 minutes before they both climaxed at the same time.

***

Yayo, TJ, and Monk crept through the darkness, finding a basement window in the back of the mini mansion, and busted the window with a piece of a spark plug, shattering the glass. TJ pushed the glass in and they climbed through the window like professional cat burglars.

***

Jug-head was laying on the bed, flicking the remote to his 60-inch Sony, trying to find something to watch. Trish was in the bathroom when Yayo and his crew entered the room, pointing their automatic weapons at him.

"You make a move, I'ma put something on your mind, nigga," Yayo said through clenched teeth.

"Aye, man. You can have all that shit, player. It's in the safe in the closet." Jug-head didn't buck. He didn't want to force their hands.

Yayo couldn't believe how scared this nigga was. Yayo grabbed Jug-head by the neck and walked him to the closet to open the safe.

"What up, fam? Just take this shit and go!" Jug-head said urgently.

Yayo slapped Jug-head in the back of the head with the Mac 11, causing blood to gush out of his head. "Shut your pussy ass up, nigga, and open the safe!"

YAYO

Jug-head proceeded to enter the combination to the safe with blood covering his face. On the second try, the safe came open.

"Aye, my nigga, come get this shit." Yayo commanded one of his henchman, then turned to Jug-head. "Get your rat ass up against the wall, faggot."

Jug-head got up off the floor and stood against the wall, scared out of his mind. Yayo looked at him, searching his eyes for answers while pointing the Mac at him.

"Nigga, I looked at you like a father figure. You were my role model, nigga. You put me on and taught me the game," Yayo said as he pulled off his ski mask.

Jug-head couldn't believe his eyes. In front of him was his protégé, his young goon, young Yayo.

"Man, shorty, listen. They was trying to send me to the joint for like 70 years. I didn't think they were going to give you that much time. Yayo, please, shorty. I can make it up to you. There's like 250 in the safe, and I got 10 keys of heroin in the basement behind the washing machine in the corner. You can have it all. Just let me have my life, shorty," Jug-head pleaded.

"Shakira, come here, shorty!" Yayo yelled.

On cue, Shakira came out of the bathroom fully dressed and stood beside Yayo.

"Bitch, you set me up! I'ma kill yo' ass, bitch!" Jug-head screamed. He couldn't believe he slipped and fell all over a bitch.

"Baby, go to the car. I'll be there in a minute," Yayo said and slapped Shakira on the butt. He turned to Jug-head and gave him the dirtiest look.

"Nigga, you violated number 1 of street law, silence and secrecy," Yayo said before he pulled the trigger five times, hitting Jug-head three times in the face, and two times in the neck. Jug-head's blood plastered the wall. After looking at the carnage of his prey, Yayo stood over Jug-head's body and styled on his opponent by emptying the clip to the submachine gun. TJ and Monk also sprayed bullets from their guns for good measure. In total, Jug-head's body received 44 bullet holes.

"You got the bread, my nigga?" Yayo asked TJ.

"Yeah. Let's get the fuck up out of here," TJ responded, holding two duffle bags full of cash.

The three men went downstairs to retrieve the heroin. Yayo went straight to the washing machine in the corner of the basement, moved it, and instantly noticed the bricks wrapped in black plastic.

"Man, let's load this shit up." TJ took two trips to load the drugs into the trunk of the Buick. While Yayo and Monk were in the basement grabbing the last of the 10 bricks, Yayo pulled a 9 millimeter from his waist and shot Monk twice in the head.

"Good looking for being loyal to Pudge, but I don't trust no traitors." He shot him once more in his neck.

When Yayo got back to the car, he jumped in the passenger seat with Shakira at the wheel and TJ in the back.

"Let's get the fuck up outta here!"

Shakira put the car in drive and slowly pulled off.

"Where the fuck Monk at, Yayo?" TJ asked from the backseat.

Yayo turned around and gave him a look that answered his question. TJ just nodded his understanding.

***

Later that same day, Yayo, Shakira, and TJ were laying low in a hotel room off of 81st and Unicess. They had burned the Buick and got rid of the weapons they used. Yayo and TJ were sitting on the floor, counting the dough.

"Y'all, what we gon do? I'm scared," Shakira said as she thought about the events of the previous night. She couldn't believe she was involved in a robbery and double homicide. Seeing all of the drugs and money in front of her made it all a reality.

Yayo got up from the pile of 100s, 50s, and 20s he was counting, walked to the end of the bed where Shakira was sitting, and placed a gentle kiss on her lips.

"Baby, everything gon' be all good. We gon' be straight from now on. Fuck that nigga, Head. He's where all rats and snitches should be, and fuck his mans too."

He turned to TJ. "Aye, TJ, check it out, fam. Ain't no turning back from this shit. We all the way in. You like a brother to me, and I always respected your gangsta. It's me and you, and that's on everything I love."

TJ stood up and embraced Yayo. "My nigga, it's whatever. I always got your back, Yayo. It's to the grave with me, G, and that's on everything, nigga."

Last night, TJ had proven himself by firing his weapon into Jughead's body. This let Yayo know that his enemies were also TJ's enemies. The brotherhood had been bonded by blood.

S. Allen

Chapter 11

It had been a year since Yayo had murdered and robbed Jug-head. He split the money he got from the robbery with TJ. Yayo got his mom a nice condo on the North Side of Chicago in the Rogers Park area. He also had her driving a nice Camaro. When Yayo tried to move his grandma from the hood, she refused. She knew Yayo's new fortune came from the streets, and wanted nothing to do with it.

Yayo and Shakira got a house in North Chicago. Yayo had a few other furnished apartments throughout Chicago for various reasons, but most importantly, he felt it would be safer to keep Shakira out of the inner city due to his countless enemies and all the haters trying to take a piece of his pie.

Within a year, Yayo had taken over the heroin trade on the South Side of Chicago. He was now the head of a crew called Get it Boy Clique (GBC), and TJ was his second in command. The two led the South Side with the closest thing to pure heroin. Yayo had a Belizean plug in Rockford, Illinois, who was giving them grams at a very low price.

Yayo had his whole hood eating. Anyone who was a part of GBC was getting money. Yayo set the bar on 69th and Wolcott all the way to the wild, wild 100s. He was a certified trap star with a squad of head-bustas following him to success. Some even named him the mayor of the dope game.

A lot of niggas were gunning for Yayo's throne. Even though the GBC had sent countless ATG gang members to Gatling's funeral home in the last year, the ATG was still a force to be reckoned with. Yayo and Fatboy, the leader of the ATG clique, had exchanged gunfire a few times.

One time, Yayo was coming out of J-Bees on the low-end. Fatboy was driving down State Street with one of his men, Payday, when he noticed Yayo coming out of the store. Fatboy made a U-turn in the middle of the street, and stuck a Glock 45 out the window and fired. Yayo ducked for cover and retrieved his FN 5.7 millimeter and opened up on Fatboy's black-on-black Denali. He pulled off as Yayo emptied his clip at the SUV. Payday died at Cook County Hospital 8 hours later.

The war between the ATGs and GBC had been a bloodbath the whole year, claiming 14 lives.

Yayo was driving down Halsted when his iPhone went off. "What up, mami?" Yayo said to Shakira.

"Nothing, boo, just calling to see what you was on. I'm just leaving Gurnee Mills, wondering if you were coming to the crib tonight."

"Yeah, I'm coming home, but it's gon' be a lil' late. I got some things I gotta take care of," Yayo said as he made a right on 83rd Street.

"Okay, baby. Be careful out there, and bring some kush home. I ain't smoked all day."

"Aight, boo, hit me up a lil' later. I got you," he said before they hung up.

***

Shakira walked out of the Gurnee Mills Mall and got inside of her new Audi A6 Yayo had gotten her a few weeks ago. Shakira had everything a woman could ask for. She lived in a four-bedroom, immaculate home, and had a closet full of the latest designs, like Deréon, Dolce & Gabbana, Gucci, Prada, Jimmy Choo, Fendi, and Coogi. Her home was furnished to her design.

After the robbery, Shakira had often seen Jug-head's face in her dreams, but after a few trips to the Bahamas, the nightmares disappeared. Not to mention Shakira was fucking one of the most feared young niggas in the Chi.

Yayo had transformed Shakira from an ordinary hood chick to a full-grown gangsta bitch.

Shakira and Yayo were Chicago's Bonnie and Clyde, and the love and trust they had for each other reigned supreme over all. Shakira knew Yayo had a few side bitches, but she didn't trip because she knew she had his heart, and she carried his seed. Yayo provided for her like a real nigga, and she was happy with her situation.

Shakira was on her way home when her Blackberry rang.

"Hey, mama. What's up?" Shakira said.

"Nothing, girl. Where you at?"

"On my way home from the mall getting this Coogi dress I had seen online. Why, what's up?"

"You heard from TJ today? I been calling his lil' butt, and he's not returning my calls," Joyce said.

"You know how that boy is, mama. He don't never answer his phone unless he want to. I'm sure he will call you later on, mama."

"Alright, tell him I was trying to find out if he was coming by the house tonight because Ricky is supposed to be coming over here for dinner, and I don't want him coming by blowing my spot up."

Shakira laughed. "Mama, you trying to get ya freak on, huh? If I talk to him before you do, I will let him know you got company tonight."

"Thank you, baby," Joyce said and hung up.

In the last year, Joyce had been doing well. Yayo and TJ got Joyce into rehab, so smoking crack was a thing of the past. The only thing she might do was have a casual drink every now and then. TJ had moved Joyce off of 53rd into a nice house on 115th and Normal, where he often stayed. Like Yayo, TJ had a few cribs in Chicago that he used for various reasons, like stashing money, drugs, and guns, and fucking bitches.

Joyce had maintained a manager position at the Jewel-Osco grocery store, which is where she met her new boyfriend, Ricky, who she was starting to fall madly in love with after only knowing him for three months, and for that reason, TJ was always throwing salt in her game.

When Shakira walked in the house, she put her bags up in the closet and started to run herself a hot bath. She put in her bubble bath and beads from Bath and Body Works, lighted a few scented candles around the spacious jacuzzi, and went to the refrigerator to retrieve her cold bottle of Bartenura moscato before returning back to the jacuzzi. Shakira slid out of her tight Deréon jeans and matching Deréon button-up shirt.

After getting naked, she sunk into the heat of the jacuzzi, letting the jet streams work her body. Shakira had drunk half the bottle and was starting to feel a little horny from the effects. She grabbed her Blackberry and dialed Yayo's number. Yayo's phone rang 4 times before the automatic voicemail came up. She hung up without leaving a message.

Shakira placed two of her fingers inside of her warmth, and proceeded to finger herself while she envisioned Yayo's tongue inside of her. After Shakira climaxed for the 2nd time, she was disturbed by her phone ringing.

"Hello?"

"What up, bitch?" Candy asked, crunk as hell.

"Girl, what up? What you on?"

"Shit, trying to see if you were coming outside tonight."

"Nah, girl. I'm in the crib. My man coming home tonight. I'm trying to get my back broken in," Shakira stated.

"Girl, let me find out Yayo got that ass on lock," Candy said with a tad bit of jealousy.

"What you on tonight, stupid?" Shakira asked Candy.

"Shit, me and Cash finna go downtown and have a few drinks."

"You still fuck with that goofy ass nigga?"

"Girl, this goofy ass nigga paying a bitch's rent and licking this pussy good!"

"I heard that. Well hit me up later, bitch."

"Aight, holla." They both hung up.

Shakira tried to call Yayo's phone once more, but came up with the same result. Shakira laid her head back and finished the bottle of moscato.

***

It was 9:30 at night when Yayo pulled up to the Rothschild liquor store to meet up with TJ. Yayo saw TJ's Range Rover as soon as he pulled into the parking lot. TJ jumped out of the Range Rover, dressed in an all-white Coogi hookup, and his long dreads fell loosely on his shoulders. The bulge on his waist was visible, letting niggas know he had that cannon on him. After the episode with Pudge, they weren't taking any chances on the streets.

Yayo jumped out of his whip and gave his comrade some dap before they walked in the store. "What up, nigga? What's the bizness, Joe?"

"You know what it is, Yayo. Getting money, and putting ho niggas in the dirt," TJ said in a serious tone. TJ was the enforcer for the gang. TJ had a love for violence ever since he had popped slugs in Jug-head's body a year ago. TJ was also public enemy number 1 to the ATG clique, and a lot of other hating niggas in the Chi. Yayo was proud of TJ, and he was the only one he trusted in the streets.

Yayo and TJ bought a bottle of Patron and a bottle of Rosé Black and were heading out of the store. On the way out, two women were coming in.

"Damn, shorty, can I go with y'all?" TJ said to one of the women, who resembled a younger version of Angela Bassett.

"Depends, baby. What's your name, sexy?" The Angela Bassett look-a-like said.

"My name's TJ, and this is my right-hand man, Yayo," TJ said, smiling and showing the white gold with VVS diamonds in his grill.

"Well, my name is Yolanda, and this is my right-hand girl, Katrina."

Yayo stood holding the bottle of Rosé Black, admiring Katrina. She was 5'4'', 120 pounds, redbone, and thick as hell. She was almost a spitting image of the porn star, Pinky, but with blond hair. All of them exchanged numbers and made plans to get up with each other soon.

"Ay, fam, follow me. I'ma park my shit and jump in the Range with you," Yayo said to TJ before getting in his Benz.

Yayo parked his whip in the hood in front of his grandma's house, and jumped in the Range Rover with TJ.

There were at least 10 young niggas on the corner posted up, selling dope, smoking weed, and clutching their hammers, watching every car coming up and down Wolcott, praying somebody comes through on some dumb shit so they could put on for their hood. TJ bended the corner of Wolcott and slowly rolled down the street. All the niggas on the corner threw up their gang signs, saluting the bosses and showing their alliance.

"Aye, Butterball! Check it out, G!" TJ yelled into the crowd. When Butterball came to the Range, TJ told him to get in the truck. Butterball got in, shook hands with Yayo and TJ, and TJ pulled away from the block.

"Damn, big homie. I was wondering when you was gon' slide through," Butterball said before handing TJ five stacks wrapped in two thick, red rubber bands.

"That's the whole thing, shorty?" TJ asked as he took a sip from the Patron bottle.

"Yeah, G, that's the whole 5." TJ went in his stash and came out with two ounces of based heroin, and passed it back to Butterball. Butterball put the drugs in his Pelle Pelle hoodie.

Yayo lit a blunt of kush and passed it to Butterball. "Aye, shorty, y'all holding the hood down or what?" Yayo asked, blowing out a thick cloud of smoke.

"Yeah, Yayo. Them ATG niggas slid through here earlier pump-faking and shit. They seen them hammers and kept it moving," Butterball said, inhaling the smoke from the kush.

Yayo turned around, looking Butterball in the face with bloodshot eyes. "Next time, instead of showing them hammers, let 'em go, nigga. It's on sight with them niggas," Yayo said, grabbing the bottle of Patron from TJ.

TJ went back to Wolcott and let Butterball out. Butterball was a young nigga TJ had put on a few months back. He was a straight hustler, and always made sure TJ's money was on point. Yayo and TJ had a lot of work in the city, but 69th and Wolcott was considered headquarters to the organization, so they had a lot of little niggas pumping work for them.

Yayo and TJ made a few more drop-offs, and after a bottle of Patron, a bottle of Rosé Black, and three blunts of kush, TJ dropped Yayo back off at his whip. TJ made his way west, and Yayo made his way to his wifey to relieve some pent up sexual tension.

Chapter 12

It had been a good year for Karen. Yayo had put her in a nice little condo on the North Side. She had a car, and was attending cosmetology classes at Malcolm X College.

Her and Darrell had separated for the time being, but they remained together to be parents to Devon and Quavon, who resided with their dad, but would come to Karen's house every weekend to spend time with her and Yayo.

Karen didn't have to work because Yayo made sure the mortgage and car notes were paid every month, along with any other bills she had. The plan was for Karen to get her beautician license, and Yayo would buy her a beauty salon.

Karen knew her son was involved in some type of criminal activities in the streets, but she never got in his business or asked questions. In reality, Karen was so proud of her son because he had been through so much in his young life, and now, he was on top.

Brenda, Karen's younger sister, was always up on the latest street gossip and was always telling her things that she had heard about Yayo. Yayo got into it with these dudes, Yayo was shooting, Yayo got this and that girl pregnant, etc. Karen knew a lot of niggas didn't like her son, but his family loved him to death.

Devon and Quavon couldn't wait to come over on weekends so they could spend time with their big brother. Yayo kept them with the freshest clothes. They had the new Jordans every time they came out, and sometimes before they came out. They had all the newest video games from Xbox One to PS4, and he kept the twins with money in their pocket. Karen saw how Yayo brought the family together. He would go to Moo & Oink and buy all kinds of ribs, chicken wings, hamburgers, and hot dogs, and invite the whole family over for cookouts.

Karen sat back in her comfortable sectional sofa, thinking about last week when Yayo and Shakira took her out for Shakira's 24th birthday. Yayo and Shakira were dressed to the tee in matching all-white Gucci outfits. Yayo was rocking Gucci like he was the co-owner. His long, French braids hung past his shoulders. The jewelry that hung from his neck captivated every onlooker as the diamonds came to life when the light shined off of them. Shakira was doing her thing with her one-piece Gucci dress, 6-inch Gucci pumps, and matching handbag. Her diamond earrings complimented her flawless skin. The pair was definitely meant to be king and queen.

Karen had gotten tipsy at Club Q as her son ordered shot after shot of Remy XO. She was a light social drinker, so it didn't take much to get her buzzed. Inside the club, Karen noticed how many young dudes walked up and shook Yayo's hand, and they all came with smiles. That's when she knew her son was somebody in the streets of Chicago, a violent city that claimed the lives of so many young men like Yayo. For that reason, every night, she prayed to God to keep her baby safe.

On the way home from Club Q, Karen was in the backseat of Yayo's Benz, happy and drunk.

"Boy, you think you're the shit, don't you?" Karen said in a slur, playfully pushing Yayo in the back of his head as Yayo sat in the passenger's side, rolling up a blunt of kush.

"Momma, chill out. You gon' mess up my braids," Yayo said with a smile.

"Boy, you look like ya damn daddy when you smile like that. I know he's looking down on you, proud as hell, because I know I am," Karen said, planting a drunk sloppy kiss on the side of her son's cheek.

"I love you, too, momma. Do you mind if I fire this weed up?" Yayo asked.

"Boy, this your car, and you're grown. I'm just the passenger," Karen said, laughing.

Yayo fired up the blunt and inhaled when he heard his mama from the back seat.

"Son, let me hit that."

"Momma, you don't smoke," Yayo said giving his mama a confused look.

"Boy, what the hell did I just say? I'm your momma, so do what I tell you."

Yayo passed Karen the blunt. When Karen inhaled the powerful cannabis, she immediately started choking. "Shit, boy, take this!" She said between coughing and passed Yayo the weed.

Yayo and Shakira started cracking up as she continued to cough. It was good times like this that Karen cherished. No matter what had transpired in the past, she welcomed their future.

***

Karen and Yayo had gotten so close over the years. Yayo was her son and her best friend, and it made her so proud to see him rise above all the adversity and mistreatment in his life and still prevail. Yayo was Karen's little soldier, and she was riding with him, good or bad. She always told Yayo, "Whatever you do in life, be your best."

Karen's reminiscing was interrupted by her doorbell ringing. When she looked out the blinds, she saw Shakira's Audi shining in the driveway.

"Hey, lil' mama," Karen said as she let Shakira in.

"Hey, mama. I was just in the neighborhood, and I wanted to come check in on you."

"Oh, girl, that's sweet, Shakira. What's that you got on?"

Shakira turned around to model her new Chanel dress she got a few days ago. "You like it, mama? Yayo got it for me. I had been bugging him for a week, and he finally gave me the money to get it," Shakira said as she put a bottle of moscato in the fridge.

"Girl, that boy know he be spoiling you. And what'd you just put in the fridge? I know you ain't coming over here to get me drunk. I got two clients coming over tonight," Karen said with her hands on her hips. Karen would do hair on the weekends to keep some extra cash in her pockets.

"Mama, I'm just gonna chill over here tonight. Yayo and I had some words last night, and I don't feel like being at home tonight."

"What y'all get into it for?" Karen asked, grabbing two champagne glasses from the cabinet.

"I told him I wanted him to get out of them streets. There's too much stuff going on out there. Every time I turn on the news, somebody got shot, and I'm always worrying about him and TJ. I don't want to get that call, momma. You feel me?"

Karen joined Shakira at the living room table with two champagne glasses of ice and the bottle of moscato.

"Baby, I understand fully how you feel. I worry about Yayo, and TJ also, and I pray every night for their safety. I don't want to lose my son, but like I tell Yayo all the time, he knows the consequences for what he's out here doing, and he gon' have to be the one to deal with them," Karen said as she poured her and Shakira a glass of moscato. Shakira took a sip.

"I know, momma, but when I tell him to slow down, he always gets mad, saying he gon' die in his hood and all that crazy shit. And when he starts talking like that, it scares me, momma. And when he's not at home, which is more and more, he don't even be answering the phone, and it will take a minute before he even call me back. I can't stand it when he does that!" Shakira said with a lot of attitude.

"Shakira, listen, baby. I was with my husband for almost 20 years, and I went through so much with him. I was mistreated and abused, mentally and physically, but I stayed because I figured he would change for the better. I can't say I loved him like that, because love does not hurt mentally or physically. I was unable to leave because I didn't have a leg to stand on. So what I am saying is if you are not happy with your man, don't let 20 years go past. Yayo's my boy, but he is hard-headed, and has his mind made up to continue doing whatever he is out there doing. If you feel like you don't want to put up with it, then don't. Put a lock on that pussy for a few weeks, and see how he acts then," Karen said as she downed her glass of wine, then poured another.

"Momma, you is so crazy."

"I hear that, girl. Do what you gotta do to tame your man," Karen said, dropping jewels on young Shakira.

The two sat up talking and drinking like two old friends. Karen's clients never came through, so they had a girls' night. They talked about everything. Karen was glad she came by.

It was getting late. Shakira knew Karen had to get up early for work, so she stood up and gave her a hug, "Thanks for your counsel tonight. I needed that."

"You're welcome, honey. Drive safe."

Karen walked her to the door and let her out. After Shakira left, their conversation remained on Karen's mind.

Before she went to bed, she got down on her knees. "God, I know my son is not an angel, but I ask you to step into his life. I ask you to rebuke the devil from him and show him the path to righteousness. God, I ask you to keep my son safe. God, please watch over Yaton. Amen."

S. Allen

Chapter 13

Yayo was on his way home from Rockford after meeting with his Belizean plug, Buddy. He had 10 keys of uncut heroin in his stash box. Yayo and Buddy had met in a club in Joliet. Buddy had been in the United States for the last 10 years getting major money, while on the run for a triple homicide in Belize. At 26 years old, Buddy flooded Rockford, Beloit, Wisconsin, Milwaukee, and Chicago with good dope. He had several lavish estates; one in Peoria, Illinois, and another in Champagne, and a mansion in Atlanta.

Yayo proved to be one of his best customers due to his consistency and ability to get money. For that reason, Yayo was getting the bricks for 40k, when Buddy could've easily charged 50-60k.

Yayo was in midday traffic in a rented Dodge Charger when he grabbed his cell phone and called TJ.

"What up, my nigga?" TJ answered on the third ring.

"Aye, Joe, meet me at the spot in 45. Let's take care of business," Yayo said before ending the call.

On every first of the month, Yayo would get the work, and him and TJ would meet up at the spot on 95th and Yates to cut and bag the heroin for distribution. Because of the purity of the heroin, they were able to turn 10 bricks into 20 with ease.

Yayo and TJ were smart with the dope game. They didn't sell their heroin in weight. To increase their profits, they bagged it all up in dime bags, made G-packs, and issued them out to their workers.

All of Yayo's drug areas were set up with structure, lookouts, pitchers, and pack runners. Everybody got paid, and that's why the streets loved him. He wasn't greedy, so everybody had a fair shake to get some money.

On the other hand, he had a zero tolerance for the bullshit. Evading on his turf or running off with money would be a sure visit to Burr Oaks Cemetery, with TJ being the deliverer. When a nigga crossed GBC, and TJ was around, he knew it was over, and there wasn't anything that could be said or done to save him. GBC's infrastructure was based on the paper from the heroin trade, and Yayo and TJ left no room for shortages.

It was 11 in the morning. As he slid the Charger through the midday traffic, Yayo's cell phone vibrated in his pocket. When he saw it was Shakira calling, he ignored the call.

Him and Shakira had been beefing for the last few weeks, and he couldn't figure out why she had been putting down her press game for him to get up out the streets. He had given her everything she asked for. He put her up in a 250k house with walk-in closets filled with all the latest designer clothes. She drove a luxury vehicle, and he had taken her on numerous trips all over the world. There were plenty of women who would kill to be in her position. That's what had Yayo baffled. He couldn't understand why she was flipping the script, especially since she had helped him get in the game by helping him rob Jug-head.

Yayo wasn't gonna be bothered with Shakira and her mood swings. He had a few bitches in line waiting to step up to the plate, like Katrina. Katrina and Yayo had hooked up a few weeks back and have been fucking around ever since. Katrina was a stripper and worked at Chocolate City, had her own crib, and attended Kennedy King College for Graphic Design. Yayo was definitely feeling that she was a Ms. Independent type.

Yayo picked up his phone and sent her a text message: "Hey Ms. Thang. I'll be sliding through there tonight to do what we do."

She texted back: "It's all good. I'll be waiting."

Yayo got back in grind mode as he got off the Dan Ryan, exiting on 95th Street. He pulled up on the block, and parked his car behind TJ's old school Cutlass. It had been a safe and profitable trip, but he still hated playing the highway. He figured he would save himself the hassle and grab his own work, and at the same time, show his connect that his hustle was impeccable.

It was 12:45 p.m., and TJ was on the porch waiting for Yayo.

"What up, Joe? I see you running late," TJ said, giving Yayo some dap.

"Yeah, my nigga, you already know how the rush hour traffic is. I should've left a lil' earlier, but this nigga Buddy was fake dragging a nigga. You know how he always wanna talk for a few hours and shit," Yayo said. "What the fuck you got under that towel?" He asked, referring to the black towel that was laid across TJ's lap.

"Nigga, this my new toy," TJ said like a kid on Christmas morning, as he pulled back the towel, revealing a Bushmaster .223 assault rifle with a 100-round drum attached to it.

"Nigga, you wild as hell, G. Let's go take care of business," Yayo said as he entered the house.

TJ and Yayo had their routine down to a science. TJ would meet him at the house, on point with a banga, making sure if anything popped off, they were ready. A nigga wasn't taking anything from the GBC, unless they were bullets, and a lot of them.

Once inside the house, they went straight to work, preparing to break down ten of the bricks. Yayo unwrapped the ten birds and placed them in a big towel that had a black plastic bag over it. He tied the towel up, took it to the bathroom, and placed it in the tub. He took a hammer and proceeded to hit the towel, in order to break the bricks down to a smaller form. While Yayo was handling that, TJ was laying out the aluminum foil in small squares all over the table. He then weighed up the cut (milk, sugar, and Sudafed). TJ put the cut in a coffee grinder and mixed it, then poured the contents into a big mixing bowl.

Both men then put on surgical masks and latex gloves, because the heroin was so potent they could easily catch a table high just by touching or inhaling the drug. They had to take extreme precautions. Yayo weighed two ounces at a time and then put it in the coffee grinder, and grinded it until it was all powder.

He then poured the heroin on the table and let TJ put the cut on it. It was 9 p.m. when the two pharmacists finished turning the ten bricks into twenty.

"Aye, my nigga, you still fucking with that bitch, Yolanda?" Yayo asked TJ while folding a dime piece of heroin in aluminum foil.

"Yeah, G, the hoe's baby daddy be on some cockblocking shit. The nigga beat her ass a couple of days ago, but you know I'm a player. Long as he keep that shit with that bitch, it ain't got nothing to do with Ol' T Jeezy," he said, trying to convince Yayo that he was a pure stomp down player.

"What's up with you and her buddy?" TJ inquired. "Y'all been kicking it real tough lately. The lil' bitch always talking about you to Yolanda, like she's wifey or something."

"On my mama, shorty definitely on my bumper. I told her I was gonna slide through later on, but by the looks of it, it ain't gonna happen. We got too much shit to bag up. I'm trying to drop these packs off by the morning. I ain't got no time to be laying up with no hoe. Even though she got that wet wet, you already know my slogan, 'Money over bitches,'" Yayo said, tossing a G-pack to the side.

"Aye, my nigga, you know they got that all-white party coming up in two weeks. They been broadcasting that shit all on WGCI. The bitch Cherokee D'Ass is supposed to be throwing it. You already know every D-boy in the city gonna be in there trying to stunt," TJ said.

"Shit, you trying to go, or are you just talking?" Yayo questioned, knowing TJ was trying to go hard.

"Nigga, I'm trying to go take a look at that shit, and let niggas know GBC runs these streets, and niggas better get their weight up. If niggas disrespect, they getting wet up."

"Fuck it then, we goin'. We gonna do this shit for Pudge. Tell the whole squad we going, and to bring them 6s out. We gon' show the whole city we at the top of the food chain," Yayo said.

They pulled an all-nighter bagging up the drugs. It was 9 a.m. when they stepped out of the house, and they still had 8 more bricks to bag up. They left the house, smelling like piss and penicillin from the heroin. They jumped in their separate cars, threw up their gang's sign, and headed out their separate ways to distribute the packs to their workers.

It was almost 1 p.m. when Yayo finished dropping off all the work, and he was heading to Karen's house for a nap. He was tired as hell, and didn't feel like driving all the way to North Chicago, and he didn't have the energy to argue with Shakira.

He was driving down Ashland when he saw a blue Crown Victoria directly behind him. He couldn't believe his eyes when he saw who was occupying the cruiser.

"What the fuck?" He thought to himself as he saw the crooked ass cops, the same ones who made Jug-head flip on him, Batman and Robin.

Yayo activated his stash box and placed his P89 Ruger inside the compartment, along with the $9,000 he had in his pocket. The Crown Vic's lights flashed and Yayo pulled over.

"What the fuck?" He said aloud.

Batman approached the driver's window as Robin stood with his hand on his weapon.

Yayo rolled down the window and asked, "Is there a problem, officer?"

"Holy shit, Robin, look who the fuck we got here! Yaton's all grown up now, and it looks like he's getting some money out here. Step the fuck out the vehicle, you fucking child killer," Batman said.

Yayo stepped out of the car, and Batman quickly searched him.

"What the fuck y'all stop me for? I ain't doing illegal shit," Yayo said.

Robin opened up the passenger door and began to search the vehicle.

"You know, Yaton, I must admit that I got a lot of respect for you. You took ya time like a man after your boss ratted you out on some sucka shit. You know they found him in his house laid out. You wouldn't happen to know anything about that, would you?" Batman inquired, showing his coffee-stained teeth.

"Nah, man, I don't know shit about that, but it's good for his snitch ass," Yayo said.

"Gangsta, gangsta. Now look, Yaton, I mean, Yayo. Word on the street is that you're getting money. And I mean a lot of money from what I hear. We've been following you all morning, and it looks like you got shit on lock. So I thought to myself, 'Batman, you need to get some of that money,' so I came up with this. Let's say you give me $5,000 a week, and I'll let you get all the money you want. And I'll tell you whenever your block is going to be raided, and I'll inform you of any snitches you might have in your circle. Oh, and I got guns for sale. It will kinda be like a 'you wash my back and I'll wash yours' type of thing."

"The car's clean," Robin said.

Yayo thought about the proposition before speaking. "Why should I trust you, pig?"

"Listen, boy, I'm just trying to eat, and like I said, I respect your G. I know you didn't mean to shoot that lil' girl, but hey, shit happens. I could easily put the feds on your ass or investigate Jughead's murder and tie you to it. I mean, the guy rats on you, and as soon as you get out of prison, he gets murdered. Let me give you a lil' word of advice, shorty. Next time you're in jail, watch who you're talking to," Batman said, and then handed Yayo a card with contact info and directions of where to drop the money off.

"Think about it, and give me a call. Have a nice day," Batman said with a sinister smile on his face. Him and Robin walked back to their cruiser and pulled off, leaving Yayo fucked up in the head.

He jumped in his whip and pondered his next move. "Who the fuck is tying me to them bodies? Watch what I say in jail?" There was only one person who knew the debts of the situation with Jughead, and what plans he had for him, and that was his old celly, Rex.

"But why the fuck would he?" Yayo thought to himself as he smoked on his Newport. Yayo knew he would be selling his soul to the devil for a cheap price. Five G's a week wasn't bad. He would be able to do what he wanted to do in the streets. He would have a license to get money and kill his enemies for a small fee. The stakes were definitely being raised with Batman and Robin on his payroll. But if the crooked cops tried to double-cross him, "The Chicago Police department will be having a memorial service with a 21-gun salute, without a doubt," Yayo thought as a wicked grin crept across his face. He made a mental note to check into Rex's whereabouts.

Chapter 14

Yayo was in his master bedroom on his king-sized canopy bed, flicking through the channels on his 70-inch projection TV. It was Sunday, and he figured he would stay in the crib and catch up on some well-needed rest. Running the streets was starting to take a toll on his mind and body.

Shakira had been out since Saturday. She went out with Candy, and didn't have the decency to call and check in on him. Yayo was seriously thinking about breaking up with her. Even though he loved her, his true devotion was to the streets.

He grabbed the half-blunt from the ashtray, lit it up, and thought about all the shit that was going on. ATG was trying to bury him, Rex had crossed him by implicating him on some bodies, and he had so much jealousy and envy coming from different angles. Yayo inhaled the weed and let the THC calm his nerves. He had over $360,000, an arsenal of weapons, and a squad of ruthless wolves itching to bang their hammers at his command. And yet, he made a crucial political move by putting the police on his payroll. There was no turning back.

His thought were interrupted by the sound of the front door closing, which meant Shakira had finally come home. She came straight to the room and hung her Donna Karan coat in the closet.

"I tried to call your phone last night. Why the fuck didn't you answer, or at least have the decency to call back and let me know you're OK?" Yayo asked nonchalantly.

"Nigga, the same reason you don't answer me when I'm trying to call you," Shakira said matter of factly.

Yayo blew a thick cloud of smoke out, and chose his words wisely before he spoke. "Shorty, I'm tired of playing these lil' games with you. Why don't you just get your shit and go to your mother's house?"

"Nigga, fuck you. Why don't you get the fuck out? You got the nerve to question me, and you're out there fucking with all different types of hoes. You stay out 2-3 nights a week, and then come home, acting like you give a fuck about what I do. Yayo, you don't care about me!" Shakira spat.

"Bitch, how you think you got all them clothes? Or how you laying your ass in this big ass house? How the fuck you think you living this life? It's because of me, BITCH. Me being in them streets and risking my life, but that don't mean shit to you, do it?" Yayo said, getting out of bed and putting on his Coogi jogging pants.

"I don't give a fuck about none of that material shit. You got me fucked up. I don't need you, Yaton."

"Well, pack ya shit, and get gone, and make sure you leave everything that I bought for you with my money."

"Fuck you, you bitch ass--" Yayo grabbed her by her hair and started slapping her. Shakira laid on the floor, balled up and crying hysterically. "Fuck you, Yayo, you murdering bastard!" She screamed out of anger.

Yayo couldn't believe his ears. Yayo quickly went under his mattress and grabbed his .40 cal.

"Oh, what, you gonna kill me now, Yayo?" Shakira asked. "You gonna shoot me?" She yelled through tears. Yayo pulled the slide back, chambered a round, and pointed the gun at Shakira.

"Say that shit again, Shakira. Go ahead and say it again," Yayo said, tightening his finger on the trigger.

"Yaton, please don't. I'm pregnant with your baby," Shakira said through tears.

Yayo stared at her for what seemed like a lifetime before he dropped the gun, then fell to his knees. He crawled toward Shakira and held her tightly. "I'm sorry, baby. I'm so sorry," he said, letting the tears fall from his eyes. "I love you."

"Yaton, I love you, too. I just want you to be around to be a father to our child."

Yayo promised Shakira he would get out of the game soon, but he had a few loose ends to tie up. He knew his intentions were good, but getting out of the street life would be easier said than done. Regardless of what he knew, he had to do what was right for his family.

Later, they were cuddled up on the sofa when Yayo's phone rang. "Hey Granny," he said, happy to hear her voice. He loved his grandmother to pieces, but felt she had been keeping her distance from him because he was in the streets doing "the devil's work," as she would put it.

"Hey, Yaton. I was calling because I haven't heard from you in a while. I saw your car parked in front of the house, but there was no sign of you. How have you been?" Honey asked, full of concern.

"I've been doing alright, grandma. I just been doing a lot of running around. I've been meaning to come over there and check on you, but I thought you might be mad at me for some reason," Yayo said as he walked out the bedroom to talk to his grandmother in private.

"Yaton, I'm not mad at you. I'm disappointed in you. I've been hearing so many disturbing things about you, and it's not for me to judge. You are my grandson, and I'm always gonna worry about you."

Yayo couldn't help but to feel guilty because he knew his grandma was always worrying about his safety, and he also knew the streets talked. His grandmother definitely knew he was out there getting down for his crown.

"Grandma, you shouldn't worry about me. I'm just doing what I have to do to survive out here, 'cause ain't nobody gon' give me nothing."

"Yaton, I'm not trying to judge you. How can I? The Bible says you will be judged by your deeds and your actions. Yaton, you are not living for God. You are doing the devil's work. Do you understand me? The devil don't care about you. All he cares about is how much evil and havoc you can cause."

The words that Honey spoke stirred Yayo's soul. He knew she was right, and he had become a savage beast, all for the love of the dollar. Yayo was starting to get emotional, so he tried to change the subject. "Hey, Granny, I'm 'bout to be a father."

"Praise God! Congratulations, Yaton!" Honey exclaimed, full of joy. "See, Yaton, God is steady blessing you. That should be more of a reason to get your life together. I want you and Shakira to come with me to church on Sunday. Will y'all be able to do that?"

"Yes, Granny. I'll do anything for you."

"Well, praise the Lord, Yaton! I love you."

"I love you too, Granny." He hung up.

Yayo got back into bed, finding Shakira sound asleep, looking like a beautiful angel. He kissed her on the forehead and pulled the blanket up to his chest. His mind was racing a million miles a minute. He had to get out of the game, but not before he milked it for all it was worth, and all of his enemies were in caskets.

He stared at the ceiling and said a silent prayer. "God, I ask you to look over me, and protect me from my enemies. I ask you, God, to look over my family and friends, and to keep us all safe and healthy. Thank you, God, for blessing me with a child. God, please forgive me of the sins I committed, and the sins I have yet to commit. Amen." He closed his eyes and fell asleep.

Chapter 15

It was 2:30 in the morning and 95 degrees, a hot summer in the city. Rex stood in front of the projects with twenty of his niggas, hustling heroin, crack, and ecstasy. Since Rex had come home from prison almost two years ago, he had the projects on lock. Rex's uncle, Skip, always had a chokehold on the projects, but after getting indicted by the feds, a 38-year sentence would end his career as a drug boss. Skip left Rex his connect, along with close to $100,000, and Rex took off from there.

"Rocks, blow, weed, park!" A young hustler hollered as drivers passed by. He was letting everybody know that Henry Hornets had whatever they were looking for. The project was a gold mine, and Rex and his crew reaped the benefits of it.

Tonight proved to be another profitable night for Rex, with him making $18,000 already, and the night was still young. Selling drugs was definitely his forte. Rex knew he was on his way to becoming a rich man.

Rex was walking toward his black Escalade truck when one of his security workers on the corner yelled out, "Ninety-nine coming down the one-way!" That meant the police were coming down the block. Rex casually got into his truck, while the other dealers walked off from in front of the building. Batman and Robin pulled up beside the Escalade and exited their cruiser.

"Put your fucking hands where I can see them!" Batman yelled, pointing his Sig Sauer at Rex.

Rex put his hands up as instructed, while Batman opened up the driver's side door of the truck, pulling Rex out by the collar of his white T-shirt. Robin stood on the sidewalk with his Taurus out, keeping the onlookers at bay. This neighborhood was known for police getting hit up with bullets, so the detectives took precautions while dealing with Rex.

Batman searched Rex, and found a bundle of bagged-up heroin and a few stacks of money.

"You're under arrest. Put your hands behind your back."

"Batman, what type of shit you on?" Rex asked, looking confused. "I paid y'all this week," he said, referring to the street tax of 10 G's a week.

"Shut up and get in the car," Batman said while handcuffing Rex.

Once they had Rex inside the car, they pulled off.

Batman pulled out a cigarette from his front pocket and lit it up.

"Damn, lil' nigga, I see you out here flamboyant as shit with your Escalade truck. You coming up in the world, huh?" Batman said as he blew out a thick cloud of smoke.

"Batman, what's all this shit about?" Rex questioned with a perplexed look on his face.

"Nothing major. I just wanted to holla at you about something. You know I had to make the arrest look legit. You wouldn't want your homeboys to know that you're my confidential informant, now, would you?"

"Aiight, then. What's up?"

"I was trying to see if you were still trying to get ol' Skip out of the feds like we discussed?"

"Yeah, I'm trying to get my peoples out. Fuck these other niggas," Rex retorted.

"Well, tell me again how you know Yayo was the one who slumped Jug-head and the other lil' nigger," Batman said while taking a long drag on his cigarette.

"I told you, I was in the joint with this clown, and he was my celly. He got some bad news about his homie, Pudge, getting laid out in a robbery, and the nigga got to crying and shit, saying he was gonna murk anybody who had something to do with it. And he was gonna murder Jug-head for sending him to prison for killing that lil' girl. Now, soon as the nigga gets out, Jug-head gets found with his head open? That nigga did that shit as far as I see it," Rex stated as if he just solved a mystery.

"Would you be willing to testify to that in open court?" Robin asked from the passenger seat.

"Hell, yeah, if y'all can work something out with the feds to let my uncle go, or at least knock that 30 ball down."

"We'll see what we can do," Batman said, looking at Rex through the rearview.

It was almost 3:00 a.m. when Batman got off on 35th and pulled up to the beach. It was pitch black in the parking lot as they parked next to a Suburban with tinted windows.

"Man, what the fuck we doing at the lake front?" Rex asked from the backseat.

Without saying a word, Batman and Robin exited the vehicle, opened the back doors, and forcefully pulled Rex out. Robin held Rex tightly by his cuffs as Batman walked around toward the driver's side of the Suburban, and handed the driver something through the window. Rex couldn't make out what was actually said, but he heard Batman laughing like something was hilarious.

"Aiight, Robin, let's roll," Batman said, and then jumped back in their cruiser.

"Aiight, lil' fella, nice doing business with you," Robin said with a smile on his face. "Tell the lil' mermaid I said, 'hello.'"

"Man, what the fuck is going on?" Rex yelled as Batman started the engine and began to pull out of the parking lot, leaving Rex scared to death in handcuffs.

Rex looked around in fear as two men got out of the Suburban, looking like ninjas.

"Rex, my main man, what the business, Joe?"

"Man, who's that?" Rex asked.

When the two men got in front of him, he couldn't believe his eyes as he stood face-to-face with Yayo. At that moment, Rex knew he didn't have much longer to live.

"Damn, Rex, I used to think you were a stomp down nigga. All that gangsta shit you used to be talking in the cell, you hot ass nigga!" Yayo said before punching Rex square in the jaw.

"Yayo, come on, homie! Batman and Robin on some bullshit. They trying to turn us against each other," Rex said, pleading for his life.

Yayo pulled the small tape recorder from his pocket that Batman had given him and pressed play. The sounds of his conversation with Batman played from the recorder.

Yayo pressed the stop button. TJ put a fishing line around Rex's neck and proceeded to choke him. Yayo kneeled down to get face-to-face with Rex. "You see, nigga, I treated you like a friend in the joint. I never crossed you, and you do this bullshit."

Rex's eyes were bulging as he tried to gasp for air. The pressure from the fishing line was cutting through his skin, causing him to bleed. Rex's pleas for mercy were idle.

Yayo continued, "If anybody knows I feel about hot niggas, it's you. Rex, I find you guilty on all charges of being an imposter and being a rat, and I sentence you to death," Yayo said as he stood up. Rex's eyes rolled to the back of his head as he took his last breath.

Yayo and TJ rolled Rex's body up in a tarp and carried him to the end of the pier, tied concrete to his ankles, and threw him over the pier. His body sank fast to the bottom of Lake Michigan.

Yayo and TJ got back into the Suburban and pulled off into the darkness.

"In the city of Chi, it's hustle or die, kill or be killed, you gotta take the pie, momma ain't lie," Speedknot Mobstaz rapped through the subwoofers inside the Suburban. Yayo turned it up and let the music put him on ten. There was nothing like looking a man in his eyes before killing him. This made him feel powerful.

YAYO

Chapter 16

It was the night of the all-white party, and every gangster, drug dealer, robber and hustler had been anticipating this players ball that was being held downtown at Luther's House of Blues.

Tonight, niggas were gonna see who was getting the most money in the Chi. Niggas were bringing out all the big boy toys and that ice. Yayo had made it mandatory that all GBC members be in attendance, and they all got diamond-encrusted pieces with the GBC logo sprayed in ice.

It was 9:30 at night when Yayo and Shakira pulled up on Wolcott in a cocaine white S550 Mercedes Benz with white and chrome 24-inch Davins. The block was flooded with GBC gangsters. There were Range Rovers, Chargers, Lac trucks, Beamers, old school Box Chevys on 6s, and plenty more. The game had been good to GBC, and this was the proof.

Niggas stood on the block, mobbed up and decked out in all-white clothing with bottles of Rosé and Remy XO. They all awaited Yayo's arrival. Yayo had wanted all his peoples to meet up on the block, so their entourage could show up at the event at the same time.

Yayo pulled up and got out of the Benz, fitted to death. He was dressed head-to-toe in Mauris. Yayo had enough carats in his bracelet to make Bugs Bunny grab a gun and try to rob something. His silk Mauris short set the jewelry off. He had his hair braided in 6 long French braids that fell to his shoulders. The diamond 40-inch chain with the GBC charm made a statement of its own.

Yayo had Shakira in an all-white silk Donna Karan dress that hugged her curvaceous body. The silk dress was almost see-through, showing her white Victoria's Secret thong. Her white Jimmy Choo sandals showed off her freshly pedicured feet. Her all-white, $2,500 Dooney and Bourke handbag would tell bitches tonight to get their weight up. She was definitely a gangster's girl.

Yayo walked to the sidewalk and shook up with his gang.

These young gangsters were loyal to him, and protected his well-being. Yayo's determination and goals had flourished into something great. Every nigga on the block would give their life for him at the drop of a hat, whether it be to the prison system, or by the hands of anybody who wasn't in GBC. Yayo would do the same for his crew.

TJ pulled up on the block in his all-white Range Rover sitting on 6s, and jumped out, ready to party. His six 12-inch subwoofers were setting off car alarms as Lil' Boosie's "We Out Chea" banged from the SUV. Butterball jumped out from the passenger's side with a bottle of Grey Goose.

"GBC, nigga! GBC!" TJ yelled as he crossed the street. He was dressed in True Religion, and his dreads were braided to the back in three long braids. He had on so much ice, one would've thought he was signed to Young Money.

"What up, bra-bra?" TJ said, embracing Yayo.

"Shit, nigga, I see you shining," Yayo said.

"Nah, nigga, we shining," TJ said, referring to the whole clique.

Shakira got out of the whip to hug her brother.

"Damn, shorty, you jumped out of the whip looking like Cinderella and shit!" TJ teased. TJ was off the chain, because he was gone off of ecstasy and was feeling like Tony Montana.

Yayo knew he was surrounded by family. The only person who was missing was Pudge. Yayo poured a half bottle of Rosé Black on the ground and said, "I miss you, my nigga. Everything I do is for us. Love you, nigga."

"Come on, my niggas. Let's go claim these streets," Yayo said and jumped in his Benz.

Everybody else jumped in their cars and trucks and followed Yayo downtown to Luther's House of Blues. Yayo looked in the rearview and saw at least 13 whips gliding behind him.

Yayo and his squad pulled up at 11:30 p.m. The line to get in was damn near around the corner when GBC pulled up with their systems banging and whips shining. Everybody else stopped what they were doing and focused their attention on the entourage. Motherfuckers were pointing with their jaws dropped.

Yayo and his clique had shut shit down, and they hadn't even stepped foot inside the establishment yet. They parked their whips across the street and walked to the club looking like NBA ball players. Yayo had already paid the owner of the club 5 G's for full V.I.P. access, which meant the GBC walked right in the club, leaving everybody else stuck in the long line.

They were led upstairs to the spacious V.I.P. lounge. A sexy waitress who resembled Nia Long took their orders.

"Let me get 8 cases of Rosé, and 10 bottles of Patron Silver to start us off, shorty," Yayo said.

"Yes, sir," She replied with a seductive smile.

Gucci Mane's "Street Niggas" banged from the sound system, getting the party crunk.

Niggas were definitely in there flossing the ice. He thought he saw Twista and his squad at the bar popping bottles, along with Derrick Rose and a couple of Chicago Bulls players. Even they had to glance and see where the bouncers were carrying all the cases of Rosé to. Yayo and his crew popped bottles and showed their asses. Every bitch in the club was trying to holler at the GBC boys.

"What up, nigga? Let's go take these flicks!" TJ said. He was drunk and high, but still on point.

The whole clique followed TJ toward the photographer, and TJ gave him a $50 bill and stood in front of the Chicago skyline. "On 3, GBC," TJ said.

"1-2-3, GBC!" They all yelled. Some held stacks of money, while some gripped their chains. Yayo stood behind Shakira, holding her while mugging the camera.

A lot of niggas were hating by the looks on their faces. Everybody knew now that Yayo and the GBC had the Chi on lock, hands down.

Cherokee D'Ass got on the mic. "What's up, Chicago? I see how y'all do it in Chi-town! Chicago, stand up!"

Everybody put their bottles in the air. Yayo and TJ toasted bottles. "This is to us, fam. This is for Pudge," TJ said.

TJ walked to the bar when he ran into Yolanda, who looked like she was trying to avoid him. "Yolanda, what up shorty?" He said, grabbing her by the arm.

"Nigga, let my arm go! Fuck wrong wit' you?" She said angrily.

"Damn, shorty, what's ya problem? You act like a nigga did something to you."

"Nah, you ain't do shit to me, but I'm in here with somebody."

"Shit, bitch, that's all the fuck you had to say," TJ said and walked off. Yolanda did the same.

"Fuck wrong wit' that hoe?" TJ thought to himself as he walked back toward the V.I.P.

When he entered the lounge, he was surprised to see Cherokee sitting her thick ass on Butterball's lap. Butterball was all smiles, with a lit blunt dangling from his mouth and a bottle of Rosé in his hand.

TJ smiled like a proud father as looked at his 18-year-old protégé. He then walked to the balcony of the V.I.P. lounge to scan the crowd for Yolanda, but he couldn't spot her in the sea of people that flooded the dance floor. "That bitch was on some weird shit," he thought to himself.

It was 2:30 a.m., and motherfuckers were starting to leave the club. A few GBC niggas had crept out of the club a little early to go to their whips to get the tools ready, just in case niggas wanted some action. Chicago was crazy like that. People can be having a good time one minute, and then next thing you know, an ambulance is picking up a body. GBC wasn't taking a chances.

When Yayo, Shakira, and TJ came out of the club, Butterball, Lil' Murda, and Tee were already outside posted up, making sure everybody got to their whips with no problems.

"TJ, what y'all getting into?" Yayo asked as he got into his Benz.

"I don't know. Lil' Butter said Cherokee and her buddy got a room at the Hilton. That lil' nigga done peeled off $3,500 to make a movie with them, wit' his lil' freak ass," TJ said, grinning.

"So, where you fit in?" Yayo asked.

"Fuck you mean where I fit in at?" TJ questioned. "In the movie, that's where. Mr. Marcus ain't got shit on me," TJ said, hitting the alarm on his Range Rover.

"Y'all so nasty," Shakira said from the passenger seat of the Benz.

"I'm nasty? You the one 'bout to have a baby with your freak ass," TJ said, climbing into his truck.

"On some real shit," Yayo said, "You gotta be careful. You know them type of hoes be trying to set niggas up."

TJ reached under his seat, pulled out a 21 shot FN 5.7 handgun, and said, "Nigga, I'm wit' that type of shit. Let 'em try me." He put the gun back under his seat.

"Aiight, then. Hit me in the a.m., fam," Yayo said as he slowly pulled out of the parking spot.

Just then, gunshots rang out in front of the club. Everybody drove off in their own directions. It was just another night in the Chi.

S. Allen

Chapter 17

It was 4:00 a.m., and Joyce was sleeping when her doorbell rang. She put on her robe and went downstairs to answer the door. First, she looked out the window as she always did before opening the door, but this time, it was pitch black outside. She definitely didn't remember turning off the porch light because she always kept it on. She heard banging at the door.

"Who is it?" Joyce said, growing agitated.

"It's Chicago police. We have a few questions to ask you about your son, Tevin," the man said from behind the door.

Hearing TJ's name made Joyce's heart pound. She quickly took the chain off the door and unlocked the deadbolt. When she cracked the door, the men kicked it in, hitting her in the nose. Two men entered the house and locked the door behind them. When Joyce finally gained consciousness, she was face-to-face with two masked men pointing guns in her face.

"Bitch, where the fuck is the money at?" One of the masked men said through clenched teeth.

"I don't have any money," Joyce replied.

"Wrong answer, bitch." He struck Joyce across the top of her head with the butt of the gun.

"You better call your punk ass son!" The masked man said and passed her a cell phone.

"Noooooo, please don't do--"

"Wrong answer again, bitch!" He said as he hit Joyce again with his gun, causing her to lose consciousness again.

When Joyce stirred, her hands were tied behind her back, and she was in an unknown location. Her jaw was fractured and she could taste blood. "Lord, please help me," she silently prayed.

***

TJ and Butterball were at the Hilton on the North Side, freaking out with Cherokee and her girlfriend, Passion. Passion didn't have an ass as big as Cherokee's, but she had some big ass titties. Butter-ball and TJ definitely got their money's worth. They had fucked both girls in every hole on their body, and watched them lick each other's pussies and assholes. It was almost 5:30 a.m., and TJ and Butterball had fucked so much they couldn't get hard again. TJ had recorded most of the sexcapades on his iPhone, and put a few clips on YouTube already.

As he was going through his phone, he noticed he had 7 missed calls. Four were from an unknown number, and three were from his mother. He dialed her number, only to find her line busy.

"Aye, Butter, let's roll up out of here," TJ said to Butterball, who was laying between the two naked women, half asleep.

After TJ dropped Butterball off on the low end, he got on the Dan Ryan and headed toward the hundreds. He kept trying Joyce's phone along the way, but the line was still busy. Something was definitely wrong.

When TJ pulled up in front of his house, he could see the door was damaged and Joyce's car was parked in front of the house. Something definitely wasn't right.

TJ grabbed the 5.7 from under his seat, chambered a round, and walked toward the house. When he got on the porch, he slowly opened the door and called out his mother's name. He immediately noticed the spots of blood on the carpet and called his mother again.

"Mama!" Nobody was there.

***

TJ was pacing back and forth in the spot on 95th, smoking New-port after Newport. He was a nervous wreck worrying about his mother's whereabouts. He had just gotten off the phone with Yayo before he pulled up, and told him to meet him at the spot, but Yayo was coming all the way from North Chicago, and that would take him another hour.

Just then, his phone rang, and he saw an unknown number. "Hello?" He said into the phone impatiently.

"Listen, nigga, this is not a fucking game," the caller said. "We need 200 G's and six of them thangs."

"What the fuck you mean, nigga?" TJ asked.

"TJ, please, just give them what they want," Joyce said through her sobs.

TJ couldn't believe his ears. It felt like his world was spinning.

"Do I have your attention now, nigga?" The caller asked.

"Aiight, man, just don't hurt my mother," TJ pleaded. "I'ma get y'all that paper."

"Listen, pussy, you got 48 hours, or we gonna start sending your moms home piece by piece."

"Where y'all want me to drop it at?" TJ asked.

"Just stay by your phone and we'll let you know. If you try any monkey shit, then you already know," the caller said, then hung up.

TJ collapsed on the living room floor in shock. "How did this happen?" He thought. TJ sat on the couch in a daze until Yayo and three goons came in.

"What the fuck is up, nigga? Why you ain't answering your phone?" Yayo asked, wondering why TJ was sitting there looking crazy.

"They got my moms, G. They said they want 200 G's and six birds," TJ said in a whisper.

"Who the fuck is they? Who got Joyce?" Yayo asked, trying to comprehend what's going on.

TJ just sat there looking into space. Yayo sat down next to him and placed a hand on his shoulder. "TJ, who got your mother?"

TJ let the tears fall from his eyes as he slapped Yayo's hand off of him. "Nigga, I don't know who the fuck got my momma, but when I find out, I'ma murder everything they love," he said with bloodshot eyes.

Yayo let his brother vent. He had never seen TJ like this, but he felt his pain, which made him cry, too. Bloodshed was inevitable for the niggas who kidnapped Joyce.

After TJ calmed down, he explained to Yayo what the caller said.

"Listen, TJ, we gonna get Joyce back. We in this shit together. Joyce is like my momma too, nigga," Yayo said, trying to console

TJ.

"Yayo, please don't let Shakira know shit. She gonna go crazy," TJ said, wanting to protect his sister from heartache.

"Aiight, bro," Yayo said as he got up and went to the next room to call Shakira and tell her to come over.

Yayo went outside an hour and a half later, where Shakira waited in her Audi.

"Pop the trunk," he said as he walked toward the back. Shakira popped it, and Yayo retrieved the two duffle bags.

"Boy, what's going on?" Shakira questioned.

"Nothing, baby. I'm 'bout to bust a move. I'll call you in a minute," Yayo said and walked back toward the house.

It was 10:30 p.m. when the kidnappers called back.

"Throw it on speaker," Yayo said as he moved closer to hear the call.

"What up, man? I got that bread," TJ said as he answered the phone.

"That's what I like to hear," the kidnapper said. "Now, listen, there's a dumpster behind McDonald's on 69th. Drop the shit off behind the dumpster at exactly 11:15 with no bullshit. If everything is everything, I'ma call you and tell you where to find your mother."

"Nigga, let me hear my mother's voice!" TJ demanded.

A few seconds later, Joyce came on the line. "TJ, baby, I'm scared. Please come get me!" Joyce cried.

"Mama, did they hurt you?" TJ asked, but the kidnapper had already disconnected the call.

"Aiight, TJ, you gonna make the drop. We gon' follow you to make sure they don't do no bullshit," Yayo said.

"Why don't you call Batman to catch them niggas?" TJ asked.

"Because we gotta make sure we get Joyce back," Yayo responded.

At 11:15, TJ pulled up to the McDonald's and did as he was instructed. He dropped the duffle bags behind the dumpsters and pulled off in his Cadillac DTS, while Yayo and his goons watched the whole play from a block away.

At 11:20, a red Cadillac truck pulled behind the McDonald's.

The passenger got out of the truck, grabbed the bags, threw them in the truck, and drove away.

An hour later, TJ received a call from the kidnappers.

"Where the fuck my mama at?" TJ said through clenched teeth as he answered the phone.

"Calm down, killa. Your mama is on 111th and Michigan. The address is 1142 South Michigan." The caller hung up.

TJ and Yayo jumped in the whip and headed toward the address. When they got to 1142 South Michigan, they noticed that the house was abandoned and boarded up. Yayo, TJ, and the goons got out the whips with their guns drawn, and walked up toward the address. When they entered the house, they were taken aback by the smell of piss and death. TJ's worst fears were confirmed when he found Joyce in the kitchen, sitting in the chair with her hands tied behind her back.

He noticed two bullet holes in her head, and he knew his mother was gone. TJ dropped his gun, ran over to his mother, and wrapped his hands around her and embraced her. The blood from her wounds stained his white tee as he held her head against his chest and cried. "Mama, I'm so sorry, mama!" TJ sobbed as he held her tightly.

Yayo dropped his head down in defeat as he watched the scene unfold. He couldn't believe what happened to her.

"Come on, fam, we gotta go!" Yayo said. TJ stood up and used his blood-stained hands to close Joyce's eyes before they parted.

***

Joyce's funeral was held at Gatling Funeral Home on Chicago's South Side. So many people came to show their respects to Joyce. Shakira, TJ, Honey, Yayo, and Karen were all seated in the front row. There wasn't a dry eye inside the funeral home. Joyce's death affected everybody, especially those who knew her struggle, and how she cleaned her life up after years of drug abuse.

TJ sat and listened as Bishop A.C. Richards gave his sermon. "My people, we must come together as a community to help stop the violence that's plaguing our city." He got plenty of amens as he continued. "God did not put us here to murder our brothers and sisters."

TJ's eyes were bloodshot red from countless nights of crying. He had given up on God. Shakira and Joyce were all he had to live for in this world, so when Joyce died, a part of him died with her. Shakira sat in a daze, still unable to face the fact that her mother was gone. Yayo did what he could do to help comfort her, but she was lost.

Joyce was buried at Burr Oaks Cemetery in a white marble casket. TJ watched as his mother's casket was lowered 6 feet into the earth, and vowed to himself that she would not be the only one getting buried. Blood was going to spill in the streets for somebody putting their hands on his family. "On my momma!" TJ screamed out in pain.

YAYO

Chapter 18

"Rocks! Blows! Rocks! Blows! Park!" The pitchman yelled on the corner of 71st and Winchester, letting the drug addicts know to park and get served some of the best heroin and crack on the South Side. It was about 20 degrees on a cold winter night, as hustlers worked to get their packs off.

"Man, it's slow as shit out here tonight," Lala said as he took a swig from his half pint of E&J to keep warm.

"Hell, yeah. It's so cold, the cluckers don't even wanna come outside to coop," Lil' Ron said to his partner.

Lala and Lil' Ron were first cousins, and soldiers for the ATG gang.

"Man, how many bags you got left, Joe?" Lala asked Lil' Ron as he twisted the cap back onto his E&J, stuffing the bottle inside his Carhartt coat.

"Shit, I got about 100 bags left," Lil' Ron said as he eyed the dark-skinned man with the dreads who was approaching him. "What's up, old school? We got that feel good," Lil' Ron said.

The man went into his pocket, pulled out a crumpled up $20 bill, and handed it to him.

"Shorty, I'm kinda short on my change right now. But I'm good for it. Let me get 3 for the dub."

Lil' Ron was so thirsty to make the sale, he didn't have to think long about agreeing to the 3 bags for $20. "Look, don't make this a habit of copping on this block wit' short paper. We ain't on that shit over here, but I'm gonna let you slide this time," Lil' Ron said as he handed the 3 bags to the man.

"Good looking out, shorty. I'm gonna spread the word that y'all got the best dope on the South Side," The dread said as he turned on his heels and started walking back up the block.

Lil' Ron added the $20 bill to the rest of his knot. It was late, and him and Lala only made about $2,500. Lil' Ron pulled his hoodie back over his head and started walking back to the corner toward Lala, not paying attention to the grey, beat-up Buick coming down the street. The sound of the tires crunching through the snow and slush caused Lil' Ron to look up, but what he saw made his whole world move in slow motion.

He saw the bloodshot red eyes of a masked man holding up some sort of assault rifle with a drum attached to it, pointing it out the window. Then, he saw the bright flash from the barrel, and then, he felt a piercing pain in his left shoulder that caused him to spin around.

Lil' Ron took off running as his adrenaline took over him and he realized the immediate danger he was in. The distraught gunman hopped out of the Buick and continued to point and fire at his intended target.

Five bullets hit Lil' Ron in the back, causing him to land face first on the frozen pavement. The gunman ran up to his prey and fired two more slugs from his rifle, silencing Lil' Ron forever.

Lala was knelt down behind a garbage dumpster as he heard the rapid gunfire echo through the night. Lala was no dummy. He had seen the Buick creeping up the block, and dipped through a gangway, seeking cover.

Lala was a young cat caught up in the life, trying to be a gangsta. Lala grew up being the only child of two hardworking parents who spoiled him and gave him everything he wanted. He started hanging with his cousin, Lil' Ron, who was heavily involved in the streets. At 13, Lil' Ron was put on as an ATG gang member.

Lala wanted to be known as a gangster like his cousin, so he joined the ATG gang. Lala had experienced a lot of violence being in the gang, but never would have thought he would be in the crosshairs of a banga. There had been a few murders in the hood in the last few weeks, but Lala paid it no mind as he chased the almighty dollar.

After the gunshots ceased, Lala knew it was time to make his getaway, and got up from behind the dumpster and started walking down the alley. He knew it was a wrap for Lil' Ron as he heard the sirens getting closer and closer. All of a sudden, the same car turned down the alley. Lala turned on his heels and started running in the opposite direction.

He felt the piercing pain in his stomach and fell on the ground.

The Buick came to a stop and Lala heard the door slam as he crawled on the ground with his intestines hanging out from the round.

"Please man, don't kill me."

His pleas fell on deaf ears as the gunman raised his rifle and fired a single round in Lala's forehead, sending him into complete darkness.

***

It was 4:00 a.m. when TJ walked into his apartment in the Dearborn projects, located on the low-end of the South Side. The Dearborn Projects were ran by the GDs, but was a fortress to TJ because him and Yayo supplied the Dearborns, the Ida B. Wells, and the whole low-end drugs. He was protected by the young killers.

When TJ walked inside his apartment, he kicked off his blood-stained Timbs and took off his black Dickies coat, and threw it on the floor. His apartment was a mess, with empty Hennessey bottles everywhere, and ashtrays filled with cigarette butts and blunt roaches. His dreads were messy with new growth, and his body reeked of must, weed smoke, blood, and gunpowder.

Ever since Joyce's murder, he had blamed himself for it, and stopped caring about his life, and he had no regard for the lives of others. He turned into a savage demon, releasing all his anger on the streets of Chicago, catching body after body.

He had hit 71st and Winchester like a Tasmanian devil. It didn't matter. If someone got caught slipping on them streets, TJ was letting it ride.

TJ moved some designer clothes off of his sectional sofa and sat down. There was a picture of Joyce on his entertainment center, and he just sat there, staring at the picture with tears coming from his bloodshot red eyes.

"Momma, I'm so sorry, momma. God, why me? Why'd you take her from me, Lord? Why didn't you take me?" TJ cried out, wishing and hoping God would answer him.

"Momma, I swear on my soul I'ma get whoever did this to you!

I love you, momma, I love you!" TJ cried out.

TJ got up from the couch and walked down the hallway to the back room of his apartment, where he retrieved a crack pipe from his dresser. He pulled out the half ounce of crack he had in his pocket, broke a small piece off, and placed it in his pipe. After lighting the pipe, the evil smoke clouded the pipe as TJ inhaled Satan's sweetness. The effect of the drug made TJ forget all his troubles as he sat on the edge of his bed.

TJ had been smoking crack since last week. It started with him being curious by sprinkling a little in his blunts to numb the pain. He eventually fell in love with the superman high, and started smoking straight crack. He felt invincible as he loaded up his guns and went out into the streets, putting in work. The more murders he committed, the more crack he smoked, and tonight was no different.

TJ placed another piece of crack on the pipe and lit it, thinking about the double homicide he had just committed not even an hour ago. After blowing out a thick cloud of grey smoke, he let out a sinister chuckle until he heard a knock at his door.

Out of paranoia, TJ grabbed his Tec-9 and hollered, "Who the fuck is that?"

"It's Yayo, nigga. Open the door."

TJ walked over to the door and looked out to confirm it was Yayo.

"What up, Joe?" TJ said as he opened the door and gave Yayo some dap.

The first thing Yayo noticed was the foul smell that invaded his nostrils. Yayo had been in the streets long enough to know what burning crack smelled like, so he looked closer at TJ and saw his eyes were wide and yellow.

"Nigga, what's that smell?" Yayo asked, giving TJ the benefit of doubt.

TJ ignored the question and took a seat on his couch, placing the weapon on his lap and rubbing it like a puppy.

"Aye, nigga, I've been trying to call you for a few days. What's up wit' you?" Yayo questioned.

"Shit, nigga, I been out here putting in work, putting niggas on the news. Have you been watching it?" TJ said with a smirk on his face.

"Listen, TJ, I loved Joyce like she was my mother, but family, you got to slow down. Batman told me the feds are trying to step in because of all them bodies and shit. Niggas is getting killed who ain't even plugged with ATG. Nigga, you trippin'," Yayo said as he took a seat on the couch next to TJ.

"Nah, nigga, you trippin," TJ said, getting angry. "Fuck Batman, and fuck the feds. I'm not stopping till they whole squad is wiped out for what they did to my momma. Nigga, if you lost your mother, you would be on the same shit, so don't come up in here with all that 'Chill out, TJ' shit!" TJ retorted with a mean mug on his face.

"I feel ya pain, my nigga, and we gonna put all them niggas on ice, but it's not what you do. It's how you do it, fam. We got to be thinkers so we don't get life behind bars for this shit."

"Whatever," TJ said as he lit up a Newport and took a long drag.

Yayo went to the bathroom, thinking about how bad his homie was doing. It was hard for Yayo to watch his homie fall off mentally, and start doing shit that could jeopardize both of their lives. TJ was moving recklessly, and he was acting like a different person. The TJ Yayo knew would listen to him, but the nigga out there on the couch was reckless and rebellious.

Yayo walked out and headed back toward the living room.

As he passed TJ's bedroom, he noticed what looked like a crack pipe on top of the dresser. His worst fears were confirmed as he grabbed the pipe and quickly walked back to the living room to confront his partner. "Aye, nigga, what's this shit 'bout?" Yayo said, throwing the pipe at TJ.

"Nigga, what you doing searching through my shit? What, you the feds or some shit?" TJ said, now standing up.

"Nigga, you smoking. That's why you been acting like this. Nigga, you done lost your mind," Yayo said, shaking his head in disgust.

"Nigga, fuck you! I'm a grown ass man, and I do what I want, nigga. What?" TJ said through clenched teeth as he got in Yayo's face.

"TJ, you better calm your ass down, fam, before I make you eat that motherfuckin' pipe."

TJ took a wild swing at Yayo. Yayo ducked the hay-maker and gave TJ a two-piece combo to the midsection. TJ tried to counter the blows, but was met by three quick blows to his face, sending him flying back on the floor.

TJ tried to grab his gun off of the couch, but was met face-to-face with Yayo's Desert Eagle as Yayo swiftly pulled it from his waist. Both men now had firearms pointed at each other.

"TJ, I love you like a brother, and I'm sorry about your mother, but we on the same side, nigga. You bleed, I bleed. You feel pain, I feel pain, but you on some other shit, fucking with that crack. I love you, but don't make me murk you, fam," Yayo said, tightening his finger around the trigger.

TJ let the tears roll down his face as he felt Yayo's words penetrate his mind and heart. TJ lowered the Tee and fell to his knees. Yayo lowered his gun and put it back on his waist. He then pulled TJ up off the floor and embraced his brother.

"TJ, you gotta pull yourself together, my nigga. I need you out here. Shakira needs you. I know you're stronger than this, bro. We gonna handle shit the right way with these niggas. Mentally and physically, we're gonna win, TJ. Joyce would want that, fam, but we gotta be level-headed out here. This shit is chess, not checkers, TJ," Yayo said, dropping jewels on his homie.

TJ wiped the tears and blood from his face and sat back on the couch. "Yayo, I'm sorry, fam. She was all I had in this world, and they took her from me. They gon' pay. They all gonna pay. On my mama," TJ said, meaning every word.

"TJ, get yourself together. I gotta go handle something right now. Take care of ya business, and hit me up later on," Yayo said as he gave TJ some dap and headed out the front door.

After Yayo left the apartment, TJ locked the door and went to the window to look over the projects. The sun had started to rise over the city. It was 6:00 a.m., and the dope fiends had already formed a line to get served their morning dose.

YAYO

Everything TJ did was in the name of the almighty dollar. He had killed, robbed, and sold drugs just to floss in fancy whips, dress in designer clothes, and be with beautiful women. He poisoned his black people and murdered black people to protect his empire. Now, as it all settled in, it hurt TJ's heart to know the life he led had claimed the life of his mother, and that alone was too much to bear. TJ walked over to the crack pipe, picked it up, and raised it to his swollen lips and lit it. He inhaled the drugs and felt instant relief. Then, all his pain went away as he exhaled.

S. Allen

Chapter 19

"It had been a long 8 years in the Menard Penitentiary. I did my time alone. Before I was sentenced for an armed robbery, my baby mama promised me she would never leave me, only to abandon me and leave me for dead in the joint.

When I was on the streets, I was getting plenty money. I had whips, cribs, and women at my feet. Niggas respected my G. My profession on the street was robbing niggas. If you were doing a brick or better, then me and my peoples were coming to take a look at you. But you know how it goes in the game when you get locked up. It's out of sight and out of mind, and you find out who your real peoples are.

I did my whole bid plotting and lifting weights. I kept my ears to the streets and learned there was a new crew of niggas called the GBC who were getting crazy money in the city. While in my cell, I formulated a plan for my rise and their downfall.

When I got released, I got right to work. I ran into this African cat who was in the pen with me by the name of Honjie. Honjie had that cake, and was always talking about puttin' me on. The nigga fronted me a brick of soft for 25k. I gave the work to my lil' nephews to make it disappear. I copped from Honjie three times before I ran in his spot and laid him down for ten keys and $40k.

I wanted to see my son, so I called my baby mama and told her to meet me at the North Riverside Mall. When I pulled up, I was in a cocaine white box Chevy with 26-inch Asantis. My baby mama was standing in front of the entrance of the mall with my son, P-nut, when I jumped out. She gave me a sob story like all bitches when they fucked off on their man while he's doing time. "Baby, I'm sorry. I was out here by myself. You left me out here with nothing. I love you and I want us to be a family again."

One thing I learned in the joint was patience and finesse. You see, I know my baby mama ain't worth shit, but I knew she could get me to some sweet licks by her being an exotic dancer at Choco-late City. So after I spent quality time with my son and spent 6 G's on him, we took him to his grandmother's house and me and my baby mama got a room at the Harrison. I banged that pussy up off a pill and a fifth of Grey Goose. The broad kept telling me that I was her king and she would do anything for me, so I told her to put me on some trick ass niggas who be coming to the club stunting. She agreed to it and started putting me up on licks.

The last 6 months had been good. I copped a red Lac truck on 6s, a Camaro on 4s, and I had a nice condo downtown.

There was this one cat who she didn't put me on. I ended up finding about this nigga from one of my guys. He told me my baby mama was fucking with this cat named TJ who drove a white Range Rover. What surprised me the most was TJ was with them GBC dudes, and was supposed to be holding on to some major paper. When I confronted her about the nigga, she denied it. So I beat her ass black and blue and threatened to take my son away from her if she didn't set the dude up.

She had told me he had taken her to his mom's house in the Hunnids, and that was all I needed to know. Me and my partner, Homicide, sat in my basement smoking PCP, plotting on how we was gon' get this money, and the solution we came up with was kidnap and ransom.

We did what we had to do, and our plan worked. The clowns dropped off the bricks and the money. I could've let the woman live, but it had been 8 years since I caught a body, so I put two holes in her head.

My baby mama called me the next day, all hysterical and shit, telling me I didn't have to kill the lady, and asked why I did it. I told her to calm the fuck down and everything was going to be okay. But she wasn't trying to hear none of that, and kept fussing. I took a pull of my blunt and let her finish venting on the other line. After that, I started to wonder, if she was ever questioned about the murder, would she be able to hold water? The way she was talking on the phone made me realize I couldn't trust her with my life or my freedom.

I called her later on that night about 1:00 a.m. and told her to meet me at one of my weed spots on Howard and June way on the North Side. Of course she was nervous and wanted to know why I *wanted to meet her up north this late, so I told her I was trying to give her $50k from the lick and of course, her greed led her to her grave.*

I watched as she pulled up on the block and killed the engine of her black Toyota Camry. It was dark, and nobody was on the block, so I slid out of the gangway with my hoodie on and pulled the .357 from my jeans. Yolanda was fidgeting with the radio when I tapped on the driver's side window. When she looked up, her eyes got big as saucers from the sight of the big Chrome pointed at her.

I pulled the trigger three times, hitting her in the head, plastering her brains and freshly done weave all over the dashboard. To make sure my work was official, I leaned in and gave her two more for good measure. The gunshots echoed through the silent night air as I turned on my heels and jogged off into the darkness of the gangway.

I felt a tinge of guilt, but it was either kill her and remain free, or let her live and risk the rest of my life in prison. That was a no-brainer for a real street nigga like myself. As long as I'm alive, P-nut would be taken care of. In these times, drastic times calls for drastic measures. In the life I'm living, it's kill or be killed!

S. Allen

Chapter 20

Shakira had not been the same since her mother's death. At eight months pregnant, she often sat in the house, crying while reminiscing about her mother. She hated the fact that her mother died without having the chance to see her first grandchild. Yayo had been trying his best to get her out of the house and do things to make her smile, but nothing worked.

She blamed Yayo and her brother for Joyce's untimely death. Shit was definitely rocky in her life, and she was starting to see less and less of Yayo as he ran the streets, got money, and contributed to the ongoing gang wars.

She heard Yayo as he pulled up and parked behind her Audi, but didn't have the strength to move. She heard him enter the condo, throw his keys on the kitchen counter as he always did, and head up the stairs toward their bedroom. When he walked into the master bedroom, Shakira was sitting on the bed with her hair a mess and her eyes bloodshot red from countless days and nights of crying.

Yayo put the Payless bag filled with money on the side of the bed and leaned in to kiss her on the forehead, but she ducked his kiss and gave him an uninviting look.

"Get away from me," Shakira snarled. "You smell like death, you murdering bastard."

Yayo ignored her comment and picked up the bag from the side of the bed. She watched him with pure hatred in her eyes as he proceeded to pull stacks from the bag, and put them inside his wall-mounted safe in the closet.

"That's all you care about, isn't it? All you care about is money. My mother is in the ground because of your selfish, drug-dealing ass. She's dead, and your bitch ass is still out here selling drugs and running the streets. You ain't no better than the nigga who killed her," she said in a hushed tone. "Yayo, I hate you and I wish I never met you," she said as her tears flowed freely.

The words she spoke touched a nerve in Yayo as he slammed the door to his safe.

"Nigga, you don't know how I feel because you're too busy

running the streets," Shakira continued. "I'm pregnant with your child, but you don't care, do you? They should've kidnapped your mother and let you see how it feels."

Yayo had heard enough of Shakira's mouth as he punched a hole in the closet wall. "Bitch, shut the fuck up! It's bad enough I gotta worry about these niggas in the streets, and then I come home and deal with you and your emotional ass. I'm sorry about Joyce, Shakira, but what do you want me to do? I love you, and I'm trying to stack this paper so I can get you and our child away from all this crazy shit. If I could turn back the hands of time, I would, and I swear I would trade my life for Joyce's if I could," Yayo said with tears running down his face.

Shakira saw Yayo's tears, and it caused her to cry even harder as she listened to him pour his heart out.

"Baby, everything I do, I do for us, for our family. You knew what type of nigga you were dealing with when you fell in love with me."

Shakira knew he was right, and she knew she was wrong for blaming him for her mother's death. She loved him until death, and she was riding for him whether right or wrong. She had been there with him since he was 16 years old, and she remained by his side during the most difficult times of his life. She knew he had an evil side, but he also had a caring side that made him go hard for his loved ones.

Shakira stood up to go comfort her man, when all of a sudden, she felt wetness coming down her leg. She grabbed her stomach in pain. "Baby, I think my water broke," she said, afraid to take another step.

Yayo sprang into action, grabbed her bags, and helped her down to the car. He didn't waste any time getting to Mercy Hospital.

**

After six hours of labor, Shakira gave birth to a beautiful, 7-pound baby girl named Shamira. Yayo stood on the side of the hospital bed, smiling like the proud father he is.

YAYO

She passed Yayo his princess and he stared into her brown eyes for what seemed like an eternity. He kissed her on the forehead and said, "Hey, baby girl, daddy loves you so much." Shamira smiled back at her father.

Yayo knew he had to lead a better life for his family, and in order to do that, he had to get out of the streets. He was on borrowed time, and the devil held the stopwatch.

While Yayo sat there admiring his newfound joy, Karen and Honey walked into the room with balloons and gift bags. Karen's eyes watered at the sight of her son holding her first grandchild.

"Come here, mama. Meet Shamira," Yayo said as he handed Karen her granddaughter.

"Oh my god, Yaton, she is so beautiful! Look at all that hair on her head. Hey, baby!" Karen said to Shamira.

Honey walked over toward her great-grandchild. Honey took Shamira in her arms and closed her eyes and everybody bowed their heads to join her in prayer:

"Praise the Lord. We would like to thank you for bringing this beautiful child into our lives. Thank you for her good health. Let everything that has breath praise the Lord. Amen."

When Yayo opened his eyes, he saw the true meaning of life, his family: Shakira, Shamira, Honey, and Karen. The only people missing were his little brothers, Devon and Quavon, and TJ.

Yayo tried to reach TJ, and got his voicemail. "What up, bro? I'm at the hospital with Shakira. You got a lil' niece, fam! Hit me back ASAP!"

***

It was 10:30 p.m., and TJ and Butterball sat across the street from the Red Fox Lounge on 119th and Halsted on the South Side of Chicago. They had followed Fatboy all the way from 81st and Vincess. Butterball had heard from the streets that Fatboy had a little broad who stayed over there, and informed TJ. When TJ pulled up on Vincess, they had caught Fatboy pulling off in his black Denali with a light-skinned female in the passenger seat. They followed him all the way to the lounge, and waited patiently for him to exit the bar.

Butterball glanced at his big homie from the corner of his eye. TJ had on a dingy, white Champion hoodie, his jeans were wrinkled, and his shoes had seen better days. Not to mention, he had lost a tremendous amount of weight. TJ pulled out a Newport, lit it up, and inhaled the tobacco smoke.

TJ caught his protégé staring at him with a strange look on his face. "What up, lil' nigga? You got a problem or something?" He asked while blowing smoke out his nostrils.

"Nah, big homie, I'm just waiting for this nigga to come out so we can handle our business," Butterball said, taking his .38 Snub out and placing it on his lap.

"Well, we ain't gotta wait much longer, 'cause here this sucka ass nigga go right here," TJ said, taking out his .45 Colt and cocking it back.

Fatboy went inside his blue quarter-length mink coat, grabbed a pack of Kool cigarettes, handed one to the light-skinned girl, and then raised one to his lips and lit it up. Fatboy lit the girl's cigarette up before he put it back in his pocket and answered his cellphone.

Ironically, TJ's cell rang at the same moment, and he sent Yayo to voicemail. He pulled his hood over his head, gave Butterball the signal, and both men exited the vehicle and walked across Halsted toward Fatboy.

Fatboy was on the phone securing an order for a half bird when TJ walked up on him with both hands in his hoodie pocket.

"Aye, fam, can I get a light?" He asked.

Fatboy never looked up, but went into his mink to grab his lighter. But when he turned around to see who asked for the light, it was as if he saw a ghost. Fatboy felt his soul leave him before the shots were even fired.

TJ had his hand on the trigger of his .45 while still inside his hoodie pocket and pulled the trigger four times. The garment muffled the sound of the powerful hand cannon as the slugs lifted Fatboy off his feet. The light-skinned female let out a piercing scream, but her scream was silenced by Butterball's .38 Special. She was shot in the face.

TJ and Butterball ran back to the grey Buick, jumped in, and pulled off into the busy traffic.

Shakira had just given life at the same time her brother had taken one.

S. Allen

Chapter 21

Candy arrived at the Ford City Mall with plans to do some serious shopping. She had $1,500 that her trick boyfriend gave her, and she planned to spend every dime of it.

Candy wasn't the average hoodrat. She prayed every day that she would get snagged and wifed up by a baller, or even a half baller for that matter. She just wanted out of the troubles that plagued her life. She didn't have a job, but she got monthly welfare checks. She knew she was a broke bitch, but if you ask any doe-boy who had been between her legs, they would all give her two thumbs up for her sex game, and most would say that the head was boss, giving her the nickname Candy Cane.

Candy a.k.a. Sasha had been friends with Shakira since grade school. They even lost their virginity together. Candy always stayed with the latest fashions and hairdos from the young hustlers in the hood who were sexing her. But like most young gangsters in the hood, they would fuck with her for a minute, then move on to the next.

However, it played out different for a sucka boy named Cash, who hit the pussy and fell in love with her. He was seriously trying to wife Candy. Cash was a wannabe hustler who only copped a half ounce of crack and fronted like he was a brick layer. Cash kept Candy's rent, cell phone, and cable bills paid, not to mention, he kept her fresh with a few dollars in her purse.

Candy walked through the food court of the mall with her Jimmy Choo stilettos clicking on the ground. Candy, who stood at 5'11" and 150 pounds, was thick in all the right places with a caramel complexion. Her ass looked like two full-sized watermelons stuffed into her Seven jeans. She grabbed her iPhone from her Gucci bag and dialed Shakira's number. The phone rang a few times before Shakira answered.

"What up, stanky?" Shakira said as she fixed Shamira a bottle.

"What's up with you, girl? I just got to the mall, and I wanted to see if you needed anything," Candy asked as she walked into the Lark fashion store.

"Nah, I'm good," Shakira said as she shook the baby's bottle.

"Girl, you sure? It's all on Cash," Candy said with a slight chuckle.

"Nah, girl, I'm cool. I see you got ol' boy tricking that cash. You must be putting an ugly head game on that nigga with yo' freak ass."

"Shit, girl, whatever I'm doing, it's working. What's up with my niece?" Candy asked while looking at a pair of Gucci pants.

"She straight. She be having me up all night though, but it's cool."

"That's what's up, girl. I'ma grab me a few outfits while I'm here, and you know them new Jordans just came out," Candy said while eyeing a dude who was looking at a pair of Ed Hardy jeans. "Damn girl, this nigga in here is sexy as hell. Girl, I'ma get at you later. I'm 'bout to holler at ol' boy."

"Whatever, hoe, call me later," Shakira said and hung up the phone.

The dude who had Candy in a trance was a 6-foot, 235-pound, dark-skinned brother with dreads that hung down to his shoulders. The Pelle Pelle leather coat he had on with the fur on the hood had to cost at least $1,500. His black Prada jeans had a slight sag, and the Nike ACG boots he had on looked brand new. The diamonds on his earlobes glittered as the light shinned on them. The dude had blemish-free skin with a hardened look to his face. He had a serious look that turned Candy on.

Candy tried to keep her composure when the dude caught her staring at him. He walked over to the clothing rack where Candy was and smiled as he spoke, exposing his pearly whites. "Damn, baby girl, you work here or something?" He asked her.

"No. Why you ask me that?" Candy shot back.

"Because you're staring at me like I'm 'bout to steal something."

"Boy, ain't nobody paying you no attention," she said with an attitude.

Candy read the tattoo on the dude's neck. "Respect few. Fear none," and was definitely turned on by this thugged out nigga. Dude looked Candy up and down and licked his lips before he spoke again. "Listen, cutie, my name is Tank. What's your name?" He asked.

"My name is Candy," she said, extending her hand to him.

He gently grabbed her hand and shook it, then placed a kiss on it before he let it go. "So, Ms. Candy, I don't see a ring on that finger. Does that mean you're single?" He asked, looking directly in her eyes.

"Yes, I'm very single," Candy replied in a seductive tone. "What about you?" She asked.

"Nah, ma, I'm a married man. I'm married to the game, but I will definitely cheat with you," Tank said. "Shorty, you're sexy as hell, and I'm trying to see what it do. Why don't you put this number in ya phone?"

Candy pulled out her iPhone, and her and Tank exchanged numbers and promised to get up with each other.

While they were talking, a young cat walked up to Tank. "What up, big homie? You ready to shake this spot?" The young cat said.

Candy looked at him, and swore that he looked familiar. Her and Tank made plans to go to the Navy pier that night, and then he walked off. She watched as Tank and the young cat went to the cashier and paid for their items in cash, spending about $4,200. Candy had just bumped her a baller, and she couldn't wait until later to get up with him.

***

Candy was in her small apartment on the West Side getting ready for her date with Tank. She had given Cash a spill, saying she was going out with her girlfriends.

Cash wasn't tripping, and he told her he was gonna be on the block hustling and he'll catch her later. She was in the mirror straightening her hair when her cell phone rang. She saw it was Tank calling and quickly answered in a seductive tone. "What up, boo?" She cooed into the receiver.

"Damn, I'm your boo already?" Tank asked.

S. Allen

"Boy, you been my boo since I first laid eyes on you," Candy flirted.

"That's what's up, shorty. I'm on my way to come scoop you right now. Are you ready?"

"Yeah, I'm finishing up my hair right now."

"Where do you want me to come get you?" Tank said, gliding his whip through traffic.

"I stay on Kedzie and Ohio, the first house on the left."

"Aiight, I'll be there in about 20 minutes."

"I'ma be looking out the window for you. What you driving?" Candy asked.

"A candy apple red Escalade on 26s," said Tank.

"Okay, boo, see you soon," Candy said before hanging up. "Damn, an Escalade on 26s. Just caught one," Candy thought to herself as she put the finishing touches on her hair.

Candy had on a one-piece Deréon dress that was way too short. Her voluptuous ass hung from under the dress, and her heavy cleavage was popping out from the front. Her six-inch Louboutin stilettos had her calves looking toned. She definitely had a "Come fuck me" outfit on. She couldn't wait to put the pussy on Tank, and have him coming up off them Ben Franklins she knew he had.

After thirty minutes or so, Candy heard what she thought was a marching band in front of her apartment. When she looked out the window, she saw a tinted-up red Escalade truck, and she hurried to grab her Baby Phat coat and was out the door. Tank was standing outside, leaning up against his whip when she exited her building.

Seeing Candy's curvaceous body walking toward his truck made Tank's dick get hard as he thought about all the positions he was going to have her in by the end of the night. He helped her get inside the truck, and admired her while doing so.

When Candy got inside the truck, the strong smell of high-grade marijuana hit her in the face. Tank looked over her once more before he spoke. "Damn, shorty, you look good as hell."

Candy couldn't help but melt. "You looking good ya'self, boo," she said as she gave Tank a onceover, admiring his all- black Ed Hardy outfit with the all-black Timberlands to match. His dreads

166

were braided in four braids to the back. His diamond chain hung to the middle of his stomach with a diamond-encrusted cross. Tank glided the truck down Kedzie Avenue.

"So, who you fuck with over here?" Tank asked her as he grabbed the half blunt out the ashtray and lit it up.

"What you mean, who I fuck wit'? I already told you I'm single, and I got my own apartment," Candy said while playing with the ends of his dreads.

"Is that so, Ms. Candy? It's still hard to believe a beautiful woman like you ain't got no nigga."

"Niggas don't be on nothing. Dudes just want a female they can fuck on, and I don't be on that. So I just do me," Candy said as she grabbed the blunt from Tank and took a long pull from it.

Tank pulled the truck to a stop at the light and noticed all the gangsters standing on the corner. He reached under his seat to grab his Glock 9 and placed it on his lap.

Candy saw the gun and nodded. "Damn, boo, what you on?"

Tank ignored her and continued to mean mug the thugs standing on the corner, throwing up their gang signs. The light turned green and Tank turned up the volume on his touchscreen TV and bumped a new song from Chief Keef. Candy knew then she was in the car with a real street nigga.

Tank and Candy drove down Lakeshore Drive, smoking kush and getting to know each other. So far, she had learned that Tank had just gotten out of prison, had one son, and was getting crazy paper. He took Candy to the Navy pier on Lakeshore Drive, where they had dinner and a few shots of tequila. When they left the pier, Tank stopped at a liquor store on the North Side to grab some Grey Goose and a box of Magnum condoms.

"What up, mami? It's getting late. What you trying to do?" He said while rubbing his hand on Candy's thigh.

"I'm with you, boo. Do you," she said while spreading her legs wider for him.

Tank pulled off and headed to a hotel on Sheridan. Candy was gone off of the weed and liquor, and her pussy got wet as she thought about Tank hitting her from the back. Once inside the hotel,

Tank kicked off his Timbs, sat on the edge of the bed, and began to roll a blunt.

Candy came over to him and planted a kiss on his lips, "Baby, you mind if a take a quick shower and freshen up?"

"Go 'head, shorty," he said as he put the finishing touches on his blunt. He lit the blunt, grabbed the remote, and started channel surfing, and stopped when he reached a porn channel. There was a porn flick with Pinky that caught Tank's attention. He watched as Pinky got her pussy eaten out by another thick broad. Tank felt his shaft trying to bust through his jeans, when his phone came to life and killed his vibe.

He looked and saw it was a call from his partner, Homicide. "What up, killa?" He said while blowing out a cloud of kush smoke.

"What's the business, Joe? Where the fuck you at?"

"I'm at the Sheridan with my new lil' move. What up?"

"I'm in the car with Lil' B. Aye, you know that nigga Fatboy got knocked off a couple of days ago?" Homicide said.

"Hell, naw, I ain't heard shit about that," Tank said, surprised by the news. "That nigga owed me 15 stacks."

"Yeah, fam, they say the nigga got hit up something raw in the Hunnids, but dig, get up with me tomorrow. I got something sweet for us."

"Aiight, my nigga, be careful out there."

"Aiight, love," Homicide said, then hung up.

Tank sat and thought about the news he just received. He made plenty of money fucking with Fatboy and the ATGs. Every time he caught a lick for some work, he would dump it on the ATGs for the low. They had a good relationship. In prison, there were a few ATG gang members at Menard, and Tank liked their rebellious attitude and the way they moved. One time, he got into it with some Latin Kings in the gym room over a basketball game, and one of the Kings called Tank out of his name. Tank ended up beating the shit out of homeboy, and the ATGs had backed him up and made sure he got a fair one. After that, he had nothing but love for the gang.

Tank's trip down memory lane was interrupted when Candy came sashaying out of the bathroom in a pair of pink boy shorts and a matching bra.

Candy walked over to the bed looking thicker than a snicker. "Here, boo, can you rub some of this on my body?" She asked as she passed him a bottle of Johnson & Johnson baby oil.

"Lay down on your stomach, shorty," he commanded as he popped the top on the bottle. Candy quickly did as she was told, as Tank rubbed the oil between his hands. He started at her thick thighs, then made his way up to her voluptuous ass.

"Mmmmmhhh," she moaned in pleasure.

"Take this shit off," Tank said while tugging at her boy shorts. She leaned up a little and took off her bra as well and let her melons loose. She laid back on her stomach and spread her legs. Tank continued massaging Candy's butt, while spreading her cheeks and oiling up her crack. After it was all oiled up, he slowly worked his finger into her forbidden hole. Candy went crazy as Tank's finger entered her asshole, and he placed two fingers in her pussy at the same time, and she let out a soft moan.

"Oooh, baby, I'm 'bout to cum."

Tank stopped, stepped back off the bed, and took off his Ed Hardy jeans. He dropped his boxers to the floor, and let his hardness free.

Candy saw his thick, long manhood, and decided to do some pleasuring of her own, as she crawled over toward him and took his erection into her warm mouth. Candy jerked and sucked on the biggest dick she had ever encountered in her life.

Tank gripped the back of Candy's head to help guide her up and down his shaft. "Damn, girl, this feels good," Tank said as he pulled his Ed Hardy T-shirt over his head along with his jewelry. He was on the verge of busting from the way she was doing her thing. "Hold up, shorty," he said as he stepped back from her.

"What, nigga? You can't handle it?" She asked with a devilish grin on her face.

Tank reached over and grabbed the box of Magnums out of the liquor store bag, opened it, and put one on.

Candy still couldn't believe what he was working with. "He got money, and he got a big dick," she thought to herself as she turned around and got on all fours, giving him full access. She tooted her ass in the air as Tank entered her from behind, and started pounding her with long, hard strokes. Candy screamed out in ecstasy as she looked back at Tank, who was looking like a demon possessed as he pounded her pussy. The light glistened off his sweaty, tattooed skin, and his eyes were bloodshot red.

Tank pounded Candy in every position known to man, but the grand finale was when he came in her mouth, making her swallow. She handled it like a champ though.

Candy laid her head on Tank's chest, spent from his dick game. She was definitely sprung. Tank was smoking a blunt as they both laid there, caught in their own thoughts. Candy's thoughts was of how she was gonna become this nigga's wifey. However, Tank's thoughts were of money and murder.

Chapter 22

Yayo pulled up behind the abandoned warehouse in Schaumburg to meet up with Batman and Robin. A lot of things were going on in the streets, and the stakes were definitely high. GBC was starting to catch a lot of pressure due to Fatboy's murder. ATG was out for blood, so the hospitals stayed busy.

Yayo pulled up alongside the black cruiser and exited his car. Batman and Robin exited their vehicle and shook hands with Yayo.

"Glad you could make it," Batman said as he took out a cigarette and lit it up. Yayo passed the purple Crown Royal bag to Batman that contained the $5,000 weekly street tax.

Batman looked inside the bag and nodded his head in approval, "Listen, Yayo, like I told you before, this fucking gang war has got to stop. You getting money is good, but all these bodies are something else. I told you they were talking about bringing in the feds, and when the feds come in, it's gonna be out of my hands." Yayo leaned up against his Cadillac.

"Yayo, I'm a fucking homicide detective, for Christ's sake. There's nobody being brought in or charged for all these murders. How do you think that makes me and my partner look?"

"Listen," Yayo finally spoke up. "It is what it is. They shed blood, and I'm just supposed to sit back and let shit ride? Fuck that! We bleed, they bleed," Yayo said.

"I'm telling you, youngin', when you end up in federal prison, just make sure you hold your weight."

"What the fuck you mean by that?" Yayo questioned, feeling offended.

"I'm just saying, when the feds get a nigga, it ain't like the state. The feds are throwing dinosaur numbers, and ain't no amount of money gonna get you out of that jam. Which brings me to my next point, this lil' $5,000 a week," Batman said, raising the Crown Royal bag, "This ain't gonna cut it. Yayo, you're getting major money, and I'm gonna need $50,000 a week, shorty." Robin stood on the other side of the cruiser with a smirk on his pink face. He knew they had young Yayo in a tight situation.

"Man, you must be crazy to think that I'ma come up off that type of money to you niggas," Yayo said through clenched teeth. Yayo knew then he shouldn't have gotten involved with the two crooked cops.

"I mean, it's like this, Yayo. I like you and all, but the rules are the rules. Either you play by them, or you lose. What's it going to be? The fifty grand or your freedom? I'll give you a week to think it over," Batman said, crossing his arms across his chest.

Yayo spit on the ground in front of him, got in his car, and peeled out of the parking lot.

"You think he'll go for it?" Robin asked Batman over the hood of their cruiser.

"If he's smart, he will," Batman said, then got back in the cruiser.

***

Yayo was driving down the Dan Ryan, thinking about how the two crooked cops were trying to put him in a trick bag. He had built a profitable empire for himself, and now, they were trying to extort him for his paper. "I got a shorty and a family to support. I ain't giving them shit," he thought to himself. They had rules to the game, and Yayo had rules of his own if they wanted to play rough. "They gonna have to come get it," he thought.

Yayo grabbed his cell phone and called TJ.

"What's up, family?" TJ answered on the third ring.

"Listen, fam, you know tomorrow is the first of the month. You gonna be ready to handle this business?" Yayo said as he exited the Dan Ryan on to 63rd.

"Yeah, I'm hip. Hit me up tomorrow, nigga."

"Aiight, bet," Yayo said and hung up.

As Yayo headed toward 69th and Wolcott, TJ was headed to Space Mountain as he picked up the pipe and took a big hit of crack.

Chapter 23

Yayo and TJ were on 95th and Yates in the kitchen, doing what they do, shaking and bagging up bricks of heroin. Yayo looked over at the pile of powder and the three handguns on the table.

He observed TJ as he bagged up the work, and noticed how much weight he had lost in the past month. TJ was never a big dude, but he wasn't that skinny, either. Yayo also took notice of TJ's demeanor, and how much it had changed in the past 10 years. TJ had at least 20 bodies under his belt that Yayo knew of, and 20 bodies could surely change any nigga.

TJ sat across from Yayo, dressed in the full army fatigue getup, looking like a master of his trade as he cut and bagged the heroin.

"What up, nigga? What you all quiet for?" Yayo asked from across the table.

"Ain't shit, nigga, just got a lot on my mind," TJ said as he shuffled some cut to the heroin.

"Aiight, but check this out," Yayo said as he placed some heroin on aluminum foil. "I met up with Batman and Robin yesterday, and they on some shit."

"Oh, yeah? What them pigs talking 'bout?" TJ said, sounding half interested.

"They bitching 'bout all them bodies that been dropping, and talking 'bout the feds 'bout to step in and start snatching niggas off the streets and shit. Fuck, they expect niggas to start a peace treaty or some shit? Fuck all that! Now, them pigs talking 'bout they raising the street tax to 50 racks a week!"

At the sound of 50 thousand, TJ looked up from the pile of heroin. "And what you tell 'em?" TJ asked with a mean mug on his face.

"I ain't tell 'em shit. I jumped in the whip and pulled off on them pigs. Listen, TJ, we ain't coming off of any money like that," Yayo said, dismissing the whole idea.

"You sho' know what to say. Fuck them pigs. How you wanna play it?" TJ asked while putting a G-pack to the side.

"Them cops got some ugly dirt on us, but we got some dirt on them, too."

"What you talking about, that Lakefront incident?" TJ questioned.

"Yeah, my nigga. I don't know if they could tie us to that, or that Riverdale shit with ol' boy."

TJ got up from the table and went to the kitchen counter to get more bags. "They say proper preparation prevents poor performance," TJ said as he grabbed the box of sandwich bags and sat back down at the table. TJ's phone started vibrating on the table. He saw Butterball's number and picked up. "What's up, shorty?"

"What up big homie? Where you at?" Butterball said, coughing from the weed he was smoking on.

"I'm at the spot on 95th taking care of that business, Joe. What's up?"

"I was just calling to let you know I got that for you, and I'm ready for the next demo," Butterball said.

"That's what's up. I'ma get up with you tomorrow in the a.m."

"Aiight, my nigga. I'm out here," Butterball said, then ended the call.

"Who was that?" Yayo asked.

"That was lil' Butterball trying to get right."

"But back to what I was saying about these pigs. We can't be walking around in these streets with our shoes untied, feel me?" Yayo said as he tied up another G-pack.

"That's all I needed to hear, fam," TJ said with a grin on his face.

Yayo had just issued Batman and Robin's death warrants, with TJ being the deliverer.

"TJ, check it out, my nigga, after we take care of this shit with these crooked pigs, we should consider getting up out these streets for a minute and turn this paper into some legit shit," Yayo said.

"Aye, that sounds all good and dandy, but I done already lost my momma to this shit, and I'm going out blazing, guns up. Police, street niggas, I don't give a fuck. I ain't got shit to live for," TJ said, staring at Yayo with bloodshot eyes.

"TJ, you trippin. What about Shakira? What about your niece,

Shamira? They need you, fam."

"Until whoever killed my momma steps from the hole, I'ma keep bleeding these streets," TJ said in a murderous tone.

"You crazy, nigga," Yayo said. He realized TJ was too far gone.

***

Shakira was at home sitting in her comfortable rocking chair, rocking Shamira to sleep. She was transitioning into motherhood very well, and she loved spending quality time with her baby.

She was happy and content with her life and her family, but she hated the fact that Yayo was still playing the streets hard. Even though he provided for his family and made sure they had everything they wanted, she still feared for him. As she counted the days down, she prayed that Yayo would keep his promise: In 6 months, he was getting out of the game, and they were going to get married and live a regular life. All Shakira ever wanted was a regular life without all the drugs and murder surrounding her. She picked up her phone and dialed his number.

"What's up, boo?" Yayo answered, using his shoulder and chin to balance the phone while he mixed the heroin.

"Hey baby, what you doing?" Shakira said.

"I'm at work, baby. What's up? Y'all alright over there?"

"Yeah, we alright. We just missing you, that's all. Yaton, tell Shamira goodnight before I put her to sleep," Shakira said as she put the phone on speaker.

"Hey, princess. What's daddy's girl doing?" Yayo said in a baby voice. Shamira heard Yayo's voice and a big smile appeared across her face.

"Daddy loves you, Mira," Yayo continued, "Daddy misses you so much and I love you. Good night and sleep tight, sweetheart," he said and blew her a kiss through the phone.

"Damn, I wish I could get a goodnight kiss, nigga," Shakira said as she grabbed the phone back.

"Baby, I'ma be there tomorrow, and I'ma give you all the loving you want. But listen, boo, I'ma see in you the a.m. I gotta finish doing what I'm doing," he said.

"Hold up, baby, is my brother with you?" Shakira asked before she hung up.

"Yeah he's right here, hold up," Yayo said as he passed TJ the phone.

"What's up, Big Head?" TJ said.

"Damn, what's up, stranger? I ain't heard from you in a minute. When you gon' come spend some time with me and your niece?"

"I've been a lil' busy, sis, but I'ma make it my business to come over there this week," TJ said, feeling guilty about neglecting the only blood family he had left.

"TJ, I just want you to know that I love you and I miss you, and don't get caught up in that shit out there. Our family needs you, bro."

"I feel you, sis. I just been going through it out here, you know, since Momma--"

Shakira cut him off. "TJ, I understand, but we have to move on from that. Momma would want that."

"Sis, I'm all good. I'ma get up with y'all this week. Give my niece a kiss for me," TJ said, hanging up the phone and passing it back to Yayo.

TJ didn't want to get caught up in his emotions right now. He had too much work to do in the streets. He got up and put six bricks in a duffle bag. "I'll be right back, fam. I'm 'bout to bring this shit down to the basement," he said as Yayo continued to bag up the dope.

***

TJ had just come back upstairs when all of a sudden, the front door came crashing down. Yayo heard the commotion and grabbed his Glock. TJ ran toward the kitchen where Yayo was, grabbed his twin Desert Eagles, and flipped the kitchen table over, sending heroin flying everywhere. Bullets came whizzing through the kitchen, splintering the wood on the table. Yayo reached over the table and returned fire.

The two gunmen took cover in the front room, while all four men exchanged gunfire in the small house, filling the dwelling with gun smoke. TJ got up from behind the table and took cover behind the refrigerator. He could tell that the shots were coming from the living room.

"What, y'all thought it was sweet, nigga?" Yayo yelled and fired a few more rounds from his .40 cal.

"Aaaahhhhhh, shit! I'm hit!" One of the masked men screamed out in pain.

TJ looked around the fridge and saw a masked man running toward the front door, and gave chase after him. When he reached the sidewalk, the masked man was already peeling out in a black Box Chevy. TJ let off a few rounds at the moving vehicle as it turned the corner.

When he walked back in the house, Yayo was standing over the other masked man with the Glock pointed at him. "TJ, go grab the work," Yayo said.

TJ ran to the basement to grab the work, and heard three gunshots corning from upstairs. As he walked back into the front room, he saw Yayo had shot the intruder three times in the chest.

"Hold up, Yayo," TJ said and bent down and pulled the ski mask off of the guy. The dead man's eyes were wide open, and he had a distinctive tattoo across his right eyebrow that said, "Homicide."

"Let's get up out of here," TJ said as they heard the sirens getting closer and closer.

TJ raised his Desert Eagle and shot Homicide in the face for good measure. TJ and Yayo ran out the house, jumped in their whips, and pulled off into the night.

S. Allen

Chapter 24

It had been a week since the shooting on 95th and Yates. Yayo had been taking extra precautions moving through the streets of Chicago. All they knew was the nigga's name they bodied in the spot. It didn't ring a bell in the streets. Yayo was stressed out from all the gun play, and felt the reaper was getting closer and closer to him. He had been having nightmares of killers invading his soul.

Yayo looked down at his sleeping daughter, who was peacefully laying on his chest. Looking at his beautiful angel gave him the strength, courage, and motivation to finish what he started, and stay alive in the process.

Yayo got up and laid his daughter in her crib, and went to the kitchen to pour himself a drink. He retrieved the bottle of Grey Goose and poured a shot of the vodka. He quickly downed the shot and wiped his mouth with the back of his hand, as the liquor made its way through his body, warming up his insides. Yayo poured himself another shot, then walked to the balcony, pulled the curtains back, and stared at the darkness of his backyard.

He was lost in his thoughts, as he thought about how he came to Chicago as a young boy with nothing. His life was dealt a bad hand from the jump. Then, he fell in love with the streets. Yayo had come up from nothing, and now, he had something to show for it. He did time in prison for murder, dodged death multiple times, and issued his fair share of death on his enemies. He made sure he put his whole hood on, letting everybody get a chance to eat. And for that, the hood loved Yayo, and Yayo loved it back.

The birth of his daughter, and the bond he felt with his family made him feel like he had a purpose in life, and he knew he had to start distancing himself from the griminess of the streets.

While Yayo was lost in his thoughts, Shakira walked up behind him and hugged him from behind. The softness of her silk Victoria's Secret gown against his skin felt good to him. "What up, baby. Are you okay?" Shakira asked while planting kisses on his shoulder.

"Yeah, I'm aiight. I just got a lot going on right now," he said, turning around to face her.

"Baby, whatever it is that's bothering you ain't worth it. Your family should be the only thing that matters," she said, kissing him on his chest.

Yayo rubbed his hands through her hair, kissed her on the forehead, and pulled her close. "Baby, in a few months, I'ma leave all this shit alone. I just want us to be happy, and I want to provide for us in a legit way. I want the best for my daughter."

"I know you do, baby," she said as she slid her tongue in his mouth, tasting the Grey Goose on his tongue.

Yayo passionately kissed her while rubbing her back, and then his cell phone vibrated in his front pocket, disturbing their moment.

Yayo looked at the caller ID and noticed it was Batman before answering. "What?" Yayo sneered into the phone through clenched teeth.

"What's up, youngin'? I'm glad to hear from you, too. I was just calling to see if you made up your mind on what we discussed," Batman said while lighting a cigarette.

"Yeah, I thought about it."

"And what exactly did you come up with, shorty?" Batman said taking a pull from his cigarette.

"I came up with you sucking my dick," Yayo said sarcastically.

"Oh, I see, Mr. Bad Yayo. You done got too big for your britches. But you listen to me, you two percent ass nigger, I got enough dirt on you and your boys to put you in the can for the rest of your life!" Batman yelled through the phone.

Yayo hung up his phone and threw it on the couch.

"What's wrong, Yaton?" Shakira asked with a nervous look on her face.

"Ain't nothing, baby. Why don't you go upstairs and relax?" Yayo said and kissed her on her lips. "I'll be up there in a minute."

Shakira headed upstairs without saying another word, leaving Yayo in deep thought. After Shakira was out of sight, Yayo got on the phone and dialed TJ's number.

"What up, family?" TJ answered.

"What's good with you, bro? I'm just calling to let you know the gloves are off with Pinky and the Brain."

YAYO

"Say no more. It's done," TJ said and ended the call.

Yayo sat on the couch and downed another shot of Grey Goose. "Who the fuck these niggas think they playing with?" Yayo thought to himself.

***

Butterball sat in the driver's seat of his '67 Cutlass, listening to a new track by Lil' Durk. It was a Thursday night, and the block was jumping on 69th and Wolcott. Butterball watched as the workers served the fiends who were in desperate need of the medication that would sooth their souls and help them function.

Butterball started out as a runner, then elevated to a foot soldier. Since he was so focused and mentally driven to succeed in the game, TJ promoted him to a block lieutenant. His job was to issue the packs to the runners, and collect all the money from sales. He had to supervise the workers. Butterball was backed by Lil' Murder, whose staff title and duties were to make sure nobody ran off with money or got out of line. He was Butterball's chief of security.

Butterball transitioned well in the dope game. He came up from a bloodline of gangsters. His oldest and only brother was murdered in a robbery when he was only 13 years old, and now, at 17, Butterball had answered the calling of the streets, and became a product of his environment.

Born into a drug-infested home, Butterball's trials and tribulations were high. Butterball's father mysteriously disappeared. His mom had a lot on her plate, unable to support her two children. She turned to the street corners, and sold her body for cash. After engaging in the life of a streetwalker, Butterball's mother, Mrs. Mary, turned to using drugs. At first, she started with painkillers like oxycodone, and then pursued the beast of all, heroin.

Butterball used to watch as his mother would inject the potent liquid in her veins and nod off for hours at a time.

His brother became the man of the house, and took to the streets to provide for the both of them. His mother died when he was nine, and after his brother got murdered, that forced him to hit the streets and provide for himself.

All the hustlers on the block who knew his brother would look out for him, and gave him 5-10 bags of crack at a time, and he would have to hustle just to keep clothes on his back and food in his stomach. His life was a rollercoaster until he met TJ.

TJ knew Butterball was a true hustler. He took a liking to the young G, and put him under his wing. Throughout the course of being part of the GBC, Butterball's bread never came up short, and he always assisted when shit popped off. Such loyal characteristics abled him to climb up the ranks, and now, he had status in the hood.

As Butterball watched the line of dope fiends being served, his phone rang. "Hello, what's the bizness, big homie?" He said.

"Ain't shit, where you at?" The caller said.

"I'm on the block."

"Aye, peeps, I'm right around the corner. Come bend a block with me," the caller said.

"Aiight, I'm out here," Butterball said, then hung up.

Ten minutes later, a Box Chevy on 26s turned the corner on 69th and Wolcott and pulled up on the side of Butterball's Cutlass. Butterball put the blunt roach out, exited his whip, and climbed into the Chevy.

***

"So what's up with the two punks and that $50,000?" Robin asked from the passenger seat of the cruiser.

"Right now, I'm going to let Yayo make the first move. He's talking all that gangster shit right now, but I have an extra copy of that confession tape of Rex," Batman said as he made a left off of Independence. "This lil' nigger gonna come up off of that money. Watch what I tell you," Batman said very confidently.

"What if he doesn't?" Robin asked.

"Then, he's going to prison for the rest of his fucking life," Batman said.

Batman knew he had Yayo with his hands tied. Him and Robin were getting major money in the streets from extorting drug dealers.

YAYO

Batman and Robin were at a stoplight on Kedzie and Van Buren, so deep in conversation they never noticed the minivan tailing them all the way from the North Side.

"What you got planned for the weekend?" Batman asked Robin as he lit another cigarette.

"I don't know, probably spend some time at the house with Tammy. We've been so busy with all these damn murderers, I been neglecting the ol' lady," Robin replied.

The white minivan pulled up alongside them and slammed on the brakes, coming to a screeching halt. The side doors opened and an AK-47 stared Robin in the face like a mirror.

"Oohhhh, shit!" Robin yelled and tried to reach for his service weapon.

The gunman pulled the trigger on the AK, spraying the side of the cruiser. The glass from the passenger window shattered, covering Robin's face. Batman floored the Crown Vic only to run into a Dodge Intrepid.

"Shit!" Batman cursed as he threw the cruiser in reverse. But the gunman hopped out of the van and continued spraying the Crown Vic with bullets.

Batman reached for the door handle and felt blood splatter on his face. He turned to his right and saw his partner slumped over with a cracked skull.

The gunman continued firing from the front of the cruiser, as hot shell casings fell on the ground. Batman felt a sharp pain in his chest. After the gunfire ceased, the gunmen hopped in their van and fled the scene, leaving a bloody mess and the air polluted with gunpowder.

Batman grabbed his walkie-talkie with his blood-soaked hands and radioed in for help. "Officer down!" Batman yelled into the radio while coughing up blood.

"Officer down!" He repeated again as his vision began to blur and his breath shortened. He closed his eyes and fell into total darkness.

***

Yayo was feeding his daughter a bottle in the lavish, furnished basement of his luxury home when the news invaded the screen of his 60-inch plasma TV.

"On today's top story, two Chicago police officers were gunned down on Chicago's West Side. Police say a gunman opened fire on Officer Lloyd Thomas, and his partner, Officer Jeffery Washington, earlier this morning as the officers sat at a stoplight on Kedzie and Van Buren. Jeffery Washington was killed in the hail of gunfire, and Lloyd Thomas is in critical condition as we speak. Police would like any witnesses to please contact the Chicago Police Department."

Yayo turned the TV off and kissed his daughter on the cheek, and she looked up and smiled at her father. Yayo was knee-deep in the game, and he was definitely playing to win.

Chapter 25

Candy and Tank were kicking back at a hotel. "What's up, baby? What you thinking about?" She asked as she ran her freshly done nails down his tattooed chest.

"Just thinking about money," Tank said as he palmed Candy's ass. "Money stays on my mind."

Tank and Candy had become an item. Candy had Tank's gangsta ass sprung off of the pussy. He gave her everything she yearned for.

He had turned it up on the streets since Homicide got killed. Tank was heartless. He trusted no one, and when it came to money and murder, anybody could get it.

Despite his coldness, Candy loved Tank, and he was everything she ever wanted in a man when he was with her and away from the streets. He kept her laced in designer clothes, and was very protective over her. She knew he was a gangster, but at times, he would turn all of that off and show her a touch of tenderness.

"Boo, you should get up with my girl's baby daddy. He got that work," Candy said as she massaged Tank's dick.

"Oh, yeah? Who is her baby daddy?" He inquired.

"His name is Yayo. He getting that money out there, and he runs the GBC. Have you heard of them?"

"Nah, what they be on?" Tank replied, playing dumb.

"Bae, they got 69th all the way down to the Hunnids on lock. They got a big ass squad," Candy bragged while rubbing his balls, causing him to get hard.

"Who he be with?" Tank asked, rubbing his hands through her hair.

"He be with his right-hand man, TJ," Candy said.

Tank couldn't believe what he just heard. He put his dick in Candy's mouth as he thought about the valuable info she just gave him. Candy started at the tip of his meat, circling her tongue around the tip. Tank grabbed the back of her head and forced her down to take all of him, which was impossible. She sucked on his dick as he fingered her sloppy, wet pussy. After a minute or two, Candy coated his fingers with her love juices. She got up, climbed on top of him, and slid down on his thick, meaty dick.

"Damn, girl!" Tank said as he grabbed her ass cheeks, spreading them wider. Candy rode him until she felt the veins in his dick swell up, letting her know he was about to explode. Once she had him where she wanted him, she sped up the pace and grinded down on him, causing him to explode inside of her tight walls.

Candy kissed Tank on his lips and went to the bathroom to wash up. Tank sat up and grabbed the half blunt he had in the ashtray and lit it up. His phone sprung to life and he quickly answered the incoming call. "What up?" He said as he blew the kush smoke in the air.

"What up, big homie? How you living?" The caller asked.

"I'm good, but check this. Remember that thang me and fam did in the Hunnids?"

"Yeah, why?"

"This bitch I'm fucking wit' say she cool with Yayo's girl, and the nigga Yayo and TJ are comrades," Tank said as he relit the blunt.

"Fam, I told you I knew that hoe from somewhere. I just couldn't put my finger on it, but trust me, I don't ever forget no face," the caller said.

"Yeah, them bitch ass niggas got away. I was trying to bum something. Homicide was faking."

Candy was coming out of the bathroom when she heard Tank talking on the phone and decided to be nosey. She stayed still and listened.

"Yeah, my nigga. When it's all said and done, I'ma whack Yayo and TJ, especially TJ's tough ass with all that killa shit. I'ma show 'em how klllas kill, and put two in his head like I did his mama," Tank retorted. "Fuck them clowns. They gon' be deceased in these streets."

Candy's jaw hit the floor when she heard Tank talk about murdering Joyce. She ran back into the bathroom and threw up. She couldn't believe what she just heard.

"Aye, check, hit me tomorrow. I'ma slide on you and blow this pound," Tank said.

"Aiight, that's a bet," the caller said and hung up.

Candy walked out of the bathroom, put on her game face, and asked, "Who was that on the phone?" as she crawled on the bed and laid next to him.

"Oh, that was my lil' man."

"Oh," was all Candy said.

***

As Candy sat in the living room of Yayo and Shakira's home, she thought of the right words to say. She called Shakira last night and told her she had something important to tell her, and now, she was nervous. She loved Tank, but Shakira was her best friend since the sandbox. Tank was expendable, so it was necessary that she told Shakira what she heard him talking about.

"Girl, what's good? Why you acting all weird and shit?" Shakira said, breaking down a blunt to smoke with her best friend.

"Shakira, sit down for a sec. I gotta tell you something," Candy said nervously.

"Okay." Shakira took a seat.

"Shakira, listen, you know that nigga I been fucking with, who got the Lac truck?"

"Yeah. What's up?" Shakira said, rolling a blunt.

"Shakira, he killed Joyce, and he was the one who tried to kill TJ and Yayo," Candy said, then told her everything else she heard Tank say on the phone.

Tears poured down Shakira's cheeks. Candy got up and hugged her friend. Shakira ran to grab her cell phone to call Yayo.

S. Allen

Chapter 26

"Aiight, Candy, say no more," TJ said as he hung up his cell phone. TJ was in a rage, and he wanted blood as him and Yayo sat in one of their stash houses in Schaumburg, plotting Tank's demise. The streets of Englewood were hot because of the shooting of the homicide detectives. Batman was still in critical condition, and was expected to survive. Yayo and TJ were moving with caution because if Batman made it through, the heat was sure to come down on them like the fury of God.

"Yayo, I want this nigga to die slow for what he did to my mother. What the fuck is we waiting for?" TJ asked as he paced back and forth on the living room floor, clutching his .223 assault rifle with the 100-round drum. He was ready for action.

"TJ, I already told you we playing chess with these niggas. This clown's slow as hell. We gon' lead his dumb ass right to us," Yayo said, trying to make sense of the situation.

"How we gonna do that?" TJ questioned.

"We gon' get Candy to set his ass up."

"You think we can trust her like that? I mean, what if she fumbles and the nigga gets suspicious and put pressure on her? She might flip on us," TJ said as he took a pull from his Newport.

"The nigga's a robber, so his greed will lead him to his termination," Yayo said, staring out the window. "We gonna get Candy to make him get some work from us, and his thirsty ass gon' think shit is sweet and try to jack like he did last time, but this time, we gon' be ready to jack his ass for his life," Yayo sneered.

TJ sat on the couch and let Yayo's words marinate in his brain, and then, it all made sense to him. Revenge is best served ice cold.

***

Tank and Candy were having dinner at the Red Lobster near the Ford City Mall.

"So, baby, did you think about what I said about messing with my girl's baby daddy on that work?" Candy said as she dipped her fried shrimp in sauce.

"Actually, I did, and I wanted to holler at you about that. I'm trying to get about 5 bricks of heroin," Tank said smoothly, then sipped on his piña colada. Tank had done his homework, and found out Yayo had major dope.

"Well, I already told him about you. I told him you was getting money, and was somebody he should do business with. He said that as long as you were 'bout that paper, he would fuck with you."

"You got a number on him?" He asked.

"Yeah, I got it," Candy said as she grabbed Tank's phone and added Yayo's number.

"That's what's up," Tank said.

***

Later that day, Yayo got a text on his smartphone that said: "What up, fam? This Candy's dude. She told me to get up with you and gave me your number. I need to holler at you on a safe line."

Yayo read the text and sent a reply. "What's good, my dude? Hit this line, 773-482-9371."

A few minutes later, Yayo's burnout phone rung and he answered. "What up, Joe?"

"What's the bizness, fam? This is Tank. Candy said you was good on that Al Green."

"Yeah, I'm definitely en route. What you trying to do?"

"How many licks can it take?" Tank asked, referring to amount of cut.

"This shit's going to six different places," Yayo said.

"Oh, yeah? Well, shit, what the number looking like on them thangs?"

"They going for 70 a block," Yayo said as he took a pull from his kush.

"What kind of play will you give me for an Allen Iverson?"

"Shit, for Tracy McGrady #3, I'ma need 2 hunnid, fam."

"Aiight, that's what's up. I'm trying to go to the store," Tank said.

"When you ready, hit this number," Yayo said, and then hung up.

TJ sat close by anxiously. "What that bitch ass nigga say?" TJ asked.

"He's down. I told you this nigga's dumber than a box of rocks," Yayo replied.

***

Tank went in his closet and grabbed his .50 cal Desert Eagle and checked the magazine. After seeing it was fully loaded with seven hollow-point rounds, he stuck the magazine back in the gun and chambered a round.

"These niggas goofy as hell. How they gon' serve a nigga they don't even know three bricks of heroin? I could've been the feds, but lucky for them, I'm a thoroughbred murderer about to rob them for their work and their lives," Tank thought to himself and grabbed his phone to make a call.

S. Allen

YAYO

Chapter 27

Karen was on her way to pick up her sons, Devon and Quavon, who were now 18 years old. Darrell had started seeing another woman, and it was getting serious. He was spending less and less time at home with his sons, and the boys wanted to move to Chicago to be closer to their mother. Karen had gotten herself together and was doing well, so it was only right for her to accept her boys with open arms.

Everything was going exactly how she planned. With Yayo being of financial help, Karen managed to open up a beauty salon named Style & Grace on the city's East Side.

Devon and Quavon were smart as hell, and Karen wanted them to attend Kennedy King College and major in something with a promising career. Yayo had already offered to pay his brothers' college tuition.

Karen pulled into the parking lot of the Pizza Hut on Milwaukee and Ashland in her Camaro LS on 22s and parked next to Darrell's S-Class Benz. The boys got out, grabbed their bags, and said their goodbyes to their father.

They gladly hopped in the car with Karen, and looked forward to their new environment. The busy streets were mesmerizing to them. All the different whips with candy paint, rims, and banging sound systems intrigued Quavon. Life in the suburbs was boring, and Darrell always kept a close leash on the boys. He was excessively overprotective of his sons.

Devon and Quavon were fraternal twins. Devon was 6 feet tall with a dark chocolate complexion. He wore his hair in a small fro that he kept neatly trimmed and tapered to perfection. His slim frame was cut up, and he had a smooth character. He was very well-mannered and naturally humble. Devon was into every sport imaginable: basketball, football, soccer, wrestling, and the list went on. Devon didn't just play sports. He played to win, and doing so, he won lots of trophies and medals in the process.

Quavon was the exact opposite of his brother. He was 5'11'' and 200 pounds of muscle from lifting weights in the basement.

Quavon was light-skinned with 360-degree waves in his hair. Unlike his brother, he didn't like attending school. And when he did, his main focus was chasing girls in between classes. Quavon's grades stayed in the C range. He had a short temper, and stayed getting into fights at school. He was a loose cannon, and was always in some drama. In return, his dad would always put him on punishment. The twins hated being locked down with so many strict rules and regulations from their father. When Karen agreed to let them stay with her, they didn't hesitate to pack their bags.

They loved going to Chicago and visiting their mother and brother. Yayo would spoil them, and make sure they were straight. Yayo would come by Karen's house on the weekends and play video games with them and take them shopping. Devon would always tell Yayo he would want to have his own business one day, so he could take care of their family. Yayo would tell him to focus on school, and with hard work and dedication, his dreams would eventually become a reality.

Quavon looked up to his older brother. He knew Yayo was a gangster, and he had an intoxicating swagger about him that Quavon tried to imitate and master. Quavon tried to walk, talk, and act like his big brother. The two even resembled each other.

One time, while visiting their mother, Yayo was in the basement of her condo, counting stacks of money from his pickup that morning. He had 30 stacks rubber banded in three 10-stack bundles on the table, when Quavon came downstairs to holler at him. He looked up from the stacks of money that he was counting and glanced at his lil' brother who walked over and took a seat next to him on the couch.

"Bro, you always got a lot of money," Quavon said while staring at the stacks of money on the table.

"This ain't no money," Yayo smoothly replied as he continued to count the cash in his hands.

"Yayo, how do I get money like that?" Quavon inquired.

"You get money like this by going to school, getting a good job, and working real hard."

"But you don't have a job, and you still got a lot of money,"

YAYO

Quavon replied.

"Quavon, everything ain't for everybody. You asked me how to get money, and I just told you," Yayo said as he wrapped two thick rubber bands around a stack of money.

"Yayo, my daddy said you're a drug dealer, and you kill people," his brother said calmly.

Yayo scowled as he went into his pocket, retrieved his blueberry kush, and started rolling a blunt.

"He said that you're a gangbanga, and you got people scared of you," Quavon continued, "He said everything you got is from drug money."

"Quavon, listen to me, bro. I do what I have to do to survive," Yayo said, getting upset. "Did he tell you he kicked me out the house at 12 years old, and sent me to the environment that changed me? No, of course not. He didn't because that was some crooked ass shit. Quavon, I'm happy with who I am, and my family is taken care of. That's all that matters to me right now," Yayo said as he lit the weed and took a long pull from the blunt, holding the potent smoke in his lungs before blowing it out.

"Yayo, can I hit that?" Quavon asked.

"Hell, naw, you can't hit this," Yayo said.

"Man, I be smoking with my friend, Thumper, at school," Quavon retorted, still reaching out for the blunt.

Yayo gave in and passed Quavon the weed. Quavon inhaled the strong marijuana, blew out the smoke, and immediately started coughing up a storm. Yayo laughed at his little brother.

"Quavon, you said Thumper is your friend, but be careful who you call your friends. Always remember that a friendship has to be built, and it's built through trials and tribulations. In the streets, it's always your so-called 'friends' who stab you in the back. Fake friends are quick to envy you in different corners and angles, so stay protected at all times."

Quavon was on an intense high as he listened attentively. Like a sponge, he soaked up all the game that was given to him.

That was two years ago when Yayo and Quavon had smoked their first blunt together. Since then, every time Yayo saw Quavon, he would lace him with knowledge, wisdom, and understanding. He was trying to prepare Quavon for the streets, in case the streets called him. Yayo prayed it didn't, but if it did, he wanted his little bro to be ready.

Chapter 28

Tank was at one of his spots on Lawrence and Winthrop on the North Side. He hollered at Yayo, and they agreed to meet at a house on Clark and Devon. He tried to contact Lil' B for the past few hours through phone calls and texts, but Lil' B never returned his calls. Tank figured he was going to have to go on the sting by himself. He made sure when he showed up, he would be prepared, so a Teflon vest was strapped to his chest.

Yayo had told him he would be sitting in a white Suburban, and to park behind it. Tank figured Yayo wanted to do business outside, and the shit would go down easy. He would just whack Yayo and whoever else was in the whip and drive off with the work. It was just that easy.

***

Yayo, TJ, and Butterball sat in one of their many trap houses on the North Side of Chicago, getting ready to meet up with Tank and take care of business. Yayo had set up a deal for 3 bricks of heroin. Tonight, Tank was getting a first class ticket to hell.

TJ sat at the kitchen table, loading up his Mac-10 submachine gun as Butterball wiped down the shells for his .44 Magnum revolver.

"TJ, I'ma be parked in the Suburban. Y'all post up in the gangway, and when that nigga pull up, y'all end this shit," Yayo commanded as he watched his soldiers load up their artillery.

"Nigga, you ain't got to tell me how to work. This bitch murdered my momma. His ass is grass!" TJ sneered through clenched teeth.

Butterball sat quietly, putting the shells in the cylinder of the Magnum. Yayo's phone vibrated inside of his True Religion jeans. He grabbed it, and quickly answered.

"What's up, player?" He said.

"What's up? I'm en route," Tank said.

"Aiight, I'm here," Yayo replied and ended the call.

"Aye, that was the nigga right there. What's up? Y'all ready to catch a body?" Yayo asked his crew.

"Nigga, I'm the body snatcher," TJ said, and all three men got up and headed out the door to go send Tank to his maker.

***

It was 8:30 p.m. and quiet as hell on the 1100 block of Clark Street, as a few crackheads walked up and down the streets, trying to cop some work. Yayo sat in the driver's seat of the parked Suburban, smoking a Newport, when his phone rang.

"Where you at, fam?" He said, answering the phone.

"I'm turning down Clark right now," Tank said.

Yayo looked in the rearview mirror and saw a car creeping slowly down the block.

"Fam, pull behind the white 'burban," Yayo instructed the caller.

"Aiight, I see you," Tank said and hung up the phone, as he pulled the Desert Eagle from his pants.

TJ was in a gangway ducked off in the darkness, and Butterball was laying low in a gangway on the opposite side of the street. TJ saw the car pull behind the Suburban and he cocked the slide of the Mac-10. It was show time.

Tank pulled up behind the suburban, killed the engine, and was about to get out the car, when his window shattered, and he heard gunfire.

Butterball's 44 rocked the Buick Regal as the slugs penetrated the car doors. TJ ran up to Tank's vehicle, spraying the Mac. Tank took a slug to his face, and tried his best to retreat from the gunfire by lying flat across the seat.

Yayo watched calmly in the rearview mirror as the hit transpired. Tank had been hit several times, and was gasping for air as blood poured from his mouth.

TJ yanked open the door to the Regal, and with one hand pulled Tank from the vehicle, and dragged him into the middle of the street. After turning Tank on his back, TJ aimed the Mac at Tank, who was hanging on to his life.

"Look at me, motherfucker!" TJ yelled with spit flying from his mouth.

Tank looked at his killer, and smiled a bloody smile. Tank was a goon, and respected the morals of the goon code. He would die a boss. "Fuck you, nigga," Tank weakly replied.

TJ stared Tank in his eyes before squeezing the trigger on the Mac, spraying Tank's head, neck, and body with the machine gun until all the shells were gone.

TJ and Butterball hopped in the Suburban with Yayo, and pulled off from the curb, leaving Tank's body smoking and his brains splattered in the streets.

After the three disposed of the Chevy Suburban, and hopped in a Dodge Magnum, Yayo dropped TJ and Butterball off on the South Side, and headed back to his kingdom to be with his family.

S. Allen

Chapter 29

TJ and Butterball sat in an apartment on the low-end of the South Side. They had been drinking 1800 tequila and smoking blunt after blunt. The tequila had both men feeling tipsy, and the murder they had just committed had them in a dangerous frame of mind. Bloodshed ignited more bloodshed.

"Man, did you see how I split that nigga's melon?" TJ asked as he downed another shot of tequila.

"Hell, yeah, that nigga's shit was so wide open, I saw what fam was thinking."

Both men laughed. TJ took a pull of the weed and passed the blunt to Butterball, then got up to take a piss. "GBC, motherfuckers! Who the fuck y'all niggas playing wit'?" TJ slurred as he staggered toward the bathroom.

TJ relieved himself, and then went to the mirror and stared at his reflection. His eyes were the color of spilled blood. His face had thinned down from constant drug use and overwhelming stress from rotating in the blood-soaked streets of Chicago.

As TJ stared in the mirror, he began to think about his mother, Joyce. "Momma, I got him," he said. "I got him for what he did to you," TJ said as tears stained his face. "Momma, I love you, and I hope you're proud of me!" TJ said, and wiped the tears from his face.

Reaching in his hoodie, he pulled out his crack pipe, put it to his lips, lit the tip, and inhaled the drug. TJ looked in the mirror again. He knew he had to get off of the drug and get his shit together. While staring in the mirror, TJ began coaching himself.

"What the fuck am I doing? I'm better than this. I'm a motherfuckin gangster, a soldier to the game, the pallbearer to these weak niggas. I'm a GBC monster!" TJ said, and flushed the crack pipe down the toilet.

When TJ staggered out the bathroom, he saw Butterball sitting on the couch, clutching his .44 Magnum.

"What's up, lil' nigga? You aiight?" TJ asked, referring to the mug on Butterball's face.

S. Allen

"Naw, I was just sitting here missing my brother, that's all. He was all I had in this world, and a motherfucker murked him. My brother was a gangsta who took care of our family. My momma and I depended on him, and these bitch ass niggas took him from us. The funny thing about it is, I know my brother is about to be proud of me. I walked up to my brother's casket at his funeral, and promised him I would kill the motherfuckers who were associated with his death. It took me a lil' time for me to put shit together, but one thing my brother always taught me was to be a man of your word," Butterball said as he raised the 44 and aimed it at TJ.

TJ sensed the danger and went for his waist, but came up short. His banga was under the cushion on the couch. He was naked.

"Man, what the fuck is you doing, shorty? You're drunk! Put that shit down!" TJ pleaded with Butterball. Butterball stood up from the couch and cocked the hammer of the cannon. Sweat poured from TJ's head.

"Butterball, what the fuck is you talking about?" TJ asked, trying to make sense of the move Butterball was bringing him.

Butterball ran up and slapped TJ with the gun, sending him to the floor.

"Nigga, shut the fuck up! You hoe-ass niggas killed my brother, Jug-head!" Butterball yelled while kicking TJ in his ribs.

TJ heard Jug-head's name and knew his life was over. He would never see Shakira again, and he would never witness his niece grow up to be a beautiful woman. TJ had a quick flashback of his past, and thought, "I became a product of the streets at a young age. I played by the rules, lived by the G code, and made a name for myself in the streets as a force to reckon with. I had put the capital M in murder, and helped the GBC climb up the food chain in Chicago. I will go down in the history books as a hood legend."

"Nigga, now you can go be with your mother," Butterball said as he raised the gun and pulled the trigger, blowing TJ's brains all over the wall. After robbing TJ for his money and a few ounces of dope, Butterball fled the apartment. TJ was the 25th homicide that weekend in Chicago.

YAYO

***

TJ rested in peace inside of his casket at the Gatling Funeral Home, the same funeral home as his mother. TJ's dreads were rested neatly on his shoulders. He was in an all-white Armani suit with platinum cuff links and Mauri cocaine white gators laced his feet. TJ no longer looked like the monster he released, but rather, an angel of death.

The whole GBC organization attended the funeral to show their respects to the chief enforcer for M.O.B. TJ was hated by many, but loved by few, and the ones who loved him were the only ones who mattered.

Shakira and Yayo sat in the front row. Shakira was shaken up by TJ's murder and shed her tears, but she was strong. She had become immune to death. Death seemed to always be near her. Karen, Honey, Devon, and Quavon also attended the funeral. Devon and Quavon had mad love for TJ. TJ was like their uncle to them, so they took his death hard.

Quavon took it the hardest. Yayo had told the twins that death was a part of the life, and to deal with death, they had to understand death. Without death, there would never be life.

TJ was buried next to Joyce at the Burr Oaks Cemetery. Yayo gave one last salute to his comrade, as tears rolled off of his face.

Back in Englewood, on 69th and Wolcott, cliques of youngsters stood on corners, pouring out liquor for TJ. Cars were flipped over, and the hood was in a panic zone. Niggas spray-painted the hood with "R.I.P. TJ: the realest nigga to ever do it."

S. Allen

YAYO

Chapter 30

Niggas think they got all the damn sense. These studs killed my brother in a robbery, and thought I was gonna let them run around Chicago getting money. Never that. This goon shit runs in my blood. I had been plotting on these cats for a few years.

I had gotten close with TJ, so it was just a waiting game. You see, I ain't no stupid nigga. I used TJ to get my money up. I made stacks fucking with TJ, and on the low, I recruited my own lil' squad of young niggas. I had work and plenty of pistols.

TJ introduced me to the murder game. He had made me go on a few moves with him to get my dick wet, and now, I was a master at serving death. In my city, head bussing is at an all-time high. There's around 500 murders every year, so you either be a predator or become the prey. I chose to become the predator.

I knew the nigga Tank from my brother. The two were cool, and had met in one of them joints up north. When Tank came home, I ran into him in traffic and exchanged numbers with him. I was the one who gave Tank his first banga when he came home. Tank was a gangsta out here, make no mistake about it. The nigga was about his business. He had told me he was getting at the GBC, and that peaked my interest.

I wanted Yayo and TJ dead, so I put Tank and Homicide on to the spot on 95th and Yates. Them niggas went in there faking, and Homicide got his shit knocked off his shoulders in the process. That's when I knew I had to take care of business myself.

I chose to ride with Yayo and TJ on the move with Tank, because it made sense to knock Tank off. He had a lot of dirt on me, so he had to go. TJ was gonna get it next, and I would save Yayo for last. Everything worked out as planned, so far.

TJ laid Tank out, and it was crazy how he decapitated that nigga with the Mac-10. That was some official shit.

TJ's only mistake was how quick he was to put his trust in niggas, and him trusting me had cost him his life. I caught him off of his square, and I made my move. When he came out of that bathroom, I manned up and took care of my business. I was the last one with TJ, so niggas were gonna be at my head. Yayo ain't stupid.

The thing is, Butterball, a.k.a. Lil' B, ain't ducking no drama. Nevertheless, when niggas come, they better not be faking.

Chapter 31

Batman was laid up in a hospital on Chicago's South Side. The slugs from the AK-47 had punctured his lungs. The IVs were doing little to nothing. Batman was in a coma as his room was being heavily secured by some of Chicago's finest officers. The streets were in turmoil because of the shooting.

The scene of the crime was horrific. Robin's body looked like a smear on the concrete as the coroners pulled the sheet over his body. It was a medical miracle that Batman made it out alive.

Mayor P. Swoley had a televised news conference about the murder. Standing at the podium, Mayor Swoley proceeded with his speech:

"My Chicagoans, we are at a very disappointing time. An officer, whose duties were to serve and protect the community, was murdered in cold blood, and the killers are still at large. Whoever fired the shots that killed Mr. Washington, I want you to know that these kind of actions will never be tolerated in my city, and you will be apprehended, so help me God. You are a disgrace to mankind, and have no business in our society. My fellow citizens, this culprit will be brought to justice, and it is advised that anyone with information on this heinous crime should notify local police. My fellow citizens, we will put a cease to this flare of violence that has plagued the city of Chicago. But we need your help. Without the help of the community, we are fighting a neverending war against these hoodlums and drug dealers. My people, these are not being used for hitting squirrels," Mayor Swoley said while holding up an unloaded assault rifle with a clip longer than a high school hallway. *"These gangsters are riding around our city with weaponry used by military personnel. Know that if you are a felon, and you get caught with a gun, you will be prosecuted at the highest extent of the law, and not even Johnny Cochran can help you. We will put a stop to all the killings in Chicago. And once again, to the killers who are involved in the death of Officer Washington, it will be in your best interest to do the right thing and turn yourself in."*

***

With Yayo issuing Batman and Robin's death warrant, he had just put everybody in the crosshairs. The Chicago Police Department had just raged an all-out war on the gangs, and the streets were about to bleed.

***

Two guys, Yellow Boy and TB, were standing on the corner of Wolcott, trying to get their hustle on. The hood had been quiet for a couple of weeks since the police was on a quest for retaliation. It was a Friday night, and the traffic was slow.

"Man, what's the bizness wit' them hoes on 59th and Dorchester?" TB asked.

"I don't know. Shorty hit me yesterday saying they was trying to get up. What, you trying to get up with them?" Yellow replied, while tying up his Timberlands.

"Hell, yeah, ain't shit shaking over here. It's slow as shit--"

"Nine-nine through the back door!" The block security member yelled out.

Yellow Boy and TB started walking toward the middle of the block when all of a sudden, an unmarked cruiser raced up the block. The two gangsters took off in separate directions, trying to elude the officers. Yellow Boy ran through a gangway, and hopped a fence. He was on parole, and would be damned if he got jammed up with the baby Uzi he had tucked inside his Carhartt coat.

The cruiser came to a screeching halt as officers bolted out of their vehicles, and went into high pursuit of the two thugs. TB hit a fence on the opposite side of the street, and ran down the alley like Carl Lewis going for a gold medal. He threw the G-pack of heroin he had on top of a building.

Meanwhile, Yellow Boy was able to get the submachine gun off of him, and ditched it in a dumpster. A cruiser turned into the alley. Yellow Boy was trapped with nowhere to run.

"Freeze! Put your hands where I can see 'em!" Officer Blondie yelled, while pointing his 9mm Beretta at Yellow Boy.

Yellow Boy weighed his options, and he had none.

"Put your fucking hands in the air!" The officer screamed.

Yellow Boy raised his hands, and then all of a sudden, one of the officers yelled, "GUN!" The dark alley lit up. Yellow Boy was shot 23 times, and was dead before his body hit the pavement. The Chicago police had just gotten an eye for an eye, and that was just the beginning.

S. Allen

Chapter 32

Yayo was sitting in his driveway in his Cadillac DTS. A bottle of Seagram's gin rested in his lap, and a blunt of kush hung from his dry lips. He was still grieving TJ's murder.

He had tried to call Butterball almost every day, only to find out he had changed his number. Yayo had found Butterball guilty and sentenced him to death by putting twenty grand on his head. If Butterball didn't have anything to do with TJ's death, he didn't care. Yayo never really trusted Butterball from the jump. There was something about him that was familiar. He just couldn't put his finger on it, so it was best Butterball was killed, plus he knew too much about the organization.

Yayo took a swig from the bottle, and let the warm liquor comfort him. As he started thinking about TJ, his thoughts flashed back to the first time they had put in work together. TJ had beaten Ameen with a baseball bat, and Yayo had shot him in the ass.

Yayo had lost two of his closest friends to the grimy streets of Chicago. Pudge and TJ were his brothers from a different mother. Since Yayo had come to Chicago, he had been constantly surrounded by death, and it was now taking a toll on his soul. The pain he was enduring was almost unreal, and it took his inner God to help him face the drama being thrown his way.

Yayo took a pull of the weed and inhaled. In the streets, it was survival of the fittest. The strong prevailed, and the weak perished. In the jungle, you were either the lion or the lamb. Yayo sat and thought about all of the dirt he did, and all of the families he broke up through killing. A tear fell from his eye.

The world was a cold and dark place for Yayo. The only thing that warmed his being was his family. Thinking about his family always gave him strength.

He couldn't lose the game at this point. His people needed him. Yayo wanted to walk away from the streets, but he had lost too much, and it was either get down or lay down. "And if you lay down, you gon' stay down," Yayo thought to himself as he took another swig from the bottle of gin.

Yayo opened the door, stepped out of the DTS, and staggered to his front door. When he walked inside his home, Shakira was sitting in the dark. Yayo flipped on the light.

"What up, boo?" He slurred and put his jacket in the closet.

"Nothing. I was waiting for you to come in. Are you alright?" Shakira asked, noticing the troubled look on Yayo's face.

Yayo went to the couch and took a seat next to Shakira. He turned the bottle of gin up to his lips, and Shakira grabbed it from him and sat it on the table. She noticed how much Yayo had been drinking since TJ's funeral.

"Baby, I just want you to know everything is going to be okay. We are going to get through this together," Shakira said as she laid her head on Yayo's broad chest.

"Shakira, shit is so crazy. I feel like it's my fault he's gone, and it's my fault Joyce is gone," he said as tears rolled off his face and fell onto Shakira's forehead. Shakira looked up and kissed the tears on of Yayo's face.

"Baby, it's not your fault. Things happen in life that we have no control over. My brother made his own decisions in them streets. Nobody put a gun to his head and made him do the things he did. My brother is in a better place now, and he doesn't have to suffer the pain of the streets anymore. He's in heaven with mama now. I need you to be strong, Yayo, and take care of your business. You are my king, and I am riding with you regardless of what happens," Shakira said, grabbing Yayo's face and passionately kissing his lips.

Yayo and Shakira held each other tightly in the warmth of their embrace. As he sat in the darkness, holding his queen, he knew he had to finish the shit he started.

He had all kind of dilemmas coming from different angles. Batman was still alive, and if he made it, trouble could come in the form of Hurricane Katrina. Butterball was still in hiding, and Yayo would not rest until he was laid to rest. His heroin plug, Buddy, had mysteriously came up missing, so the work was definitely getting low. Yayo had enough paper to step out of the game, but not before he tied up all of his loose ends.

YAYO

***

Yayo had called a meeting with every member from the GBC. The meeting was held at Triangle Park on the city's North Side, and it was mandatory everyone attend. Yayo was head of the crime family, and he had just promoted TB as his chief enforcer. TB had always been loyal to the gang, and was quick to put in work. He was infatuated with the gun play, and was always respectful to his superiors.

There were at least forty men at the park in attendance, all from off of 69th and Wolcott. Only a few had rank, but most were the foot soldiers to the gang. Yayo stood in the middle of the big circle, along with TB, Murder, Clementa, and Jhon Jhon.

"GBC, what up!" Yayo yelled. All the members of the mob yelled salutes and threw up their gang signs.

"My niggas, we are at a troubled time. As you know, we have just lost one of our strongest soldiers, but make no mistake, his death will not go unpunished. First and foremost, I am shutting 69th and Wolcott down. There will be no serving on that block. Anybody who gets caught serving on Wolcott will be in violation."

As Yayo scanned the eyes of his soldiers, he noticed a mean mug on Murder's face, and continued his lecture.

"There's a lot of heat on that block, so I want extra security set up." Yayo glanced at TB, and TB nodded. "Them niggas on 71st are in violation. There's a code blue on them niggas, meaning shoot on sight. A couple of weeks ago, Yellow Boy was killed by some crooked ass pigs. Fifty stacks to whoever drops Blondie." Whispers could be heard throughout the crowd.

"My niggas, if these muthafuckas want war with GBC, then we gon' turn up and give them what they want," Yayo said.

"Man, how the fuck we gon' war and get money at the same time? Y'all about drama. I'm about a dollar," Murder sneered.

Yayo calmly walked over to Murder, pulled his .40 from his Girbaud denims, and shot Murder point blank range in his face, causing blood to spray from the back of his head. The loud boom from the 40 echoed through the night air. When Murder's body hit the pavement, Yayo spit on his corpse.

"Anybody found to be insubordinate to authority will be treated as an enemy of our people, and dealt with in that fashion," Yayo said, tucking the hot .40 back in his waist.

"If there is anybody else who has a different opinion, please step out of the circle now, so I won't have to murk you later." Nobody made a move. "With that being said, it's clean up time for y'all who don't know. My niggas, it's murking season. Meeting adjourned!"

Chapter 33

"Nigga, this is gonna be the quickest 4 you've ever seen. Fo'-fo', make sure yo' kids don't grow," Kilo said, shaking the two red dice in his hands.

"You ain't hit a point all night. You don't hit for another 50," Burner replied, throwing a $50 bill in the pot.

The two gangsters were in a heavy dice game in a house off of 71st and Marshfield. The trap house they were in was owned by the ATGs, and Kilo and Burner were loyal members to the gang. The house was filled with weed smoke and about six other ATG gangsters. Rap music banged from the Bose speakers in the living room.

"Nigga, bet," Kilo said, rolling the dice on the floor. One dice landed on a 1, and the other dice landed on a 3.

"Ace, Trey!" Kilo yelled, and picked up the $300 pot.

"Nigga, you lucky as shit!" Burner retorted.

"Shorty re-rolled that bitch," D-nice, the oldest of the thugs, replied.

"Aye, when y'all order that Italian Fiesta? They shoulda been came. I'm hungrier than a muhfucka," Monkey Man said.

"I ordered that shit about an hour ago," Kiesha stated. Kiesha was a thick redbone who resembled a light-skinned Pam Grier. Kiesha was fine and thick, but make no mistake about it, she was ATG crazy, and known for busting them thangs. She was a gangbanga to the heart.

The gang continued to talk shit and get high until they heard a knock on the door.

"It's about time," Smurf said, getting up to answer the door for the pizza man. When Smurf answered the door, the pizza man stood there, looking scared as hell.

"Man, I know we get a discount as long as you took!"

The pizza man was pushed aside, and four men rushed inside the house, holding sawed-off shotguns. Monkey Man reached for his banga, and was met with buckshots covering his upper torso. The sound of the loud gun made everybody freeze. The masked men ordered everybody to the basement of the house, where the men duct taped everybody, including the pizza man. They were all shot execution style, and left in the basement with the roaches and rats. The killers then fled the house. This crime would later be known as the Marshfield massacre.

***

It was 1:00 a.m. as Yayo cruised down the North Side in his '87 Malibu with Quavon in the passenger seat.

"Roll this up," Yayo said, passing him a half ounce of sour diesel, as the two cruised down Lakeshore Drive. "So, what's up with school? When do you and Devon start?" Yayo asked while looking in his rearview mirror.

"Mama said we gonna start next semester," Quavon replied while breaking down the weed.

"What you majoring in?"

"I don't know. I haven't decided yet."

"You gotta make sure it's something you like doing, and also something that's gonna pay you a nice salary," Yayo stated while looking at the text he just received in his phone: "Watch the news, my nigga," the text read.

Yayo smiled a devilish grin at the text, and put his phone back in his Pelle Pelle.

"For real, Yayo, I wanna get some money. I ain't with that school shit right now," Quavon said and fired up the blunt.

Yayo let his brother's comment marinate for a second. He thought back to when he was 16 years old, and he practically begged Jug-head to teach him the game. He didn't want Quavon to go through what he did just to make a few dollars. Getting in the game was easy, but Yayo knew getting out was hard, and it could ultimately cost a nigga his life. He wanted the best for his brothers, but Quavon was 18 going on 25, and no matter what he thought or said, Quavon would end up doing whatever he wanted to do. And if his brother was going to be in the streets, he at least wanted him to be mentally and physically equipped to deal with the bullshit. Yayo grabbed the blunt from Quavon, and made a left on Howard Street.

YAYO

"Quavon, just think about school for right now," Yayo said, not wanting to pressure his brother.

Yayo pulled the Malibu up to the corner where a dude was posted up with a black hoodie covering his head. Yayo rolled the passenger window down as he took a pull from his blunt. "Aye, Limbone, let me holla at you right quick."

Limbone didn't budge. "What's up?" He said, still not walking over toward the window.

Yayo passed the blunt to Quavon and said, "If this nigga don't come to this window and holler at me, I'ma smash his ass. This nigga been owing me money for 'bout three weeks now."

"Aye, Limbone, come over to the whip real quick!" Yayo yelled from the window.

"What's up, Joe?" Limbone said, still not moving.

Yayo opened the door, walked over to Limbone, and punched him square in the jaw, causing Limbone to fall against the fence. Yayo rained blow after blow on him until Limbone was laid out on the ground. When he hit the ground, Yayo proceeded to stomp him in his head and face until he lost consciousness. Yayo then went through his pockets and relieved him of his cash.

"You niggas gon' respect my land!" Yayo said, out of breath as he walked back to the Malibu, jumped in, and pulled off.

"Rule number one," Yayo said to his brother, "Never let a nigga get over on you about your paper. If you let him get away with it once, he'll do it over and over again." Quavon inhaled the weed smoke, and soaked up the game his brother was giving him.

S. Allen

Chapter 34

Inside a run-down building on the city's South Side, Butterball stood at the microwave, watching the cocaine bubble inside of the mayonnaise jar. Butterball was in hiding since he had ended TJ's life. He found out Yayo had put twenty grand on his head, and his main man, Murder, had been killed by Yayo.

Butterball wasn't scared to let to let his gun bust, but at the same time, he knew the GBC was loyal to Yayo, and they would stop at nothing to split his head to the white meat. It was a no-win situation, and he couldn't go to war with a whole mob.

Butterball took the mayonnaise jar from the microwave, and dropped an ice cube in it. He then took the end of a clothes hanger and started to whip the substance inside the jar as it began to lock up and turn into crack. He dumped the work on a dinner plate after grabbing the sandwich bags off of the counter. Then, he began to slice the crack up with a razor, making dime-sized rocks.

Butterball was on his last two ounces, and his money was getting low. He couldn't sell his drugs on 69th and Wolcott, or anywhere near 69th for that matter. His life was on borrowed time. For the first time in his young life, he was scared to die. He needed to make a move, and he needed to make it quick.

***

Two unmarked squad cars were posted up in the alley off of 51st and Peoria. Police had received a tip from an informant that a murder suspect was at a house on 51st. The police had the whole block under surveillance, and knew for a fact the suspect was there.

Homicide Detective Royce sat in one of the squad cars, looking at 19-year-old Telly Fields' mugshot, waiting for the SWAT team to arrive so they could raid the premises. The feds had stepped in to help the local agencies bring down the infamous GBC. This would be the start of a snowball effect.

***

Butterball's phone vibrated on the table next to his Glock 26 handgun. It was one of his henchmen, Black. "What's the bizness?" Butterball said, while tying up a boy of crack.

"What's up big homie? Where you at?"

"I'm at the spot on 51st. Why, what's up?" Butterball asked while bagging up the drugs.

"I'm trying to see if you want an M-16 I just came across?" Black asked.

"Hell, yeah. What you want for it?" Butterball replied, sounding as if he had just hit the lottery.

"Dude said he wants $300 for it. This muthafucka's nice, fam. It has a suppresser and a 200-round drum on this bitch," Black informed him.

"Bring it through," Butterball said, while slicing a rock on the plate.

"That's what's up, fam. I'm on my way," Black replied and hung up the phone.

***

U.S. marshals sat in the back of a white van, gearing up for the raid. "Now listen, men, this young man is considered armed and dangerous. He is believed to be involved in at least three murders," Marshal Reid said, putting the clip in his Hecklert & Koch MP5 machine gun. The officers were putting on their bulletproof vests and strapping on their helmets.

"Those gangbangers are heavily armed and known to fire at police. Take all caution while pursuing the suspect. We will be backed by the Chicago Police Department. Ten minutes until show time, ladies and gentlemen. Let's make the government proud," Reid said.

***

Butterball was counting out the $300, when all of a sudden, he heard the window in the front room break, and then, a loud noise. *Boom!* As the smoke invaded the house, he heard another explosion. *Boom!* Butterball's ears went numb from the flash grenades being tossed in the house. The front door was knocked off the hinges by the marshals.

"U.S. marshals! Let me see some hands!"

Butterball could hardly see through the thick, dark smoke. The smoke had him coughing hard. Then, the back door was kicked in.

"U.S. marshals! Don't move!" The marshal yelled, pointing the AR-15, placing the red beam on Butterball's head. The feds stormed the house like roaches in the projects. Butterball put his hands up and dropped to his knees. The gig was up, and Butterball had nowhere to run. He was going to jail.

One of the marshals handcuffed and searched him. Marshal Reid walked over to Butterball, holding a picture of him, as he spoke into his walkie talkie.

"This is Reid. We have Telly Fields in custody."

Butterball was taken to the 51st precinct and placed in a holding cell. The cell reeked of funk and piss. Sitting on the cold, concrete slab inside the small cell, he knew he was in trouble. The police took the Glock, along with the drugs inside the house. The officers confiscated the six thousand dollars he had in his pocket. Looking up, Butterball saw two detectives standing at the bars.

"Mr. Fields, are you okay? Do you need medical attention?" Detective Royce asked.

"Naw, I'm straight," Butterball replied.

Detective Royce unlocked the door to the holding cell. "Mr. Fields, come this way."

Butterball was led to a small room inside the police station and handcuffed to a chair. The room was dimly lit, and the only thing in the room was a large table with a black tape recorder in the middle.

"Now, Mr. Fields, I must say you are in a lot of trouble. You were caught with two and a half ounces of cocaine and a loaded handgun." Sweat formed on Butterball's forehead.

Detective Royce noticed it. "Mr. Fields, the guns and drugs are the least of your worries." Detective Royce slid three pictures over to him. Butterball looked at the first picture. It was a photo of TJ with his brains leaking on the floor. A knot began to form in Butterball's stomach. The second picture was of the ATG shot caller, Fatboy, sprawled out on the concrete. The third picture was of the light-skinned woman who was with Fatboy the night he was murdered. She was plastered to the cement with a large hole in her face.

Butterball put his head down. He knew he was in deep shit. Detective Royce lit his Newport cigarette and took a seat across from Butterball.

"Listen, Mr. Fields, you are looking at some serious charges. Not to mention you are involved in a federal investigation with the GBC. You are looking at a RICO charge, youngster, and I can almost guarantee you will get a life sentence. But the thing is, you are in a position to help yourself. We don't want you. We want the head of the GBC."

Detective Royce took a pull from the Newport hanging from his lips, as he slid Butterball the picture of Yayo. "Mr. Fields, we know you have been dealt a bad hand in life. We know about your brother being violently murdered, and we know about your mother and the life she led. That's why we are giving you a chance to save yourself."

Detective Royce paused to let Butterball think. He felt like his soul had just left his body. He had never been to prison, and the thought of spending the rest of his life in the feds made his skin crawl. He definitely wasn't built for the Bureau of Prisons.

"So if I tell you what you want to know, I won't have to go to jail?" Butterball asked.

"Like I said, we know you're just a foot soldier, and you were just following orders. You give us Yayo, and I'll try my best to make sure you don't get over ten years in prison," Detective Royce replied.

"Alright," Butterball said, putting his head down in defeat.

"You just made the best decision in your life." Detective Royce pressed record on the tape recorder. "Now for the record, what is your government name?"

"Telly Fields."

"And what do you go by in the streets?" Detective Royce asked.

"Butterball."

"And what gang are you affiliated with?"

"GBC," Butterball answered. Detective Royce smiled like the cat that swallowed the canary.

"What can you tell us about a cop getting shot on the West Side?"

Butterball talked in the recorder for 8 hours straight. The feds had everything they needed to get the GBC. They had a nice, cold cell for Yayo at the Lewisburg Penitentiary.

S. Allen

YAYO

Chapter 35

It was Valentine's Day weekend, and Yayo had planned on taking Shakira downtown on a horse and carriage ride. Karen had come to pick up Shamira for the weekend so the two could have the weekend alone. Even with all the drama Yayo was involved in, he felt he still had to keep some kind of balance in his home. The streets were blazing hot. Yayo was engaged in one of the bloodiest gang wars since the Al Capone days, and was determined to reign supreme over his adversaries.

"Shakira, come on, shorty. We gotta get downtown before rush hour traffic hits," Yayo said while lacing up his ACG Nike boots.

"Here I come, bae. Damn, you always trying to rush me. You can't rush greatness," Shakira replied, coming down the stairs.

Shakira was doing her best to move on from the mourning of TJ's death. Some nights, she would wake up from her sleep in a cold sweat. With so many people around her losing their lives to gun violence, she was always worrying about her child's father. When Yayo wasn't by her side, she was a nervous wreck. Yayo was always in her prayers at night. She would pray to God to keep Yayo safe, and pray for his safe return.

Yayo and Shakira left out the front door and got into Yayo's '96 Chevy SS with 26-inch Giovanni rims. He rarely brought this vehicle out, but today was different. He wanted to stunt and shine with his wifey on his side. Yayo put the key in the ignition and brought the Chevy to life. When he put it in reverse, he looked in the rearview mirror and saw at least seven squad cars blocking him from getting out of the driveway. Officers stood outside of their cruisers, pointing assault rifles and shotguns at his whip.

"Shit!" Yayo cursed out loud.

"Driver, turn the car off, now!" The officer said over the blow horn.

Yayo looked at Shakira, whose eyes started to water. Yayo thought about going out guns blazing, knowing his Glock was under the seat, but then, he quickly thought about Shakira's safety. If he busted his gun, both of them would surely be killed.

"Driver, take the keys out the ignition and throw them out the window with your right hand." Yayo did as he was told.

"Passenger, put your hands where we can see them!" The officer barked. Shakira put both of her hands above her head as instructed.

"Driver, slowly step out the vehicle."

"Shakira, I love you, shorty," Yayo said, staring at Shakira, whose tears had started to pour from her big, brown eyes. Yayo slowly opened the driver's door and stepped out of the car.

"Let me see some hands," the officer demanded. Yayo put his hands on top of his head.

"Step back to the sound of my voice," the officer commanded.

Yayo slowly walked backwards toward the officers. Then all of a sudden, he was rushed and forcefully shoved to the concrete. Shakira was also pulled from the car and placed in handcuffs.

"Yaton Anderson, you have the right to remain silent. Anything you say can and will be used against you in the court of law." The arresting officer continued reading Yayo his Miranda rights, while placing him inside of an unmarked Crown Victoria. Yayo was hauled off to the county jail.

The feds had a search warrant for Yayo's home. They went through the home like the Tasmanian devil. The feds recovered a PLR-16 assault rifle, an AK-47, two handguns, and two military-issued bulletproof vests. The master bedroom was torn apart as the officers recovered over a half a million dollars in cold cash. Yayo was going to be a hell of a candidate for the RICO act.

***

Shakira sat in a small room inside of Cook County Jail, nervous as hell, when two federal agents walked inside the room.

"Ms. Johnson, how are you doing? My name is Agent Michaels, and this is Agent Thomas. We would like to ask you a few questions about your boyfriend, Yaton," the agent said, while handing Shakira a cold water bottle.

"First and foremost, Ms. Johnson, I want you to know the severity of this situation. Your boyfriend will be indicted on federal weapon charges and murder charges. We have proof Yaton is the head of the Get it Boy Clique, GBC. We also know the house you reside in was purchased with drug money. Ms. Johnson, Yaton has allegedly orchestrated the murder of a Chicago police officer, and if found guilty, he could be put to death by lethal injection. We know you knew about Yaton selling drugs. I mean, how else would you be able to afford the lifestyle you two live? Half a million dollars was found in your bedroom. With that being said, you could be charged with conspiracy."

Shakira's facial expression remained the same. Agent Thomas intervened.

"Ms. Johnson, do you really want to risk going to prison for his deeds for the next 20 years? And what about your daughter, Shamira? Who's going to take care of her while you're doing your time in a women's federal prison? You have to think about you and your child, Ms. Johnson," Agent Thomas said, taking a sip from his coffee.

Shakira shifted her eyes from the officers. "I want my lawyer." That was the only thing Shakira said.

"Okay, Ms. 'Ride or Die bitch,' don't say we didn't try to help you," Agent Thomas replied as he led her back to the holding cell.

***

Back inside the Cook County Jail, the feds had Yayo in an interrogation room, playing Good Cop, Bad Cop. Yayo was a seasoned vet in the streets, and he thought the feds were truly wasting their time with the questioning. He knew there was a rat in the picture, but he couldn't pinpoint who it was.

When they asked him about the cop getting hit, he knew it had to be a GBC member who spilled the beans on the move. The only person who came to mind was Butterball. Butterball was still in hiding, and he knew TJ had told Butterball about the slaying, if not involved directly. But right now everything was just speculation.

"Yaton, you know you're going to die in the Bureau of Prisons, you cop-killing son of a bitch," the agent sneered.

"You're going to be indicted on the guns. Then you are going to be superseded on the RICO act, Mr. Gang Leader," Agent Ross said, pulling out a pack of cigarettes from his vest jacket. Yayo was unfazed by the clown ass agents.

"Mr. Anderson, we have a witness who's going to testify that he was a part of your organization, and you sanctioned and ordered the murders of at least four men, including Officer Jeffrey Washington. It's in your best interest to cooperate with us, and make it light on yourself. And just know your girlfriend is going to be indicted with conspiracy to distribute heroin and tax evasion," Agent Zimmerman stated.

Yayo thought about his wifey and how she was holding up. He knew he groomed a thoroughbred bitch. He smiled to himself, knowing Shakira would not be the weak link in the case. Nothing could break their loyalty to each other, not even the feds.

"Yaton, we are willing to make a deal with you right now if you tell us what we want to know. Tell us what we want to know about the GBC, and we can maybe get you a sweet plea for thirty years. You're in your early twenties. When you get out, you'll be in your fifties. You can still have a life after prison. It's better than dying in the feds, and getting burned in a prison cemetery, don't you think?" Agent Ross reiterated.

"You pigs never amaze me. You ain't got nothing but an oversized rat formulating a falsified story. Maybe y'all promised him an orgy or some shit, but for real, y'all wasting time and government money. I'ma go to court and smash that weak ass shit," Yayo taunted.

"You got shit all figured out, huh? You drug dealing nigger, let's see how smart you are when you end up in the gas chamber. Get this piece of shit out of my sight!" Agent Ross hissed.

Yayo was dressed in Cook County brown khakis. He was taken to Division 11. Division 11 was for medium custody inmates. Most of the inmates in Division 11 were gang chiefs who had high profile cases, and were sure to get a boatload of time.

YAYO

Yayo was assigned to the lower tier, in cell #34. When he walked in the cell, there was an older Puerto Rican man sitting in the cell at a small desk, writing a letter. Yayo took his bedroll and threw it on the top bunk. The old school cat stopped writing and watched Yayo attentively as he made up his bed.

"What's up, youngin'? My name's Rivera," he said.

Yayo turned to face Rivera, who looked to be in his late fifties. "My name's Yayo."

"Where you from, Yayo?"

"I'm from the South Side," Yayo replied, wondering why Rivera was all in his business.

"You ever been to the joint, my friend?"

"I was at St. Charles when I was young. Why?" Yayo asked.

"Well, you have graduated now, youngster. Welcome to Cook County."

Yayo looked at Rivera, confused. The old timer went under his mattress, retrieved a small bag of tobacco, and rolled a cigarette. "You smoke, youngin'?"

Yayo nodded and Rivera passed him the cigarette and a book of matches. Yayo lit the cigarette, inhaled, and immediately got a head rush. The cigarette seemed to relax him for a minute.

"Youngin', who you run with in them streets?" Rivera asked Yayo.

Yayo blew out a thick cloud of smoke. "I own GBC!" Yayo informed Rivera.

"Well, in this unit, there's a lot of different gangs. You have the Gangster Disciples, Black Disciples, Vice Lords, Latin Kings, and a few Spanish Cobras from Humboldt Park. There was a lil' dude in here who was a GBC, but he kited off the deck," Rivera said.

Yayo's interest peaked. "Who was he?" Yayo asked.

"I don't know the youngin's name. He was only here for a couple of days. He was young and light-skinned with French braids. I think shorty had a feds case, if I'm not mistaken. You might wanna holler at the GDs. They were hollering at shorty," Rivera relayed.

"Who do I talk to?" Yayo asked.

"Go holler at Wo-love. He got the deck for the GDs."

"Lock in for count! Lock in for count!" A short, dark-skinned guard yelled as she walked down the tier, locking inmates in their cells. During count, Rivera continued to school Yayo about the unit and who was who. Yayo's only thought was about GBC member Rivera mentioned. He was going to get to the bottom of this.

***

Shakira walked out of the Cook County Jail after Karen posted her $1,000 bond. Shakira was originally charged with the gun inside the Chevy SS since the car was in her name. The gun had turned out to be stolen, so she was charged with a misdemeanor for concealing a weapon. When Shakira walked out of Cook County Jail, she looked a mess. Her hair was tangled, and her eyes had dark circles from crying for the past 13 hours. Karen walked up and put her arms around Shakira.

"Shakira, everything's gon' be alright. It's gon' be alright," Karen assured her while rubbing her back.

The ride to Karen's condo was an emotional one. Shakira told her everything the feds told her about Yayo and what he was facing. Karen couldn't believe how the feds were treating her son. She had heard a lot of stories about him and what he was involved in, but never in a million years would she have thought Yayo was this monster the feds were portraying him to be. Regardless, she was going to support her son in any way she can.

When Karen and Shakira walked in the house, Devon was at the kitchen table filling out a few job applications, while Quavon sat on the couch playing Call of Duty on the PlayStation 4. His eyes were bloodshot red from the blunt of sour diesel he fired up as soon as his mother left.

Quavon looked up from the TV. "Mama, what's up with Yaton?" He asked, concerned about his big brother.

"I don't know right now, Quavon. We have to wait and see if they give him a bond," Karen said.

YAYO

Shakira sat on the couch next to Quavon, as Devon got up to join the family in the living room. Shamira was in her swing, sound asleep.

"Shakira, are you alright?" Devon asked.

"Yeah, Devon, I'm okay," Shakira replied. Her eyes began to water.

"Man, these snitch ass niggas got my people jammed up!" Quavon hissed.

"Quavon, watch your damn mouth. I didn't raise you to talk like that," Karen scolded. Quavon got up off the couch and went to his room, slamming the door behind him.

***

Back at prison, the four o'clock count had just been cleared, and the doors were popped, releasing the inmates from their cells. Yayo walked out and went over to the pay phone. Looking around the dayroom, he saw how all of the other inmates were looking at him with mean mugs on their faces.

He had heard a lot of horror stories about Cook County. Taking the phone off of the receiver, Yayo dialed his mother's number. Karen answered the phone and accepted the charges.

"Hello," Yayo spoke into the phone.

"Yaton, baby, are you okay?"

"Yeah, mama. I'm good. I was calling to see if y'all were good," Yayo said, as he watched his celly talking to a rough-looking dude with a six-pointed star tattooed under his right eye.

"Yes, Yaton. We're all good. I bonded Shakira out this morning. She's been over here waiting on your call," Karen said.

"Mama, put her on the phone right quick." Karen laid the phone down and to get her.

"Shakira!" Karen yelled. "Yaton's on the phone."

Shakira rushed to the kitchen and picked up the phone. "Baby, are you okay?" She asked urgently.

"Yeah boo, I'm good. What about you?"

"I'm alright. Yaton, I'm scared," Shakira said.

"Baby, remember when we used to lay up and talk at night, and what we would talk about?"

"Yes, baby."

"Well it is time to exercise what I taught you. Remember what I said about law number one in street laws?"

"Uh huh," she replied.

"So with that being understood, it shouldn't have to be explained," Yayo said. "So, how is my lil' princess?" Yayo asked, knowing the call was being monitored.

"She's good, baby. I think she misses you because she's been in a lil' funky mood lately," Shakira stated.

"Well, when I figure out what's going on, I'ma set up a visit so I can see y'all. I need to talk to you face-to-face."

"I know, boo. I need to see you so bad."

The automated voice recorder came over the line. "You have one minute remaining."

"Baby, I love you, and I'ma call back later tonight."

"We love you, too, Yaton, and I will be waiting on your call," Shakira said, just before the phone went dead. Yayo hung up the phone and walked to his cell.

He had just finished taking a piss when three men came in the cell, including the one with the six-point star under his eye. He spoke up.

"What up, Joe? You wanna holler at me about something?" The two men who accompanied him had mean mugs on their faces, and they both had their hands in their pockets.

Yayo was a little shaken, but he kept his composure. "Who are you?" He asked.

"My name's Wo-love. What's the bizness?" Wo-love sneered.

"My celly said I should holler at you about the GBC cat who was in here a few days ago."

"Why, he's your people or something?" Wo-love questioned, while stepping completely into Yayo's cell. His henchmen were behind him.

"I don't know. That's what I'm trying to find out," Yayo responded.

"What you is, nigga? What you claim?"

"I'm Yayo, fam. I run GBC," Yayo replied.

"I heard a lot about you, shorty. I hear you a real nigga."

In the midst of the interrogation, another inmate came in the cell. He was also a GD.

"What's good, Yayo?" T-Bone greeted while stepping inside the small cell.

"Ain't shit. What's good?" Yayo said with a stern look.

"You know shorty, T-Bone?" Wo-love asked.

"Hell, yeah. That's TJ's right-hand man. Them the niggas who had the guys on the low end eating with the dog food heroin. I used to fuck with TJ hard before he got killed. RIP TJ," T-Bone said.

"Chow time! Chow time!" The guard yelled, letting the inmates know dinner was being served.

In the county jail, different gangs sat at different tables. The *folks* had their own table, and the *people* had their own table. The folks were the GDs, BDs, Spanish Cobras, and the Insane Gangstas. The people were the Vice Lords, Stones, 4-Corner Hustlas, and the Latin Kings. The other tables were for the neutral dudes who weren't affiliated with any gang.

Yayo had built his own clique in the city of Chicago, which was looked down upon by others. The ATG was also a clique formed in the city's high gang culture. Yayo's clique was a force to be reckoned with in the streets, and a lot of GDs and BDs respected GBC because they made sure the folks ate, and ate good, too.

"Yayo, you can eat at the folks' table as a guest," Wo-love said. The five men stood in line waiting for their food, which consisted of a dry hamburger and a few soggy French fries.

"So, you wanna know about the lil' nigga?" Wo-love asked, picking back up on the conversation.

"Yeah. Who was he?" Yayo replied, eyeing the other inmates.

"The nigga came up in here saying he was a part of GBC, and said he was out there putting in a lot of work. The lil' nigga had a federal detainer and shit." Wo-love grabbed his tray and waited for Yayo.

"There was something funny about the lil' nigga. Every night, late as hell, the pigs would come and get him at like two in the morning." Yayo grabbed his food and took a seat at the table with Wo-love.

He continued, "It seemed like the nigga was on some police shit, so I went to his cell with them shanks and told shorty to raise up outta here, or we was gon' put the knife in 'em. Shorty put a kite in, and told them people he couldn't be in here," Wo-love said as he put ketchup on his burger.

"What was his name?" Yayo asked.

"His name was Lil' B. They called him Butterball."

Yayo couldn't believe what he had just heard. If Butterball made it to the stand to testify, he was surely in a fucked up predicament.

It all made sense. Butterball knew way too much. He knew about the drugs and the bodies. Shit was about to get real shaky. Yayo and Wo-love finished eating. Wo-love told Yayo to meet him at his cell in ten minutes.

When he got to Wo-love's cell, he was sitting at the table. In front of him were two sharpened pieces of steel wrapped in shoelaces. Wo-love stood up, grabbed the weapons, and handed them to Yayo.

"Here, my nigga. You gon' need these around this muthafucka." Yayo grabbed the two tools and placed them in his pocket. "Yayo, there's a lot of shit that goes on around here. The deck always going up. All it takes is for some homies in another unit to go up, and then, boom! This unit gon' blow, so it's best to be ready, so you ain't got to get ready. You feel me?"

Yayo nodded his head in understanding.

"I know you ain't one of them folks, but we respect y'all movement out there, so we respect it in here. Your enemies are our enemies, and it should be vice versa, don't you think?" Yayo nodded. "You gon' be on the AA with the folks, aid and assist," Wo-love explained.

The two gangsters sat in the cell getting acquainted. Yayo found out Wo-love was a GD from 55th and Garfield, an infamous hood on the South Side named Wo-love City. Wo-love was 34 years old on his way to do a lengthy prison sentence for a double murder. He was the shot caller for the GDs in Cook County Jail. He controlled everything from the gang's finances to their weapons. Yayo had heard Wo-love's name mentioned a few times in the streets, and each time, it was always connected to some murder shit.

Yayo kicked it with Wo-love for about 30 minutes before he went back to his cell. His celly was nodding at the table with a needle in his veins. Yayo closed the door and climbed up on the top bunk. "Shit is crazy. Niggas come to jail, and still can't stop shooting dope," he thought to himself.

Yayo's thoughts began to wander as he lying on his bunk. He was thinking about how he could get out of the dilemma he was in. He had to find a way to get at Butterball because if he made it to the stand, it was over.

Yayo thought about all the bodies Butterball knew about. There were too many to count or pinpoint. Butterball was TJ's protégé, so TJ had trained him with hands-on experience in the art of bodysnatching. Butterball knew about the distribution of drugs, the runners, the security men, and the stash spots. He was a black lieutenant, so it was his duty to know that kind of information. With TJ resting in peace, Yayo would have to answer singlehandedly to all the terror the GBC released on the streets of Chicago.

"Yayo," his celly slurred, coming out from his dope nod. "You gotta be a master of art. You gotta beat deception with deception. When you playing the game of the streets, you have to be willing to do the unexpected."

Yayo sat up and gave Rivera his undivided attention.

"Yayo, problems can be big, or they can be small. The problem has to be eliminated totally, by any means necessary. If you are not willing to risk your life in this game, then you are playing the wrong game. Always remember, Yayo, never love this game because it will never love you back."

Yayo digested the lesson Rivera had just given him. In order to win and get another chance at his freedom, he had to find a way to knock Butterball's head from his shoulders in jail.

S. Allen

Chapter 36

TB was in the liquor store on 56th street. He had been trying to lay low since the Marshfield Massacre. Plus, he knew Yayo had got knocked by the feds, so he was definitely taking caution while he played the streets. The streets of the South Side were quiet, and the weather was piercing cold. TB paid for his bottle of Crown Royal Black and exited the store. Once in the comfort of his Chevy Tahoe, TB opened the top and took a swig from the bottle. The dark liquor warmed his chest. The stakes had been raised in the streets with ATG. There was a body getting dropped in the Englewood area almost every night.

The police had beefed up their presence, but not even that seemed to keep the gunplay down from the gangs. By TB holding down the GBC since Yayo was away, TB was an intended target for both the ATGs and the Chicago police.

TB pulled the SUV in traffic and was sitting at a red light on 55th when his phone sprung to life. Seeing it was Maniac calling, he answered. "What up, killa?"

"Ain't shit. Trying to see what the move is for the night."

"You already know, duck hunting," TB said, referring to hunting his enemies. TB made a left on Halsted Street.

"That's what's up. I'm in the whip with Psycho and Twon G. We on the same shit," Maniac said.

"A peep game. I gotta slide through my baby mama's real quick to drop some bread off for my seed. When I'm done, I'ma hit your phone. I got a lil' broad on Moe-Town. She got some buddies we can slide through there, and run they asses. You down?" TB said, not noticing the Astro van following him since he pulled off.

"Hell, yeah, my nigga. Hit the phone when you're ready to slide through there."

"That's a bet," TB said and ended the call. TB turned his music up and let Yo Gotti blast through his subwoofers. The Crown Royal plus the music had TB on ten, and ready for some drama. Little did he know the drama was about to be brought to his front door.

***

Quavon was at home in the basement watching Gangland on Yayo's 60-inch Vizio television. He liked watching the show because it showed all kinds of gangs in the United States. Quavon always thought the thugs on the show were soft because they exposed all of a nigga's business.

Quavon had signed up for school at Kennedy King College. He wanted to take up Business Management, and Devon wanted to major in Graphic Design. Devon liked video games, and always wanted to design them. Quavon took up Business Management because his plan was to make a lot of money in the streets. When he got his bread up, he wanted to turn it into a legit empire.

Both twins were scheduled to start school next semester. Quavon pulled half of a blunt from his Perish limited jeans and fired the tip. Karen was at her shop doing hair, so the coast was clear for him to smoke.

He puffed on the strong kush, and continued to watch Gangland. This specific episode was about the Milwaukee Ghetto Boys Gang, a ruthless drug crew in Wisconsin. Quavon listened as the gang told all their business to the world.

"These got to be the fakest niggas ever," Quavon thought to himself as he took a pull from the blunt.

Tired of watching the niggas fake at an all-time high, he changed the channel. After flipping through, he turned the TV off. Smoking the blunt down to the roach, he put it in the ashtray and walked over to the bar. Quavon found a bottle of 1800 tequila, and poured himself a shot. Quavon was never big on drinking, but out of boredom, he downed the smooth liquor and put the top back on the bottle.

When he sat the bottle back behind the bar, he found a Nike box at the bottom of the shelf. Staring at the box, his curiosity got the best of him. When Quavon opened the box, a Springfield Army 45 ACP stared him in the face. Picking up the chunky, Glock-style weapon, he admired it. He had seen Yayo with numerous guns, but Quavon was never allowed to hold one. After putting the 14-shot extended magazine in the butt of the gun, he pulled the slide back, putting a hollow tip round in the deadly chamber. A powerful feeling washed over his being.

Quavon felt devious, and he wanted to go outside and do something with the gun. It was 8:30 at night, and Karen wouldn't be home until 11. He put on his shoes, tucked the .45 on his waist, and slid out the back door into the crime-ridden streets of the North Side, also known as the North Pole.

***

TB pulled up on 69th and Bishop and parked his truck. It had been two weeks since he had seen his newborn. With all the action he was involved in, he wasn't able to come visit. Plus, he wanted to smash his baby mama, Tiffany. The Crown Royal had him horny, and Tiffany's thick ass would be his thirst quencher. As TB got out of the Tahoe, he saw an Astro van creeping down the block. The van had the side door open, and TB saw someone hanging out with a gun in his hand. TB reached for the FN tucked on his waistline as the driver of the van sped up.

"What's the bizness, doe?" The man holding the pistol sneered before he lit up the street with gunfire. *Blocka! Blocka!* "ATG, nigga!" *Blocka! Blocka! Blocka!*

TB ducked behind the Tahoe and let the FN speak. *Cho! Cho! Cho! Cho! Cho! Cho!* The two men exchanged deadly gunfire for sixty seconds.

The Astro van sped off, making a left on Bishop Street, as TB continued to spit rounds at his enemies. The gun smoke in the air looked like fog as TB jumped in his truck and pulled off, leaving the streets littered with hot shell casings. He would have to see his son another day.

***

Quavon walked down Sheridan Street. His destination was the White Hen Pantry. It was blistering cold outside, so he wore a hoodie. The weed he had just smoked had him feeling good, and the shot of tequila had him amped up. Quavon walked inside the store and went to the counter to purchase two cherry Black & Mild cigars. After he paid for them, he walked out of the store and stood on the corner. Across the street was the Sheridan movie theater. It was a Friday night, and one of the movies had just let out.

Quavon saw a few females in the crowd, and figured he would get his mack on. Waiting for the light to turn red, Quavon made his way across the street.

A group of dudes his age had been watching him. All of them had their hats turned to the left. The Conservative Vice Lords ran the neighborhood on Sheridan. Even though Quavon wasn't a part of a gang, he looked like a thug due to his baggy jeans and Timberlands.

Quavon had just finished hollering at a sexy redbone by the name of Roxy. The two had exchanged numbers by the time the crowed started to thin out. Roxy got in a car with her friend, and told Quavon to give her a call. Quavon started walking back toward his house when the five Vice Lords started to follow him. One of the young thugs called out to Quavon.

"Aye, Joe, let us holler at you real quick."

Quavon looked over his shoulder and saw the thugs pursuing him, and he put some pep in his step.

"Aye, nigga! Come here right quick!"

Quavon felt the adrenaline rush, as he turned down a dark alley. The individuals caught up with Quavon.

"What's up, doe? Vice Lord, nigga. What you is?" One of the thugs asked with a mean mug on his face.

"I ain't in no gang," Quavon smoothly replied.

The gang knew Quavon wasn't from their hood. "Nigga, what you got in your pocket?" One of the dudes tried to reach for him.

When Quavon pushed the dude off of him, another took a swing at Quavon, landing on Quavon's jawline. All five guys began throwing blows at him. Taking a few punches to the head, Quavon reached for the gun on his waist. Coming off of his waistline with the hammer, the youngsters took off running at the sight of the cannon. Aiming the .45, Quavon closed his eyes and squeezed the trigger. *Bloc!*

Hitting one of his attackers in the shoulder, the youngster fell to the ground, clutching his shoulder. He was trying to stop the blood from pouring from the large hole the .45 had inflicted.

"Ahhh! I'm sorry, man. Ahhh!" The dude yelled in agony. Walking up to him, Quavon went through his pockets and relieved him of a couple hundred dollars. Tucking the hot gun back on his waist, he jogged off into the night. That gangster shit definitely ran in his blood.

S. Allen

Chapter 37

Yayo stood at the sink inside his cell, washing his face. The hot washcloth against his smooth skin seemed to relax him. Today would be the day he went to court to see if he could get a reasonable bond. Yayo grabbed his khaki pants from under his mattress and slid them on. After he was dressed, he went to Wo-love's cell.

"What up, fam?" Yayo greeted. Wo-love looked up from his Holy Quran and motioned for him to enter the cell.

"What's the lick, killa?" Wo-love said, giving Yayo some dap.

Ready for these people to come and get me. I got IA court today."

"They gon' start calling for court around ten," Wo-love told him, and started to roll a joint.

"I hope these people give me a bond so I can touch."

"Yayo, I'ma keep it real with you, fam. They gon' have a federal detainer on you. That's gon' make sure they don't let you out." Wo-love lit the joint and passed it to Yayo.

"I know, but how do they have a federal detainer on me, and I ain't been indicted on shit?" Yayo asked, taking a pull from the joint and passing it back.

"I feel you, my nigga, but those feds are a whole different breed. They do shit different from the state. They leave a nigga in here for five years before they indict," Wo-love said, filling his lungs with smoke. "For real, Yayo, you need to touch that nigga, Butterball."

"How I'ma get that rat ass nigga? I don't even know what block his rat ass on," Yayo replied.

"Don't worry. You will soon, G. I got an APB out on that rat. Just a matter of time before I get a kite with the info you need," Wo-love stated.

"That's exactly what I need, my nigga." Yayo gave Wo-love a gangsta pound.

* * *

"Yaton Anderson, Marcus Hall, and Kevin Brent, get ready for court," the guard yelled over the intercom.

"That's me, family."

"Aight, good luck. Smoke the rest of this cap when you get back," Wo-love said and continued reading his Quran.

Yayo was led to the crowded bullpen, where at least fifty other inmates were waiting to see the judge. They were all stuffed inside the tiny cage. The smell was musty as hell, and there was no place to sit. Yayo took a spot in the back of the cage and put his back against the wall. He scanned the faces of the different men in the cell. There was a combination of blacks, Puerto Ricans, and Mexicans. Yayo knew it was going to be a long day.

A familiar face maneuvered his way through the crowd toward Yayo. He knew the guy from somewhere, but he couldn't remember.

"Yayo, what's good, fam?" The man said. His dreads fell below his shoulders, and his teeth was laced with white gold and diamonds.

"Where I know you from, my nigga?" Yayo asked.

"Off of 69th and Wolcott. I be with Skeeterman and Pablo and them. My name's Peewee."

"Oh yeah. I think I remember you now. You drive that black bubble Chevy?" Yayo remembered.

"Yeah, that's me," Peewee said, giving Yayo some dap. Peewee was a nickel and dime hustler who ran with a few of the foot soldiers from the GBC. Peewee wasn't a part of the organization, but he rotated hard with the gang.

"What you in here for, lil' homie?" Yayo asked.

"I got a heroin case. I was on the block, and the jump out boys came through and planted some bags on me," Peewee informed him. "Man, the whole hood talking about how you got knocked by the feds. It's going down out there, fam. TB and Maniac are out there shooting shit up. They on the ATG niggas' line. It's like Iraq in the hood, straight up," Peewee told Yayo.

It made Yayo feel good knowing his men was out there applying pressure where it was needed.

"What are they talking about with your case?" Peewee probed.

"I don't know. It's some bullshit. I should be out soon," Yayo answered, minimizing the conversation. The two continued conversing for an hour or so until a guard came to the holding cell.

"Yaton Anderson, court." Yayo was led out of the bullpen and through a door. When he stepped into the large courtroom, he noticed how packed it was. Yayo sat next to his court-appointed lawyer, Mark Brown. Looking back and scanning the crowd, he saw his family in attendance. Karen, Honey, Shakira, and the twins all came to show their love and support, as they anticipated the verdict.

"All rise for the honorable Judge Crane," the bailiff said. Judge Crane came from the chambers and took a seat on the podium.

"Thank you. You can all be seated," the clerk informed the court.

"Case number 05-CF-1574, State of Illinois vs. Yaton Anderson. May we have the appearances, please?" The judge asked.

"Rita Gibson for the state," the district attorney replied and sat down.

"Thank you."

"Your honor, Mr. Anderson appears in person by Attorney Mark Brown," Yayo's lawyer said.

Rita stood and stated her case. "Your honor, we are here for the initial appearance of Mr. Anderson. In this case, Mr. Anderson is charged in the state of Illinois for possessing an illegal firearm. Mr. Anderson was on parole or probation for homicide at the time of this charge. He is the alleged leader of a drug crew on the South Side of the city that is now under a federal investigation for charges ranging from drug distribution, money laundering, tax evasion, and multiple murders. It would be in the state's best interest to deny Mr. Anderson bail at this time. I feel Mr. Anderson is a danger to the community, as well as a flight risk. Thank you."

"Mr. Brown, is there anything you would like to say on behalf of the defendant?" Judge Crane asked.

Mr. Brown stood up to address the court on behalf of his client. "Yes, your honor, thank you. Your honor, Mr. Anderson has already taken responsibility for the weapons found in his home. My client is allegedly involved in a lot of different crimes, but is yet to be indicted by the government. Mr. Anderson is ready to deal with the situation at hand. So, I feel he should be able to obtain a reasonable bond, as he is not a flight risk, nor a danger to the public. Thank you," Mr. Brown stated and took a seat next to Yayo.

"Thank you, Mr. Brown. First and foremost, for the record, I disagree with you. I feel Mr. Anderson is definitely a risk and a danger to our community. He has been convicted of murder in the past, and was on parole at the time of this offense. The weapons found in his home were the kind of weapons used to fight wars. Mr. Anderson, you do have a federal detainer from the United States government, as well as a parole and probation hold. You have some serious issues at hand, and to protect the safety of the citizens of the community of Chicago, I am denying your bond at this time."

A tear fell from Shakira's eyes. She couldn't believe they weren't going to release Yayo.

"Mr. Anderson, your next scheduled court appearance will be June 12th."

The judge slammed the gavel as his bailiff came over to Yayo to escort him back to the depths of Cook County Jail. Yayo looked over his shoulder and mouthed the words, "I love y'all" to his family as he was led out of the courtroom.

When Yayo got back to Division 11, it was quiet as hell. The tension in the air was so thick. Walking in the unit, Yayo spotted Wo-love with about ten GDs standing on the top tier with mean mugs on their faces. Wo-love motioned for Yayo to come up to the top tier and join them. When Yayo got up top, Wo-love greeted him with some dap.

"How'd court go, family?" Wo-love asked.

"Shit went fucked up. They gave me no bond. Said I got a federal detainer, too." Wo-love gave him the "I-told-you- so" look.

"Yeah, that's fucked up, but shit gon' work itself out. But check it out. I need to holler at you real quick," Wo-love stated.

Yayo followed Wo-love back to his cell. Once inside, five GDs stood posted up in front of the cell on security. Yayo noticed the strange movement and asked, "What the fuck is going on around this bitch?"

"Check it out, Yayo. While you were at court, one of the folks got into it with a couple of Stones over the TV. This is the third time we done bumped heads with these niggas and we always worked it out through politics. I told myself last time if we got into it with them again, we was gon' blow this bitch. These niggas think it's a game or something, so I sent a kite to every division in here. At six on the dot, we gon' punish everything that got to do with the finball? all at the same time," Wo-love explained.

Yayo nodded his head in understanding. He was already upset from the outcome of his court date, and he had some built up tension, so some drama with the Stones was right up his alley. His only wish was that he could inflict some of that pain on Butterball. But little did he know, in due time, his wish would ultimately come true.

"That's what's up, Wo-love. I'ma show y'all what this Yayo shit about," Yayo stated, and walked out of the cell to get his knives.

***

It was 5:52 p.m., and Yayo was in his cell letting T-Bone tape magazines and telephone books to his chest. In the county, that was equivalent to having a bulletproof vest on.

Yayo and the GDs were about to use the element of surprise on the Stones. Wo-love had told the shot caller of the Stones that the earlier incident was put to rest. And the GD who was involved was in violation, and would be disciplined for his disrespectful conduct. The head of the Stones agreed with Wo-love. Little did he know that the incident was far from over, and a few of his homies were about to be a part of a serious demonstration.

Most of the unit was outside at recreation. Most of the security for the GDs stayed back in the unit. After the first wave of the attack, whatever enemies left would be disposed of after they took the unit off of lockdown status.

At 5:55, the unit started filing in from the rec period. Most of the inmates rushed to their cells to get their things for shower time.

Yayo had already chosen a target. He was a light-skinned dude with long French braids, who went by the name Teflon. He was from the East Side of Chicago, called Terror Town.

Yayo didn't like Teflon because he felt he was always talking kill shit. Coming up, Yayo was always taught that killers don't talk. They kill. He knew Teflon was pure pussy, and he was about to prove it. Yayo watched as all of the GDs and BDs came out of their cells and posted up all around the walls in the dayroom. When the clock read 5:58, Yayo made his way over to Teflon, who was attempting to make a call.

When 6:00 hit, Yayo hung the phone up on Teflon.

"What the fuck?" That was all Teflon could say before he turned around to see who had come at him with disrespect.

Yayo's knife punctured his face. The GDs and BDs rushed almost every inmate who wasn't a part of them. Teflon fell to his knees, using his forearms to protect his face from the assault. Yayo stabbed him viciously in the head, back, and chest, as the GDs chased their enemies with shanks that looked like mini swords. The assault lasted three minutes before the C.O.s rushed in the unit with their riot gear. The GDs and BDs tossed their weapons, and were cuffed and lined against the wall.

The Stones laid sprawled out all over the unit in puddles of blood, waiting to be carried to Cermak hospital in critical condition. Wo-love and Yayo locked eyes. Wo-love nodded his head at Yayo and Yayo nodded back. The two goons had just bonded, and it was bonded by blood.

***

Quavon sat at the kitchen table with a notebook and a pen. He had missed his brother dearly, and started to write a letter to him.

Yayo,

What's up, big bro? I saw you in court today. Man, you getting skinny as hell. You look like Wacka Flocka on the pipe, lol. For real tho, bro, them people bogus as hell for not letting you bond out. I wish I could have broken you out. Bro, we all miss you. Shamira doing good. You already know we gon' make sure she's good by all means. Shakira's been looking for a job. I think mama will let her work in the shop until she finds one. Devon is straight. All he talks about is starting school with his nerd ass. Granny sends her love, and says for you to pick up the Bible. Other than that, it's the same shit. I am sending you two hundred dollars with this letter. It should get you some commissary up in there. I know you're wondering where I got the money from. It's a long story, but just know I represented. I love and miss you.

Love always,
Your lil bro Quavon

***

Two days after Yayo and the GDs sent up the deck with the Stones, Yayo laid on his bunk, reading the letter from Quavon. Yayo had much love for his brother, but he knew he would answer to the lure of the streets, if they ever came calling. That's why every chance he got, he laced Quavon with the street knowledge he would need to succeed. Yayo wanted the best for his brother, but it was in Quavon's blood to be a thug.

Yayo knew all too well of how the streets of Chicago would turn the most humble into the most venomous, and Quavon was no different. Yayo started to wonder where and how Quavon got the money to send him, and what he meant by representing. In Chicago, representing meant an act of violence on another. Yayo wished he had mentored his brother in a more positive way.

Yayo took the letter and put it under his mattress. He had been in the hole for two days. They had Division 11, 5, 2, and 1 on lockdown status. In all, 42 inmates were stabbed in the incident. The entire hold was packed to capacity with gang members who participated in the riot. Shit had definitely gotten real.

S. Allen

Chapter 38

It had been three weeks since the riot. Yayo and everyone else who had been involved had been assigned back to their original division. Yayo walked in the unit with his bedroll and property slung over his shoulders. The GDs had laid down a vicious move that the whole jail respected. Walking into his cell, Yayo saw his celly making some jailhouse food.

"What's up, youngster?" Rivera said, getting up and giving Yayo a hug.

"Good to be back," Yayo replied, tossing his property on the top bunk and taking a seat on the foot of Rivera's bunk. Rivera knew Yayo was getting out of the hole today and had prepared him some hot food.

Rivera had been doing time since the 70's. He was a beast in the cooking area, so he made Yayo his specialty of burritos and rice. The Kool-Aid he mixed up was the sweetest Yayo had ever tasted.

Yayo and Rivera sat in the cell feasting while Rivera brought him up to speed on the current events in the unit. Yayo learned they moved all the fin-balls, a.k.a. peoples, off the unit to keep the violence down. Wo-love came into the cell while Yayo was still eating.

"Yayo, what it do, gangsta? I saw you come in a while ago," Wo-love said, shaking hands with young Yayo. Wo-love had been out of the hole a week before Yayo. He was the last to get released because the camera saw him starting the fight.

Rivera put the top on his food. "I guess I'll let you two youngsters chop it up." Rivera got up and walked out of the cell, giving them some privacy. Wo-love took a seat in the chair as Yayo continued to finish his meal.

"A nigga hungry as shit," Yayo said with a mouth full of food.

"Man, I know. When I got out of the box, I definitely got my grub on." Wo-love began to roll a fat joint of some chronic.

"I got something that's gon' float your boat, lil' nigga," Wo-love said with a smile.

"What's that?"

"I got the info on where that rat ass nigga Butterball is at." Wo-love now had Yayo's attention.

"Where he at?" Yayo asked, putting his food on the desk. His appetite was now nonexistent.

"He's in Division 6. One of my coordinators just sent word."

"Oh, yeah? How the hell I'ma get to Division 6?"

"Yayo, you a chief. You no longer have to put in work in the battlefield. You have to learn to network with other gangsters. The way you rode out with us on that move, I am forever indebted to you. You just say the word, and the business will get handled," Wo-love replied, lighting the joint and inhaling the potent weed.

Yayo didn't hesitate. "Make it happen."

"Check it out, lil' homie. This is the move." Wo-love then explained to Yayo how everything was going to go down, and sent a kite to Division 6.

***

Butterball was watching *The First 48*. They had just served the afternoon meal, and the unit was on chill mode. He had found out Yayo was in Division 11, and had just gotten into a riot. Butterball was grateful he had been moved off the unit before Yayo came to the block. Butterball didn't feel bad about snitching on Yayo. In his mind, it was either him or Yayo, just like his brother, Jug-head. Butterball was on a mission to whack Yayo anyway, so in his mind, he was still winning. Whether Yayo did life in the feds or was killed by his gun made no difference to him. He would have revenge for his brother one way or the other.

"Aye, Butterball, what the fuck you watching this snitch ass show for?" Muso asked.

"Ain't shit else on TV," Butterball replied, but in actuality, it was one of his favorite shows.

"Man, fuck that TV. The guys and I are about to get fucked up. We got wine, weed, and cigarettes. We up in Bo-Jack's cell," Muso said, heading back to the party. Butterball followed, not wanting to miss a free high.

When Butterball got to Bo-Jack's cell, it was packed with GDs, Pig G, Muso, Twin, and BD Skeetdog were all getting their drink on and passing joints around.

"Come on in, my nigga," BD Skeetdog said, passing Butterball the bottle of jailhouse wine. The first bottle had Butterball feeling tipsy. Along with the weed, he was sloppy. The crew stayed in the cell for about an hour, with BD Skeetdog being the center of attention, as he bragged about all the work he put in on the street. Everybody had their own war stories. Butterball's head began to spin from all the alcohol he consumed.

"Aye, Dog, let us holler at dude real quick," Bo-Jack said, referring to Butterball. Butterball didn't sense the danger surrounding him. Pig-G and Twin also left the cell. Bo-Jack rolled another joint and passed it to Butterball, who lit it and inhaled the smoke into his lungs.

"Man, I'm fucked up, y'all," Butterball slurred.

Another thug entered the cell. He was 6'6" and 280 pounds of muscle. His name was X-man. He was on his way to Statesville Penitentiary with a life sentence.

"Aye, Butterball, you feel good, my nigga?" Bo-Jack asked.

"Hell, yeah, G. I feel good," Butterball responded.

"Let me see how good you feel," Bo-Jack slurred, putting his hand on Butterball's thigh.

Butterball drunkenly slapped Bo-Jack's hand off of his leg. Bo-Jack jumped up and put Butterball in a chokehold. Muso closed the cell door, while X-man proceeded to yank Butterball's pants to his ankles. Butterball could hardly breathe as he tried to scream for help.

"Shut the fuck up, you snitching bitch!" Muso said through clenched teeth, as he pulled the shank from his waist.

X-man stuffed a dry cloth in Butterball's mouth to muffle his pleas for help. Muso and Bo-Jack held Butterball down while X-man lubricated Butterball's asshole with petroleum jelly. Satisfied with his work, X-man pulled his pants down and forced himself inside of Butterball's ass. The smell of shit invaded the cell as X-man continued to pound Butterball, splitting him in two. The pain was too much to bear, so Butterball passed out. After climaxing inside of Butterball, X-man pulled out, and wiped the blood and shit off of his dick.

"Let me see that banga." X-man commanded. Muso passed him the 10-inch shank with the jagged edges. X-man spread Butterball's cheeks and pushed the knife in his ass. He then drug Butterball's body to the tier, spit on him, and walked off.

"Rat ass nigga," Muso said, while stepping over Butterball's unconscious body.

***

Yayo was on his bunk reading a novel, Trust No Bitch by Ca$h, when all of a sudden, he heard, "Yaton Anderson, get ready for court." Yayo sat up.

"How the hell I got court? I don't have court for another two months," Yayo mumbled as he jumped off of his bunk.

"Yaton Anderson, court," the officer said again over the intercom.

Wo-love came to Yayo's cell. "What's good, fam? You hear them calling you for court?"

"Yeah, I heard 'em. They must got me mixed up. I don't have court 'til June," Yayo said.

"That's probably them people, the feds," Wo-love retorted.

"Anderson, you ready for court?" The officer at the door asked.

Yayo walked over to the guard. "Man, I don't have court 'til June."

"Mr. Anderson, you have federal court," the officer replied.

"Damn," Yayo thought to himself It was now time to face his worst nightmare, the United States government. Yayo was taken to the intake part of the jail, when he was met by two white U.S. marshals.

"Yaton Anderson, we are with the U.S. marshals. Put your hands behind your back, please," one of them said.

Yayo was handcuffed and led to a tinted-up Yukon Denali. He was headed to the MCC Federal building downtown. Looking out the window, he watched the streets pass him in a blur. He was starting to wonder when he was going to be a free man again. In his mind, his future was up for grabs.

Yayo started to think about his family, mainly his daughter. The thought of her growing up without him was unbearable. Yayo's eyes began to water. He was going down for the love of the game. The money, cars, and clothes would all be taken away from him. He already lost Pudge, Joyce, and TJ. He thought of what Rivera said, "The game would never love you back."

Sitting at a stoplight on Michigan Avenue, Yayo noticed a young black man crossing the street with a baby in his arms. The way things were looking, Yayo would never get to hold his daughter again.

The Denali pulled inside of the garage of the MCC building. Four U.S. marshals stood waiting for them to deliver Yayo to the building. He was led to a holding cell, where he was handcuffed and given a bag lunch, which consisted of a sub sandwich, a soda, and a bag of chips. Yayo was starving, so he went at the bag lunch. While eating his meal, a federal agent in a dark, pinstriped suit came into the cell.

"Mr. Anderson, put your hands behind your back."

Yayo was cuffed again and taken to a small room, as a U.S. marshal sat on the other side of the room. Yayo was asked a slew of questions: name, age, address, Social Security number, and his gang affiliation. After the questionnaire, he was led to another room where he was fingerprinted. He was given his FBI registration number, 07505-424. After being booked into federal custody, he was walked into a federal courtroom. The marshal led Yayo to a cushioned blue chair next to an older white man, who he assumed was his court-appointed lawyer.

"Mr. Anderson, I'm Attorney Davidson, and I will be representing you on your case," the lawyer stated.

Yayo looked at the judge's podium, which sat high in the sky like a mountain. Yayo knew he was in deep shit. The magistrate judge came from the chambers.

"All rise for the honorable Judge Matthews." Everyone stood.

"Thank you. You can all be seated at this time," said Judge Matthews.

Yayo went through the initial appearance procedure. At the end, he was indicted on federal weapons charges, tax evasion, and continuing a criminal enterprise. With his serious charge and extensive criminal history, he was definitely looking at a life sentence.

Chapter 39

It had been a whole year since Yayo was indicted by the feds. He anticipated his trial date. Butterball was due to testify at his trial, and he was being held in protective custody.

Yayo was a stone cold gangster, and was ready to accept his fate, whether it be life or death. It was noon, and he had just gotten a visit from Mr. Davidson. He had told Yayo that his chances of winning the trial were slim to none. Butterball was going to testify that he was a soldier of the GBC, and he was involved with drug distribution and the enforcement for the gang. He would also testify that Yayo was the commander-in-chief for the organization, and orchestrated and participated in the deaths of Jerome Fields (Jughead), Latrell Pope (Homicide), Kenny Charleston (Tank), and Jeffrey Washington. Butterball was also going to state that GBC was a criminal-organized gang that followed a chain of command, and disciplined members through beatings and murder. Yayo was definitely feds bound, and the thought of it all had him in his feelings.

As Yayo walked back in the unit, a lot of inmates stared at him as he walked back to his cell. They knew he was just coming back from an attorney visit, and was trying to read his facial expression. In jail, niggas would try to dissect character, looking for a weakness, so they could exploit it to the highest level. Yayo was a vet in the game, and kept a stone face.

"What up, big homie?" Tay-Tay asked as Yayo came in the cell and plopped down on his bunk.

"Ain't nothing, fam. Lil' faggot about to take the stand on a nigga," Yayo said angrily.

"Yeah, that's messed up bro. He gon' get his day, trust and believe that."

Tay-Tay was 18 years old, and was about to be shipped to the feds for a spree of bank robberies. He wasn't a gang member, and always stayed out of the way of their business. Yayo took a liking to Tay-Tay. He thought he was a criminal mastermind with the ambition of a go-getter. If he was released from the feds right now, he would be running up in somebody's bank the same night.

S. Allen

"Let me beat your ass in Casino to get that shit off your mind," Tay-Tay laughed, while grabbing a deck of cards from under his mattress. Yayo and Tay-Tay played cards in the cell for an hour before Yayo got up and went to use the phone to call Shakira.

Shakira was driving home from the Jewel grocery store, with Shamira in the backseat, when her iPhone 6 sprang to life with Kelly Rowland's "Motivation" ringtone. She answered the phone, knowing it was Yayo.

"Hello."

"You have a collect call from, Yayo," the voice recorded operator stated. "To accept the call, press five. To deny the call, or have this numbered blocked, press seven." Shakira pressed five quickly.

"What's up, boo? I miss you," Shakira purred into the phone with a huge smile on her face.

"How you doing, beautiful?" Yayo flirted.

"I'm good, baby. Shamira and I just came back from the grocery store. Now I'm headed home." Shakira said as she got on the expressway.

"That's what's up. I was just calling to let you know how shit went with the lawyer."

"How did it go, baby? What's he talking about?" Shakira asked with great concern.

"Baby, he says it ain't looking good. They got dude in protective custody, and he gave it to them people raw. With my charges, if I get found guilty, baby, they gon' throw me away," Yayo informed her.

Shakira's smile instantly faded. "Yayo, your destiny is not with the racist judge. Baby, it's up to God. It's all up to Him, so we gon' put it in His hands. Just know that whatever the outcome is, I'm going to be here through thick and thin. I love you."

Yayo let her love, dedication, and devotion sooth his emotions. "I love you, Shakira. I want the best for you and our daughter, and I don't want to be a burden on you with all this shit. If you want to move on with your life, baby, I understand."

"Nigga, you got me fucked up! I don't give a fuck if they send you to the moon. Nigga, I'm gon' find a way to get there. You need to stop worrying, Yaton."

"Baby, I'm sorry. I didn't mean to upset you," Yayo apologized.

"You have one minute remaining," the recording stated.

"Listen, baby, stop stressing over this shit and handle it. Call me later tonight. I love you, Yaton." The call ended.

S. Allen

Chapter 40

Quavon walked down the hall of Kennedy King College on his way to lunch. His Coogi jeans sagged over his brand new Jordans, and his tight, white tee clung to his physique. The GBC chain hung from his neck. Quavon and Devon had transitioned into the college atmosphere well. Devon loved his classes and was learning a lot.

Quavon used college for different reasons, the bitches and the money. His swag was dripping so hard, every woman in the school wanted a taste of Quavon. He always stayed fresh, and graced the halls like he ran the joint. Quavon was also hustling in the school.

He had been fucking with TB within the last year. TB had stacked his money in the streets, and was now a heavyweight in the game. The ATGs were practically nonexistent, so TB's new focus was the money instead of the murder.

Quavon met TB when he would stop at Karen's to drop off money for Yayo, or he would just look out with him. Quavon was always asking TB to put him on his feet with the work, but TB refused to put dope in Quavon's hand. After months of begging TB for drugs, he broke down and started giving Quavon pounds of kush. Quavon would break the weed down into forty-dollar grams, and take them to school. After a few months, Quavon's clientele was so official that he went from grams to pounds.

Selling drugs was easy for him. He had good social skills. Everybody wanted to fuck with Quavon. He would pull up in his blue box Chevy sitting on 26-inch rims, stunting. He was on a money-making mission.

TB watched Quavon's bank grow as he flooded him with weight. On weekends, Quavon would hit the club with GBC. They all treated him like he was superior to the crew. They respected him on the strength of Yayo, one of the coldest gangsters to come out of the Chi.

Quavon was at the lunch table, glued to his iPhone, browsing through his Facebook page. Devon came and sat down.

"What's good, bro?" Devon said, while eating a French fry.

"Shit, you ready to leave, or you got lab class tonight?" He asked Devon.

"Nah, but I gotta stay late today because I got study class," Devon replied, putting ketchup on his burger. The two brothers sat eating their lunch when three fine chicks walked up.

"Hey, Devon. Hey, Quavon," Missy greeted. She was a thick little redbone who was in Quavon's Business Management class. She was on a 24-hour mission to get the dick from Quavon. Missy was an uppity chick who always had her nose in the air like her shit didn't stink, and for that reason, he never really paid her any attention. He was a player to the bone. His motto was, "Never chase the hoes. Let the hoes chase me."

"What's good, Missy?" Quavon said, not looking up from his phone.

"Nothing. I was just wondering if you wanted to go see that new Tyler Perry movie on Friday." Missy and her two friends took a seat at the table.

"Nah, shorty. I ain't got time for that shit. I got thangs to do."

"Boy, you always got something to do or something going on," Missy said with an attitude.

Quavon got mad. "Bitch, my brother just went to fed, and is on trial for his life. Ain't nobody got time for your bougie ass. Matter of fact, move around," he snarled, still not looking up from his phone. Missy's jaw dropped to the floor, as she got up and walked off with her friends, feeling stupid.

Devon laughed. "Boy, you stupid as shit."

"Man, fuck them hoes." Quavon got a text, and after reading it, a smile lit up his face.

"What you smiling for, goofy?" Devon asked.

"Man, I'm about to bounce. You gon' need a ride later?" Quavon asked, grabbing his backpack.

"Nah. I'm good. I'll catch you at the crib later." The two gave each other a pound. Quavon rushed off to go supply the order for the five pounds of kush that just got ordered.

After conducting his business, Quavon pulled up to TB's house on the East Side. He had just made 27 racks from offing the five pounds of weed. Quavon also had weed on 69th and Wolcott. He was getting money. Quavon jumped out of the whip and knocked on the door. It was answered by a thick, chocolate sister, who wore tan booty shorts and a lace Victoria Secret's bra.

"What up, lil' mama?" Quavon said, while walking past the sack chaser. The house was filled with weed smoke. TB, Maniac, Chopper, and Reggie G were all in the front room fucking with the Xbox.

"What up, my niggas?" Quavon asked, grabbing the blunt of sour diesel from Maniac.

"What's good with you, Schoolboy Q?" TB laughed.

"You niggas always talking that school shit. Don't let that shit fool you. I just look like this, my nigga." Quavon blew out a thick cloud of weed smoke.

"Damn, pump your brakes, killa. We know how you get down," Reggie G joked.

The five gangsters got high and talked nation business. There was a lot going on in the streets. Everybody knew it was just a matter of time before they came through serving indictment papers.

Yayo's trial was in two days, and the crew was trying to mentally prepare themselves to support their leader. They hated seeing Yayo in cuffs. They missed his leadership, friendship, and his presence on the streets. Without Yayo, there was a huge void in the squad. Quavon vowed that no matter the outcome, he would be there for his brother. Yayo would live like a king inside the belly of the beast by any means necessary.

An hour or two later, Quavon got up and gave his niggas some dap. "Man, I'm about to bounce up outta here. I'ma holler at y'all in a minute," Quavon said, clipping his phone on his belt.

"Aight, Quavon, hit my phone later when you ready for me, lil' homie," TB said, referring to Quavon's re-up.

"Alright, that's a bet," Quavon replied, as he slid out the front door. After jumping in his Chevy, he pulled out the driveway, blasting his music. He didn't notice the black Crown Victoria doing surveillance on the house. Quavon just got his first snapshot as a GBC gang member.

S. Allen

Chapter 41

Yayo went to trial and lost. Today, he would face his fate at the hands of the U.S. government. Butterball had crushed him in the courtroom. Butterball told the feds how Yayo would go to Rockford to cop bricks of cocaine and heroin. He also told them about taking the work to the trap on 95th and Yates to process and bag the drugs. Butterball also confessed that he killed Homicide because he tried to rob him. Butterball testified that Yayo shot and killed Tank because he murdered Joyce in an abandoned house on the South Side. The whole infrastructure at the GBC was broken down to the feds.

Butterball told them about the lookouts, the enforcers, the block lieutenants, as well as the security detail for the gang. Butterball gave the FBI all the pieces to the puzzle. They knew about Batman and Robin being on Yayo's payroll, and how Batman tried to extort Yayo for money, which ended with Yayo orchestrating the shootings of the two cops.

Butterball gave them all the stash houses in the city where the drugs, guns, and money were held for the gang. He admitted to going on the mission with TJ on the Fatboy murder, which was a double homicide. Butterball said TJ forced him to commit the murder.

Yayo's family sat in the courtroom, not able to believe how Butterball was getting down on the stand. Quavon sat there, staring at Butterball through bloodshot eyes, as Karen had tears rolling down her cheeks. Honey sat there silently praying for her grandson, while Shakira's blood boiled as she thought about all the times Butterball would come around, and how they would treat him like family.

Butterball continued to break the code of silence, giving the court murder after murder. Butterball was emotional as he told the court how Yayo and TJ killed his brother, Jug-head.

Fifteen minutes passed after his testimony. The jury came back with a guilty verdict.

Today, Yayo's future was held at the hands of the judge who now stood before him. Even at his worst, Yayo remained in boss mode. He was dressed in a gray, pinstriped Armani suit, Mauri gators lacing his feet, and his diamond pinky ring held enough ice to freeze Africa. Yayo wore his hair in six long French braids to the back. Taking a sip from his bottled water, he sat back and attentively listened to the district attorney paint the picture to try and close his casket.

"Your honor, this individual is a violent criminal to the highest extent. He has taken life after life, leaving families to mourn the loss of their loved ones. This man sitting here in this courtroom has no remorse toward his victims. He has sold drugs that have poisoned our community. Mr. Anderson is the leader of the GBC, a murderous drug gang from the South Side, whose objectives were to distribute drugs, and shoot and kill rival gangsters. We must make an example that this type of lifestyle will never be accepted in our city."

Yayo grinned as the D.A. continued.

"Your honor, it is recommended from the United States of America that Mr. Yaton Anderson be designated to the Bureau of Prisons for the rest of his natural life. Thank you."

The judge shifted his eyes to Yayo's lawyer. "Mr. Brown, would you like to say anything on behalf of the defendant?" His attorney stood up from his seat, loosening up his tie.

"Your honor, we have a witness who was arrested and charged with a loaded handgun and a few ounces of cocaine. This individual was on his way to a lengthy prison sentence. He couldn't just accept responsibility for his own actions. To take the weight off of his own shoulders, he fabricated a story against the defendant to take the spotlight off of himself. I'm not going to say the defendant is an angel, or he didn't have a troubled past. But he has already served his time for his crimes. Your honor, the testimony from the witness is not credible. He has admitted to being involved with murder and drugs. Mr. Anderson has a family who loves and supports him. He is a good father, and if pointed in the right direction, could be a pillar to our community. Thank you," Mr. Brown stated as he sat back down beside Yayo.

"Mr. Anderson, is there anything you would like to say to the court before I impose sentence on you today?" The judge asked Yayo, shifting his eyeglasses on his long, crooked nose.

Yayo stood up and straightened his pants leg, looked at the judge, and turned his back on him. "Yeah. I would like to apologize to my family and friends. Mama, I'm sorry for the decisions I have made, and just know you are my world and I'm proud to be your son. Shakira, you are my heartbeat, and I'm sorry for leaving you out here." Shakira's tears flowed as she held Shamira in her arms. "Quavon and Devon, always know you can achieve anything in life through discipline, determination, and dedication. I love y'all niggas. Granny, I love you. You made a man of me when I came into your home as a young boy. Thank you for loving me, and please keep me in your prayers. I love y'all, and trust and believe, I will return here a better man." Yayo turned to face the judge.

"Alright, Mr. Anderson, thank you. You may have a seat." Yayo sat down.

"Mr. Anderson, I totally disagree with your attorney. You have been involved in violence since you were 13 years old. You were released from prison, only to get out and start a violent gang that has terrorized the city of Chicago. You have no remorse for your actions, and I find that heartless. Mr. Anderson, the United States Penitentiary was built for men of your caliber. The world should be protected from men like you, and it is my job here today to make sure of that. As for count nine of your indictment, continuing a criminal enterprise, I sentence you to life in prison. As for count two of the indictment on tax evasion, I sentence you to life in prison. As for count three on the indictment 924C, being a career criminal, I sentence you to thirty years in prison."

Karen fell out in the courtroom, as the judge snatched her son's life away.

"As for count four on the indictment, intimidating a witness, I sentence you to twenty years."

Yayo was shocked when Butterball ratted the assault in Cook County Jail. The judge continued. "All sentences are to be served consecutively. Good luck, Mr. Anderson," the judge said, as he slammed the gavel, concealing Yayo's fate with two life sentences, plus fifty years.

Yayo was led out of the courtroom with his head held high, leaving the streets in blood, and his family in tears.

***

Batman was in the comfort of his home. He had retired from the Chicago Police Department. He had just popped a TV dinner in the microwave. Grabbing the Chicago Tribune, Batman read the headline, "Chicago gang leader, Yaton Anderson, gets two life sentences plus fifty years in federal court for murder and drugs." Batman tossed the newspaper on the couch when he heard his food was done. Batman walked over to the microwave, using his crutches. The nerves in his legs were severed from the shooting.

Batman pulled the Salisbury steaks from the microwave and placed them on the counter to cool off, when all of a sudden, his front door came crashing in, and a SWAT team invaded his living room.

"Lloyd Thomas, get on the ground, now!" One of the masked officers yelled, pointing the AR-15 assault rifle at his hat rack. He was dumbfounded as he laid on the floor on his stomach. The SWAT team moved through the house, making sure no one else was on the premises.

"Mr. Thomas, you are under arrest for extortion and tampering with evidence." The officer held out the indictment and search warrant signed by a federal judge. Batman was cuffed and taken to the MCC federal building.

***

Butterball was standing at a bus stop on Cottage Grove. He was given immunity for his charges, and released from the county a week ago. He had a new job as a full-time confidential informant. He would be a snitch for the rest of his life, helping the government get gangsters like Yayo off the streets, and into the confines of the federal penitentiary.

Butterball was lighting his Newport, when a black Yukon pulled up, and three men hopped out with ski masks covering their faces. Not having time to run, Butterball was snatched up like a rag doll and forced into the truck at gunpoint. The driver sped off as the four passengers punched him like a punching bag until he blacked out.

When Butterball woke up, he was tied to a chair in the middle of a basement with five men surrounding him. He knew all of them: TB, Maniac, Chopper, Booty-man, and Quavon. TB walked up and punched Butterball in the jaw, breaking it on impact.

"Wake up, bitch nigga. Thought you was gon' get away from the mob?" TB said through clenched teeth.

"Snitch ass nigga," Maniac hissed, spitting in Butterball's face.

He pleaded for the gang to let him live, but his pleas fell on deaf ears. Tired of hearing the rat beg, Quavon snatched the Glock 40 from TB's waist, pointed it at Butterball's head, and pulled the trigger. His brain splattered on the cold basement floor.

"Tell it to God, pussy," Quavon spat, as he wiped the tear that had fallen from his eye.

***

Yayo had just gotten off the phone with Shakira, setting up a visit for next week, when he bumped into a cat from Detroit named Fat Pat.

"Aye, my nigga. What's good, lil' nigga? Plug me with a phone call."

Yayo had never spoken to Fat Pat, and found it odd he asked him for a phone call. "Nigga, you ain't got no phone call coming from me," Yayo replied and kept it moving.

Fat Pat didn't like his response and got on straight bullshit. "Nigga, fuck you, soft ass nigga. Don't get mad because your weak ass squad ain't hold up. Bitch ass--" Yayo rushed him blow for blow.

Fat Pat hit the floor and got in the fetal position as Yayo proceeded to stomp his head, face, and chest on the dayroom floor. Blood stained his khaki pants.

Officers rushed the unit and forcefully restrained Yayo. Fat Pat was left in the middle of the floor, drowning in a puddle of his own blood.

When Yayo got to the hole, he laid his blanket on the concrete slab and laid on his back, staring at the ceiling.

"Damn, I'm going to the feds. Fuck!" He said in frustration. His thoughts and his heartbeat were still racing from the work he just put in on Fat Pat. He closed his eyes to try and get some sleep.

At 4:30 in the morning, a U.S. marshal came to Yayo's cell. "Yaton Anderson, number 07505-424, let's go. Time to go to prison."

Yayo got up, wiped the crust from his eyes, and grabbed his blanket. He was led out of the cell without the opportunity to wash his face or brush his teeth. He was taken to another holding cell with at least 15 other inmates. They were all loaded on a bus, headed to Terre Haute airport in Indiana.

While on the bus, Yayo got to see downtown Chicago. He would never see those streets again. He was going to miss driving nice cars and smoking good weed. But most importantly, he would miss his family. Yayo started to feel homesick the moment he left MCC. It took four hours to get to the Terre Haute airstrip. When they pulled up, the plane was already there.

The U.S. marshals were posted all over the landing strip with assault weapons and shotguns, just in case a prisoner tried to escape. They only shot to kill.

Yayo had heard about the feds his whole life, but he never thought he would fall victim to their system. Now, he was being loaded on a plane with some of the United States' most elite gangsters, killers, and drug lords. Yayo was told at MCC that he was designated to a penitentiary called Pollock in Louisiana. It was rumored to be one of the bloodiest penitentiaries in the country, which had him a little nervous.

YAYO

Yayo had assured himself if anybody ever disrespected his G, he was going all in. And he meant it from the heart. He had a fresh life sentence, and nothing to lose.

Yayo asked a dude who was sitting next to him where the plane was going. The man with the long dreads and strong accent said, "We going to Oklahoma, man. That's the holdover until you go to your prison. What joint are you going to?" He asked.

"I'm going to USP Pollock," Yayo replied.

"Me boi, you gon' to a fucked up place. Be careful there, brother. A lot of killings in that prison. It's like a cloud of death ova that place. Let God be with you."

The plane landed, and Yayo was in Oklahoma for two weeks before he was hauled off to USP Pollock. While on the bus, Yayo tried to mentally prepare himself to enter the concrete jungle of the Federal Bureau of Prisons.

To be continued…
YAYO 2
Coming Soon

Submission Guideline

Submit the first three chapters of your completed manuscript to ldpsubmissions@gmail.com, subject line: Your book's title. The manuscript must be in a .doc file and sent as an attachment. Document should be in Times New Roman, double spaced and in size 12 font. Also, provide your synopsis and full contact information. If sending multiple submissions, they must each be in a separate email.

Have a story but no way to send it electronically? You can still submit to LDP/Ca$h Presents. Send in the first three chapters, written or typed, of your completed manuscript to:

LDP: Submissions Dept
Po Box 870494
Mesquite, Tx 75187

DO NOT send original manuscript. Must be a duplicate.

Provide your synopsis and a cover letter containing your full contact information.

Thanks for considering LDP and Ca$h Presents.

YAYO

oming Soon from Lock Down Publications/Ca$h Presents

BOW DOWN TO MY GANGSTA

By **Ca$h**

TORN BETWEEN TWO

By **Coffee**

BLOOD STAINS OF A SHOTTA **III**

By **Jamaica**

STEADY MOBBIN **III**

By **Marcellus Allen**

RENEGADE BOYS IV

By Meesha

BLOOD OF A BOSS **VI**

SHADOWS OF THE GAME II

By **Askari**

LOYAL TO THE GAME **IV**

LIFE OF SIN **III**

By **T.J. & Jelissa**

A DOPEBOY'S PRAYER **II**

By **Eddie "Wolf" Lee**

IF LOVING YOU IS WRONG… **III**

By **Jelissa**

TRUE SAVAGE **VII**

By **Chris Green**

BLAST FOR ME **III**

DUFFLE BAG CARTEL **IV**

HEARTLESS GOON **II**

By **Ghost**

A HUSTLER'S DECEIT III

KILL ZONE **II**

S. Allen

BAE BELONGS TO ME III

SOUL OF A MONSTER III

By **Aryanna**

THE COST OF LOYALTY **III**

By **Kweli**

A GANGSTER'S SYN III

By **J-Blunt**

KING OF NEW YORK V

RISE TO POWER III

COKE KINGS III

BORN HEARTLESS II

By **T.J. Edwards**

GORILLAZ IN THE BAY IV

De'Kari

THE STREETS ARE CALLING II

Duquie Wilson

KINGPIN KILLAZ IV

STREET KINGS III

PAID IN BLOOD II

Hood Rich

SINS OF A HUSTLA II

ASAD

TRIGGADALE III

Elijah R. Freeman

MARRIED TO A BOSS III

By **Destiny Skai & Chris Green**

KINGZ OF THE GAME IV

Playa Ray

SLAUGHTER GANG III

RUTHLESS HEART

YAYO

By Willie Slaughter

THE HEART OF A SAVAGE II

By Jibril Williams

FUK SHYT II

By Blakk Diamond

THE DOPEMAN'S BODYGAURD II

By Tranay Adams

TRAP GOD

By Troublesome

YAYO II

By S. Allen

GHOST MOB

Stilloan Robinson

KINGPIN DREAMS

By Paper Boi Rari

CREAM

By Yolanda Moore

S. Allen

YAYO

By **Meesha**

A GANGSTER'S CODE I &, II III

A GANGSTER'S SYN II

By **J-Blunt**

PUSH IT TO THE LIMIT

By **Bre' Hayes**

BLOOD OF A BOSS **I, II, III,   IV, V**

SHADOWS OF THE GAME

By **Askari**

THE STREETS BLEED MURDER **I, II & III**

THE HEART OF A GANGSTA I II& III

By **Jerry Jackson**

CUM FOR ME

CUM FOR ME 2

CUM FOR ME 3

CUM FOR ME 4

CUM FOR ME 5

An **LDP Erotica Collaboration**

BRIDE OF A HUSTLA **I   II & II**

THE FETTI GIRLS **I, II& III**

CORRUPTED BY A GANGSTA I, II III, IV

BLINDED BY HIS LOVE

By **Destiny Skai**

WHEN A GOOD GIRL GOES BAD

By **Adrienne**

THE COST OF LOYALTY I II

By **Kweli**

A GANGSTER'S REVENGE **I II III & IV**

THE BOSS MAN'S DAUGHTERS

THE BOSS MAN'S DAUGHTERS II

S. Allen

THE BOSSMAN'S DAUGHTERS III
THE BOSSMAN'S DAUGHTERS IV
THE BOSS MAN'S DAUGHTERS **V**
A SAVAGE LOVE   **I & II**
BAE BELONGS TO ME I II
A HUSTLER'S DECEIT I, II, III
WHAT BAD BITCHES DO I, II, III
SOUL OF A MONSTER I II
KILL ZONE
By **Aryanna**
A KINGPIN'S AMBITON
A KINGPIN'S AMBITION **II**
I MURDER FOR THE DOUGH
By **Ambitious**
TRUE SAVAGE
TRUE SAVAGE II
TRUE SAVAGE **III**
TRUE SAVAGE **IV**
TRUE SAVAGE **V**
TRUE SAVAGE **VI**
By **Chris Green**
A DOPEBOY'S PRAYER
By **Eddie "Wolf" Lee**
THE KING CARTEL **I, II & III**
By **Frank Gresham**
THESE NIGGAS AIN'T LOYAL **I, II & III**
By **Nikki Tee**
GANGSTA SHYT **I II &III**
By **CATO**
THE ULTIMATE BETRAYAL

YAYO

By **Phoenix**
BOSS'N UP **I , II & III**
By **Royal Nicole**
I LOVE YOU TO DEATH
By Destiny J
I RIDE FOR MY HITTA
I STILL RIDE FOR MY HITTA
By **Misty Holt**
LOVE & CHASIN' PAPER
By **Qay Crockett**
TO DIE IN VAIN
SINS OF A HUSTLA
By **ASAD**
BROOKLYN HUSTLAZ
By **Boogsy Morina**
BROOKLYN ON LOCK I & II
By **Sonovia**
GANGSTA CITY
By **Teddy Duke**
A DRUG KING AND HIS DIAMOND I & II III
A DOPEMAN'S RICHES
HER MAN, MINE'S TOO I, II
CASH MONEY HO'S
By Nicole Goosby
TRAPHOUSE KING **I II & III**
KINGPIN KILLAZ I II III
STREET KINGS I II
PAID IN BLOOD
By **Hood Rich**
LIPSTICK KILLAH **I, II, III**

S. Allen

CRIME OF PASSION I & II

By **Mimi**

STEADY MOBBN' **I, II, III**

By **Marcellus Allen**

WHO SHOT YA **I, II, III**

Renta

GORILLAZ IN THE BAY **I II III**

DE'KARI

TRIGGADALE I II

Elijah R. Freeman

GOD BLESS THE TRAPPERS I, II, III

THESE SCANDALOUS STREETS I, II, III

FEAR MY GANGSTA I, II, III

THESE STREETS DON'T LOVE NOBODY I, II

BURY ME A G I, II, III, IV, V

A GANGSTA'S EMPIRE I, II, III, IV

THE DOPEMAN'S BODYGAURD

Tranay Adams

THE STREETS ARE CALLING

Duquie Wilson

MARRIED TO A BOSS... I II

By Destiny Skai & Chris Green

KINGZ OF THE GAME I II III

Playa Ray

SLAUGHTER GANG I II

By Willie Slaughter

THE HEART OF A SAVAGE

By Jibril Williams

FUK SHYT

By Blakk Diamond

280

YAYO

BOOKS BY LDP'S CEO, CA$H

TRUST IN NO MAN

TRUST IN NO MAN 2

TRUST IN NO MAN 3

BONDED BY BLOOD

SHORTY GOT A THUG

THUGS CRY

THUGS CRY 2

THUGS CRY 3

TRUST NO BITCH

TRUST NO BITCH 2

TRUST NO BITCH 3

TIL MY CASKET DROPS

RESTRAINING ORDER

RESTRAINING ORDER 2

IN LOVE WITH A CONVICT

Coming Soon

BONDED BY BLOOD 2

BOW DOWN TO MY GANGSTA

YAYO

www.ingramcontent.com/pod-product-compliance
Lightning Source LLC
Chambersburg PA
CBHW060527260626
47161CB00003B/785